MIKE WEST

Special Forces Super-Soldier

D1730494

EX MONTIBUS MEDIA

26 Caledon Street, Darling 7345.

Text © Hannes Wessels

Images © Mike West.

Cataloguing-in-publication data is available from the SA National Library.

Cover design: Mike Cruywagen.

Editing: Steve Lunderstedt

Proof reader: Jerry Buirski

First edition, first impression 2023

ISBN: 978-0-7961-1546-1

For a complete list of **EX MONTIBUS MEDIA** titles, please contact:

Email: admin@exmontibusmedia.co.za

Telephone (27) 83 251 3359

www.exmontibusmedia.co.za

MIKE WEST

Special Forces Super-Soldier

Hannes Wessels

Contents

Dedication

To John Barry; my brave best friend who died by my side. There are times when it is easier to have fallen than to be the one still standing.

Rest in Peace my 'brother'.

Author's Note

The outside world, in its collective determination to simplify events in Africa, has long accepted the erroneous view that white people living on the continent are inherently privileged. Mike's story is potent proof that that is absolutely not the case. Brought up poor and little loved, in a racially and ethnically divided society, that was inherently hostile, his fists were often his first and last line of defence. And being of English ancestry in an Afrikaner neighbourhood, his early enemies were white, not black.

As the writer, it has been heartwarming for someone from that country to learn that the first time he felt he had found a 'family' where he was wanted and warmly welcomed, was when he came to Rhodesia on a whim, and joined the Rhodesian army.

That is where his life as a warrior begins with a blast and lasts another action-packed 12 years that would see him launch himself at the enemy with great gusto, from the air, the sea and on foot, in Angola, Rhodesia, Mozambique, Namibia and Zambia.

Like his mentor, Captain Darrell Watt, he was never far from the cauldron and there can surely be only a few soldiers in modern history who have fought so long, so fiercely and in so many roles, against such daunting odds, and survived. And again, like Watt, he was disliked by his superiors, and received little recognition, despite his enormous commitment and courage.

And as is so often the case with these extraordinary soldiers, his devotion to duty was never motivated by racial animosity; beneath the rugged veneer, there was, and remains a thoughtful man, kindly disposed to all who are in need of help, with a deeply ingrained sense of righteousness; Mike believed then, as he does now, that the forces he fought so hard to destroy, offered no better to those they claimed to be liberating, and so he fought on to the end.

Taking stock of the situation in South Africa and Zimbabwe today, it appears he was right.

Prologue

My aim with this publication is to try to get on record some of the operations I was involved with in Rhodesia and then to tell the story of my part in the various South African Recce operations I was involved in between 1980 and 1989. To not have these written would, I believe, be a loss to history since soon I and my fellow soldiers will have left this life and these stories will fade into obscurity. I hope, in time, our grandchildren and their children will read this and remember us for what we were, and not how the world portrayed us. Today the world has been led to believe that all people of European ancestry are and always have been 'privileged'; well, I do hope some of the people repeating this fiction read this and understand this is a completely false generalisation. Although born white in apartheid South Africa my childhood was tough and I was far from alone in the white community in having to deal with tremendous adversity virtually my entire life.

Many believe the wars we fought in and for Rhodesia and South Africa were about racial supremacy, but this is simplistic and wrong; I did not fight for white domination or for white rule, but I did fight for a living, and I do not apologize for that. After spending time in Rhodesia I fell in love with the people and quickly realised I was happy to die for them and their cause. Unfortunately, we have been proved right; and what we feared would happen has indeed happened; Zimbabwe is a failed state and South Africa is on the same downward path.

In the writing of this book I do not seek glamour or glory, nor compassion, I simply wanted to tell my story, warts and all, as I remember it. Some of the operations were successful and some were not. Either way, it still took a huge effort to complete the tasks we were given, and most were characterized by excellent soldiering, finesse, fortitude and bravery. What I hope we (the production team) have succeeded in doing, is producing a colourful tapestry reflecting the lives and times of some truly remarkable men and the extraordinary challenges they faced. This is not only about us soldiers on the ground, but also the airmen and the sailors who provided us with such fantastic support and were always there for us in times of need.

I also want to pay a special tribute to the man who changed my life; Darrell Watt. He was, without a doubt, the best and most experienced tracker and bushfighter that I ever met and surely in a class of his own in the history of counter-insurgency wars. Rhodesian Operators raved about the man. Everyone wanted to be on one of his teams. I was one lucky bastard, as I caught his eye on selection and he gave me the chance other officers were not prepared to do.

He was the kind of soldier who looked at every deployment as a reason to find a fight and he would search ceaselessly until he found trouble. He didn't rest on his laurels waiting for trouble to come to him. Much like in 'Civvie Street'. If you went into a pub with Darrell, you could be sure a fight would erupt. Darrell loved action.

No one could track and find terrs (terrorists) like he could. He had tracked game (wild animals) since childhood, so finding the enemy was always an enjoyable challenge to him. Yes, we had great trackers in the Selous Scouts and the Rhodesian African Rifles (RAR), but nothing like this man. Darrell would react to any challenge no matter how daunting, with a cool and calm demeanour. Ask me, I know. I've been in some incredibly volatile situations with him, and thanks to him, after having survived these extremely close shaves many times over, he would have a good chuckle at my moment of recovery, uttering:

"Hey West, did you shit yourself?"

I would reply: "Fuck it, Darrell. That was close…"

Again, he would chuckle. To him, it was just another day of the week. He was a year younger than me, but he was my Father in War.

I think it's important for you, the reader, to understand that this man was not only my mentor, but my hero and idol. I emulated him in every way possible. I absorbed every move and tactic. I used all of this in my future successes, because my motto was:

WWDD – What Would Darrell Do? Keep this in mind when reading the rest of my story.

Having served under his command repeatedly and being involved in countless combat situations with him, he was, and always will be, the embodiment of the God of War to me.

One thing we can say, my friend, we gave it our best shot and lived a life few can and will never experience.

PAMBERI NE HONDO[1]

I hope you enjoy my story.

---

1   Pamberi ne Hondo – translated as Forward with the War.

CHAPTER 1

Growing Up

As little boys we played with weapons of war.
Pellet guns and water pistols but nothing too sore.
As kids it was about learning to be a man,
and hitting the bull's-eye whenever you can.
Then we became boys with killing machines,
exposed to blood and heart-crushing scenes.
We did it because we all had to fight
to protect our country from attacks in the night.
Inside our young hearts we were just a little boy
thrust into a world with very little joy.
But we did it with courage, we did our best,
and we know we excelled when put to the test.
Sometimes the memories awake us at night,
especially the bad ones, the fears and the flight.
And then the morning comes with the sun shining bright
to remind us we're alive… we're going to be alright.
Diana Clare Cairns

Mike West writes about his early life in South Africa:

"My grandfather was a Commissioner in the old South African Police (Zuid-Afrikaansche Republiek Polisie)[2] and for a while was in command of the force in what was then the Bechuanaland Protectorate (now Botswana). I never ever saw him smile, and my father told me that he had murdered my grandmother.

---

2   The ZARPS closed down in 1900. They were replaced by the South African Constabulary (Transvaal and Orange River Colony) in 1900 who remained as such until 1913 when all four colonies/countries that made up the new Union of South Africa of 1910 became the South African Police.

"I have photographs of my grandmother and she was a very beautiful woman with a kind face. Maybe he was jealous of her but I think he was also mad. No children were spared the sjambok. He was very cruel, a bad man. We were petrified of him. There was a large black and white portrait of my grandfather, in full uniform, sitting on a horse and holding his sword. When sitting at the table with him, we could not look at him. If we wanted something from the table we had to ask him, but we were not allowed to look up, and had to eat with our heads down or else suffer a blow to the head with a breadknife. On one occasion, when I was a little boy, he attacked me for no reason and was giving me a severe beating. I had to run and call my dad. My father had to intervene and actually knocked my grandfather unconscious.

"My father, one of four brothers, left South Africa to fight in the Second World War (1939-1945) when he was 16 years old. My great uncle, also Mike West, was killed in the First World War. Their father told them to go and make themselves 'useful'. He served with the Imperial Light Horse/Kimberley Regiment[3] in Italy and was posted as missing in action after a severe bombardment, but he turned up later in hospital in Milan. This is where he met my mother, Louisa Cariotti, and when the war finished she returned to South Africa with him. I have newspaper clippings of the two of them standing together at Durban harbour. All four brothers fought in World War II. His brother Herbert, who was a massive man standing at 6' 8" was also wounded, but they all survived and returned to South Africa. Herbert was also a heavyweight boxer and fought in the ring during the war. In one bout he knocked out a guy in the first round. He was also a cruel and merciless man, a true brute who would flatten anyone who dared cross him.

"On their return they all went to work in the gold mines and all of them contracted tuberculosis from the damp air underground but that did not stop them brawling. Fighting was really a way of life in the world that I grew up in. By that stage my father only had a quarter lung. That bastard would never have died. He was a fighter and trouble-maker.

"My mom had no parenting skills whatsoever. I remember my mother taking

---

3   An amalgamated Regiment that served in the Sixth SA Armoured Division in Italy from
     1944.

us into the passageway, and when I cried, she bashed my head against the wall. I hated her as she rejected and abandoned us, beating us beyond the point of no return.

"I was only four years old when she went back to Milan, Italy. I was placed in a home for boys called Nazareth House with my older brother. It was run by the Sisters of Nazareth at that time and had been going for more than 100 years, supporting and caring for those in need at all stages of life and not just for orphans. These values were supposed to be shared by the staff who worked there, making it places of peace. It was anything but. Instead, it was a place of uncontrolled brutality run by extremely cruel people. I was beaten virtually every day of my life. Our dormitory had wooden floors that creaked. Horsehair mattresses so sensitive to noise that you had to turn over very carefully, or the prefects (more like wardens) would make you regret it. We had to have permission to leave the dorm to urinate. Days were tough and tedious, and we children spent many hours on our knees scrubbing floors until our bodies ached.

"Water was always cold and we had to bath with a towel around the waist, the same as what Christ was wearing when he was crucified. No less than three in a bath, the same dirty water over and over; a deluge of water under wooden slats over concrete floors. When they scrubbed us with a brush and carbolic soap it really hurt. My father had taken a new job with Iscor (Iron and Steel Corporation) and we did not see him for a very long time.

"One time when my father visited us, he brought a large paper bag, filled with 'Smarties'. When he left, it was already late. We had to go and bath, so we carried it with us, but it was stolen whilst we were being scrubbed. And nothing could be said, or we would have faced further abuse. We were lucky enough to get a few handfuls in before we were dunked in the bath.

"We were always hungry and we would rummage in the dustbins looking for scraps of food. On one occasion my brother stood on a plank full of nails which went deep into his foot. The treatment for this was to rub the wound with a raw tomato. Every morning we would stand barefoot at attention in the cold while on parade and be inspected by the prefects. A clout came quickly if we so much as breathed wrong. Then we would get a cup of sugarless coffee, a thick slice of brown bread with white margarine, then off to church for morning prayers.

Having to dip your hands into this filthy water, my brother and I were so sold on this faith we even tried drinking the water, hoping that Mary and Jesus would come and help us, take us anywhere but just get us out of there. This is where I learned about the dark side of religion and the hypocrisy of those who preach it.

"I remember being sick and feverish, walking up the stairs to the nun's office for medicine. I looked out the window and saw a kid riding a bicycle outside. I wished I could have one. The only remedy I remember for any sickness was castor oil.

"I can recall how we were asleep in a dormitory and a cat shat there. I was ripped out of bed and flung on the floor then beaten over the back and I had to clean it up while the senior guys were kicking me. I was only five years old.

"When my father came to visit we all had to stand in a row down in the basement which was dark and cold. I just tipped my head slightly to the right looking for him while waiting, and they hit me so hard I saw stars. Once they were finished with us we were allowed out to see our father.

"That's where I learnt to hate religion. Every morning we had to go to church and take holy water, where we had to kneel for such a long time that our knees were sore. It made me obstinate, and I learnt to hate. My father eventually managed to get us out of that hellhole. How, I do not know.

"We started our first-grade school next to the railway line in Pretoria West, the Burgher Right Primary School. Everything continued to go wrong in our lives. Endless fist fights with Afrikaans children, who moved in cowardly packs. They lived next to the Pretoria West Showgrounds on Church Street.

"It was while I was at Burgher Right when I was walking on the street outside our house and a black man pushed me for some reason. I remember I was carrying a balloon at the time and somehow I fell without bursting it, but my father saw what had happened and he was enraged. He came out and hit the black man with such force that he knocked him out and then smashed his head into the road. The police were called. I remember they simply drove up, loaded the black man in the back of the van and drove off; that was the end of that.

"When I was at Burgher Right my Italian mother came back into the picture and my dad was very protective. He was drinking at the Iscor Club in Pretoria West one night when some Italian guy must have made a move on her. He knocked him clean through a glass window. The Italian lay unconscious outside until an ambulance arrived. I think my father was arrested. I have vague memories of him causing grievous bodily harm to other men. I don't know how many of them were able to walk away from that, because my father was unhinged, and mad with hatred because of my mother's infidelity.

"I was seven when we were taken to St Peter's Hostel on Murray Street in Pretoria and that would be home for five years. The Matron's name was Mang Bayford, who had a son named Brett, who bullied us ruthlessly. He was a big fat spoiled brat and used to eat all the food. We used to play with dinky toys and this fat bully would kick our cars and fuck us up. If you complained you had to stand in the corridor for hours.

"We attended Brooklyn Primary School, which was directly across the road. There were many good days, and many bad days, but it was a world away from our horrible start at the Boys' Home. It was here that I popped my first 'cherry', and many others, in the bushes of Brooklyn Park. We were all on the lookout for each other. I may not have had toys, but I had a lot to play with. There was no compassion in our lives, and I grew up with hate in my heart. The problem was we were growing and never had enough food. We used to steal milk that had been delivered to peoples' houses. Like any child, I wanted to see my mother again but I was unable to find out where she had gone to.

"I did Standard 4 at Brooklyn then moved to Welkom. By this time my mother was living with a German baker. We left St. Peters when my dad met and married Sophia Phillips, and he was then allowed to take us to his home to Welkom, but it was not a happy place as we were very poor, plus Sophia had two of her own kids. In Welkom we were sent to Rheederpark Combined Primary School.

"Every class was dual English/Afrikaans, and the war between us, the English, and them, the Afrikaners, began once again. The hatred was unparalleled. There were three rows in the class for Standards 3 – 5. We English kids were the 'rooineks', the 'soutpiels'. For woodwork we had a 'Dutchman'[4] teacher who used to hit me on the head when I made a mistake.

"When we came to the school gate, we would see Afrikaans-speaking guys waiting to fuck us up. The beatings that I had to take from the large Afrikaners,

---

4   Derogatory name for an Afrikaans-speaking male

moving in their hyena packs, instilled a hatred in me that will never be quelled. Getting to the shops to buy bread was always a big challenge. The 'Boertjies'[5] were always out there in their packs stalking us. We used to carry stones in our hands and let the stones go when throwing punches. I was always fighting; a very hard life. I had the odd Afrikaner friend but mostly so I could get lucky with their sisters. However sport turned things around for us.

"Fighting was the weekend sport for all the children on the gold mines and the parents encouraged it. We would be paired off and they would bet on who would win the bouts. There was also constant fighting between the Afrikaner children and those who were English-speaking. It was as if the Boer War had not ended. We used to launch mobile attacks with me on the crossbar of a bicycle with my brother on the seat riding the pedals. I was armed with a broomstick and we would ride at speed into the Afrikaner boys with me beating the hell out of them with the stick. We normally got the shit beaten out of us but always went back for more; this sort of ethnic conflict was a way of life for us.

"We used to swim in the Cyanide dam, which is bad for you, which flowed under the railway from the mines. We even derailed a mine-train after lifting the lever that changed train tracks, such that the train went off the track and rolled over. They chased after us but we hid at home, with dad protecting us.

"Aged 13 years I was sent to Welkom Boys High. There I was put in Standard 6C for all the stupid kids; I'm not sure why because I had been in the top set at Rheederpark. For some reason I was put in the bottom stream for the dunces despite having been doing well. There was an initiation, but they knew I could box so the seniors left me alone.

"At the same time my dad had me join the Western Holding Boxing Club. The coach was Sarel de Beer who also hated the English-speakers. There were three clubs and there were always fight challenges. With all the animosity between the miners, they would get their kids to fight and bet money on them. I never lost.

"So they put me up against a boy who always won. He would punch one, two, and over with his punch. As he came out of his corner, and before he could throw a punch, I hit him and knocked him out. Then his father jumped into the

---

5   White Afrikaners were called 'Boers' (farmers) and the young white males 'Boertjies' – little farmers.

ring and hit him with a leather skipping rope because he had lost his money. My father was very happy with his winnings though. On our way home the 'Boertjies' were waiting for us, so we had to fight again.

"Back from school we cleaned everything from floors to toilets to walls and then washed our clothes and bedding. We walked barefoot to school in the mornings, and in winter it was icy cold. To warm our feet we used to stand in warm cow dung then run like hell before our feet froze again. There was no meat to speak of, but my father had his own chickens, so every Sunday we had a bit of chicken for lunch. The step-siblings did absolutely squat. My brother and I would hunt birds with catapults in the veld, and in the trees by the mines. The birds would be cleaned and cooked. We had to make a fire, daily, to warm the geyser. We would walk along the railway lines, picking up loose pieces of coal for the stove and hearth. The shunters had such a soft spot for us, after a while, that they would fling a bit of coal, here and there, as they passed by.

"I was making a name for myself as a boxer and as a goalkeeper for the provincial Northern Free State soccer team. I boxed barefoot because we could not afford shoes, but one night I remember being loaned a pair of shoes from a friend, which I rubbed resin into so I wouldn't slip. I became the Northern Free State Champion, and was given a shiny red shirt with Western Holding on it. I was so proud of it that I used to sleep in it

"Every night that my father wasn't working, my brother and I would be made to fight each other, under the light my father rigged outside. We would even work it out, beforehand, because we didn't like hurting each other. We were getting ready for the 'Boertjies'!

"No one complained. Everyone was aggressive and angry, looking for someone to hurt. At home we would have to do the washing in Persils Washing Powder by stomping on the washing before hanging it out, and then washing the lino floors, while my stepmother's kids simply watched. She used us as labour, which interfered with what we wanted to do.

"At home my father used to leave at 04h30 to go to the mine, and only return two days later. We could not go anywhere until we had prepared the vegetables and peeled the potatoes; again while my stepmother's son and daughter just watched.

"We would then run five kilometres to school, then back again, make a fire, then off to boxing and back, and never complain to father. There was a guy at school whose parents were rich, and he had an empty swimming pool where we would go and fight. I just liked it. It was good for me.

"We had a science teacher – a Mr Haylet, and I hated him. Once I was messing around and he hit me so hard with a cane that the welt was bleeding badly. Dad walked me back to school shouting and going mad, so much so that the teacher locked himself away and refused to come out and face my dad. The police came and took my dad away.

"I was still only 13 years old when my father knocked me out cold. The fighting between Afrikaner and English continued and the Afrikaners were tough and extremely dangerous. My brother and I learnt the trick of having a stone hidden inside our fists to add weight to the blow and help us land more powerful punches. My brother and I, along with a few English friends, would walk around four kilometres, in the dark of night, to the only drinking spot in town: the Welkom Hotel.

"There were always fights between the Afrikaans miners and the Italians. We walked all the way there, and back, just to watch the blood flow and, on more than one occasion, an Italian pulled a gun. They would really get stuck into each other. This was our Reality TV. We loved it. Here is where we learned just how guys get stuck into each other with kicking when someone drops. Some added further play by adding broken bottles to the live entertainment. The police really had their hands full, and we had ringside seats. My dad was something of a celebrity at some of these matches, bringing his own flair and flavour over card game disputes. My father once drilled a guy so hard during an argument he stumbled across his sitting room, and straight into his glass-fronted showcase. I remember accompanying my father home from some of these matches, missing his shirt, and covered in blood.

"We would also go to Rainbow Valley where we learnt how to ride horses, hunt birds, and have clay fights. We would shoot ducks and take the meat home to be cooked as we couldn't afford to buy meat. And once a month we would watch the black guys fight with knobkieries and shields. It used to be so bloody, and we loved it.

"Duncan Weiss was a good friend, he was in my class and came from an affluent family. They had cars, a nice house and life's luxuries. Many fights took place in his empty swimming pool, which was nearby. After that entertainment, we would sit and smoke cigars in his dad's cigar lounge. Mills cigarettes were packaged in yellow tins. Duncan kept us in the smokes.

"I was even caned by the police for riding abreast, on a bicycle. Two of us were pulled off and I got three of the best. I am not blaming the system. A hard life had moulded an angry, undisciplined kid who had become ruthless.

"I hated my stepmother, there was nothing for me to do at home, so I decided to run away. I left with the idea of going to see my girlfriend who had moved away from Welkom with her parents.

"I walked and hitched rides for days from Welkom sleeping in the veld, under banana trees, and mixing with hobos. It took me around two weeks to walk and hitchike to Illovo where they were staying in a hotel on holiday.

"They couldn't accommodate me but let me sleep in the boot of their station-wagon and gave me some tinned fish. In those days all we were doing was chasing women. Then I got a job washing dishes for food in a caravan park, and the use of a fishing rod from one of the campers to catch some fish, but I was swept off the rocks and lost all the equipment. I high-tailed it out of there.

"I lived rough on the streets, scavenging for food for a few weeks, sleeping in railway stations and under the subway with the hobos. Eventually I made my way to my aunt Doris in Pretoria. Obviously I was an annoyance to her, and eventually she contacted the police who were looking for me after my father had reported me missing. They got me back to Welkom, but because my parents did not want me at home I was placed in the care of Child Welfare.

"Aged 15 years, I climbed into a Hollander who had a big mouth and gave him a severe thumping. So it was back to the headmaster's office. His name was Mr East. My surname is West. The school joke was: 'The cane rises in the East, and sets on the West.' That's how often I frequented his office. He beat me the usual six but he had had enough of my nonsense and I was expelled. Nobody really knew what to do with me. I wanted to go and work on the mines but they would not let me go underground, and I failed their entrance exam.

"Dad said I had to go back to school, but Mr East refused to allow me to come back, and made me leave. When I was told to get off the premises and never return, I was cheered on through the classroom windows, as I exited the school gates. I was so goddamn happy; I passionately hated school.

CHAPTER 2

Prison Service

"After a few weeks, welfare came and took me away to the Prison Services Training College in Kroonstad, to train as a warder. It was as if nothing had changed there because the fighting continued almost as a way of life. I was still causing 'kak'. Because I was a potent boxer they treated me differently. I wasn't scared. Our recruit course ended and I was posted to Zonderwater.

"We would watch movies on a Friday night, chase the ladies, and get into fights. At this time I was moonlighting; available for any tasks. We were only paid R30 a month, and I could make R20, R40, or even R60 a job. I managed to buy an Alfa Giulietta for R300. I put down R30 deposit and paid it off at R10 per month. Boy did we have fun with the girls then. I ended up causing a lot of harm.

"In the years at Zonderwater prison my father worked in various mines. When I was in Carletonville I went to find him. On the way I stopped at the '007 Roadhouse'. I was dressed like a 'skollie', and the guy behind the counter swore at me. I hit him, and was locked up again in a cell. The next morning I was released, and went to see my dad. Once back at Zonderwater, I got nicely smashed with my mates, and promptly wrote off my newly acquired car. No worries – I simply went and bought a second-hand Fiat 1500. She was red and gorgeous. I was so proud. But that's when the questions arose. Where was Mike getting the money from?

"Eventually the Fiat 1500 started to smoke and give problems. I sold it, and bought myself my first brand new anything – a Honda 500cc motorcycle. I was called in by my superiors, because I was being investigated. My income versus expenditure was out of sync. Major Snyman, known as '007' at the time, headed up the investigation. He found *bupkis*.[6]

It was decided that I would be transferred to Pretoria Central Prison because,

6   Bupkis – Nothing at all

although I was under suspicion, I was an excellent rugby player and well versed in the way of the fist. At Pretoria Central Prison, I found my niche: Maximum Security and the Gallows.

"At this stage I was playing good rugby at fullback, so Brigadier Buurman van Zyl, the legendary Northern Transvaal (later the Blue Bulls) coach, liked me and put up with my nonsense.

"There I met 'Moaner' van Heerden who would go on to become a great Springbok rugby lock forward from 1974 to 1980. He appeared in 17 Tests, including the series against the 1974 Lions where the Boks got a hiding. He is well remembered for his saying when asked about an unsavoury incident on the field that 'cowboys don't cry'. He said this after being laid low by a right-hook from the great British and Irish Lions fullback JPR Williams who had sprinted 60 metres to hit him after a '99' call at the now infamous 'Battle of Boet Erasmus Stadium', in Port Elizabeth.[7] Actually, the truth is 'Moaner' was a real gentle giant and did not like hurting people.

"Within the complex there were three separate clusters of prisons: Pretoria Central Prison, Pretoria (Local) Prison, and a third known only as 'Maximum' or 'Beverley Hills'. The latter was the ultra-maximum-security section. The facilities were split according to race and gender. Pretoria Central Prison was where the gallows were; it was the official facility for capital punishment in South Africa during the apartheid era. The black political prisoners were held on Robben Island.

"I was then transferred to join Moaner to work with the hard-core long-term prisoners and those on Death Row. This was very difficult work at time. Moaner, although immensely strong, did not like getting involved in fights with inmates.

"This is when I started boxing with Jimmy Richards at the Phoenix Boxing Club. Jimmy was from Boksburg, undefeated in his first 11 fights, with a 26-11-4 record, and held the South African Heavyweight boxing championship from 1972 – 1973 before losing it to Mike 'The Tank' Schutte. He then lost his two

---

7   Ironically the pair met in 2005 and JPR spoke fondly of their more 'friendly' encounter. He told the Guardian: "Funny enough, I bumped into him on a train from London to Cardiff last year and he asked 'do you remember me?' I had to admit that I didn't and he just said that he had played against me in South Africa in 1974. We had a lovely chat. When I got home I looked in the match programme and saw that it was the guy I had punched – and he never mentioned it during the whole time we were talking on the train. What a gentleman."

following fights to Gerrie Coetzee, the future world heavyweight champion. I also trained with Frikkie Ludick, a welterweight with a 9-12-1 win, loss, draw record.

"When I was moved to where the condemned prisoners were held I met Dimitri Tsafendas who I came to know well during this time. He was the man who had stabbed South African Prime Minister Hendrik Verwoerd to death in Parliament in September 1966. He was conveniently found to be insane, and did not stand trial, but was locked up for the rest of his life.

"I spent some time with him trying to get to know him better and I don't believe for a moment that he was mad. He knew that his cell was stuffed with listening devices so when he was inside the only sound he would make was when he farted and he seemed to have a lot of wind to blow out. Outside the cell he would talk, but no matter how hard I and others tried, we never managed to get him to say anything about the assassination.

"I was on the gallows section for a while. Before their execution we would take them to an office where the Messenger of the Court was present. The Messenger was the hangman. Here all the paper-work was done and they were weighed before being told they were to be hanged in seven days. The lighter the condemned man the longer the rope.

"Then they were given time with a priest or religious leader from their respective denomination and then into a soundproof room where they were given their last wish. Some said nothing. One Indian asked who was going to look after his family and he was told the government would.

"The night before being executed they were given a meal of their choosing. Most asked for chicken. Moaner, I and others had to go and get the condemned men out of their cells in the early morning and get them ready for their last day. Some became violent and we had to subdue them to put the handcuffs on. On the walk from the cells to the gallows the black men would sing and the prison went silent. There was a phone near the gallows to take the call if there was a last minute reprieve. I never heard it ring. Then the condemned were led out on to a platform where they would see the ropes.

"We had to stand and watch as the hoods were placed on their heads by the hangman. Once the noose was secured, the executioner would pull the lever and the trap-door opened. Below the drop was a pond to catch the human fluids and solids expelled on sudden death. The shock of the snapped neck and spinal cord caused an instant discharge of bodily fluids. The hangman was efficient, he could hang a maximum of seven people at a time.

"As it happened, one of the guys on death row was a former policeman by the name of Frans Vontsteen who had killed Francois Swanepoel, a police detective and former Springbok athlete in a fight over Swanepoel's wife Sonjia. He was then sentenced to death. On a particular night a warder who was inexperienced gave him permission to come out of the cell onto the catwalk between the blocks to collect a Coca-Cola. Vontsteen was very athletic and he leaped over the wall, out the yard, and he was gone.

"At the time I was off-duty driving taxis, moonlighting for a bit more money with Willie du Toit, a pal of mine who was also a warder when we saw this guy in prison gear running through the railway station and we knew immediately he was on the run. I took off after him and had no problem catching him and dragged him into the back of the car whereupon he fought back and I had to subdue him.

"When we got back to Pretoria Central there was pandemonium with people shouting and screaming and all the alarms were going-off. I calmly walked him through those doors and there was jubilation from all the prison staff. Nobody had ever escaped from death row before so this was potentially a huge embarrassment, and I had saved the day.

"I then became a bit of a hero and my picture was in the newspapers. Unbeknown to me, Vontsteen and I had been friends and played together when we were little kids. I had forgotten about him until a relative reminded me. Unfortunately this guy had lots of friends in the underworld and they were not at all happy with me having recaptured him and I started to get death threats. When they hung Vontsteen on 4 October 1972 things really started going wrong for me so I was transferred to Durban.

Back on the Street

"Some months later I was sent back to Pretoria, but I never earned enough so I left the Prison Service, bought myself a Hillman, and went off to become a taxi driver. I got locked up for assault at the Pretoria Police Station, spent the night, paid R10 bail the next morning... and never heard of it again.

"Taxi driving was one way of meeting a lot of women. While driving, a certain guy crossed my path. He claimed to have been in the Congo with Mike Hoare's mercenaries. He was as wide as he was tall, and was the kind of tough guy who had already had a shootout with police. All the other taxi drivers tended to avoid him, temperamental SOB (son of a bitch) that he was.

"He owed me more money than I owed him, but he was demanding his money. I told him to take it off what he owed me, and to cough up the difference. A number of the other drivers were watching this dispute play out, and he obviously wanted to make an impression, because he charged at me, swearing. As he came within range, I hit him with a solid right cross, which propelled him over the bonnet of a car. I followed up, drilling him with a right fist. I was pretty angry now. Another driver came running over to try and stop me, because there was blood everywhere. I stood back and the taxi driver that I was fighting ran, screaming like a pig, all the way to the Railway Police. It took about 30 minutes, before he came out of the building, pointing at me, saying 'Dis hy...'.

"Apparently, when he was in the station, and washing his face in the bathroom, accompanied by another driver, he tried to rinse the blood out of his mouth only to discover that it was exiting out of his cheek. I clearly hit him hard. I'm still proud of this phenomenal blow – and well done to the fat bastard for not checking out while I thumped him.

"The Railway Police called me over to come to the station. I told them where to put it, and to come and get me. They left me alone but the driver then went to Central Police Station to go and lay a charge. Fortunately for me, there was a jurisdiction problem, as the incident had occurred on railway property, he had already laid a charge there, and the police could therefore not get involved. He then went for medical treatment, and tried to sue me for assault and medical costs, via a lawyer. I made sure it went no further.

"There was another incident, where a passenger decided to exit the vehicle before paying me – not something uncommon at the time – but I was rather attached to my fees, and thus pursued him. He took a swing at me, when I grabbed him. That was a mistake. There was a police investigation around this incident, which was also being coupled to a few other incidences involving other taxi drivers.

"The railway decided that the only way forward was to close the taxi rank, as there were too many problems. They did it under the guise of needing the property for further development. I was running out of options.

"At this time I was transporting miscellaneous parcels for Indian businessmen in Church Street, who were trading with certain goods under the table. There would be a car parked with the keys on the wheel. I would simply drive the car to the destination, place the keys back on the wheel and leave.

"One time I was asked to deliver a 'hot' car parked in Bosman Street. I drove it to Waterkloof. I had the address on the inside of the old page-matchbox, and I drove inside the gate. It was a beige-pink double-storey house. I stopped by the garage and three guys came out. They were much older than me. They greeted me in Afrikaans, and got into the car. They scratched around but not sure what they found. They said '*wag net*' (wait a while) as they went inside.

"A little while later they came out, and the one guy suddenly threw a punch at me, and all I remember is that they were swearing. I still don't know what went wrong or what was missing, and what the hell had been done because most of the jobs I did, I didn't know what was inside, but I guessed something valuable was hidden in the car. They were older lads than me, but I wasn't lazy with my fists. They were swearing at me, 'fucking cunt...', and I retorted 'fuck you' back at them. I got quite damaged, but I fought my way out. My nose and ears were bleeding, but I put up a good fight against them. But I still didn't know what was going on. I remember later catching a taxi and going back to check it out. The next day I went to see the 'Chara', the coolie, and he apologised although I was still upset. He still said to me; 'Boss, I did a favour for a friend of mine. I'm sorry about this. I don't know what was in the car.'

"I tried to find his friend, but he was missing. I still don't know to this day. All I know is that I got a couple of good shots to the head. I could take a hiding. Still to this day I am baffled. I normally dropped off the car and left, but these fuckers told me to wait while they took something from the back and all I got was R20. Pissed me off a lot, but I never took it out on the Indian. These jobs were very lucrative although I never knew what I was moving.

"My natural aggression was key to my success. Chris Schulenburg, who I would get to know better in Rhodesia, owned this pub in Church Street, called Van Der

Stel Pub. They hired me to fuck up the railway workers whenever necessary, and also act as a bouncer and in return I would get a beer from the barman; his name was Richard. They would phone me when they had problems and I would come down and fuck them up. Clearly I was going down the wrong track, becoming a career criminal and it was just a matter of time before I ended up in Pretoria Central on the wrong side of the bars. It was 1974 and I now had a wife and two children to think about. There was no use me being in the slammer with a family to support. I decided to join the South African army.

"I went to Poynton's Building in Church Street, Pretoria, where the SADF (South African Defence Force) headquarters were situated. I applied to join the Recces, which I had heard of, but I was rejected because of my lack of Matric and complete lack of religious interest.

"I tried my hand at a few things, could not find work, nor could I put a CV together with positive references, and then realised that there was only one solution.

"I had heard about Rhodesia and the fact that there was a war on. It seemed like a good place to make a new start. They needed fighters and I was pretty sure I could help. Within two weeks, I received my letter of acceptance, and off I went to join up with my new family."

Hi Ho, Hi Ho,
It's off to war I go
With hand grenades and lemonade
Hi ho, Hi ho, Hi ho!

"Look, I know that my ways didn't help things. I blame nobody, but my unusual upbringing certainly did not help matters. Poverty, fighting, struggle, suffering and constant rejection. Homes, hostels, stepmothers. You may look at someone who survived this and feel pity for them. Don't pity me. These broken building blocks shaped a soldier, whose name is now known. I am no victim. I am a survivor. From the gutters, to the sunlight. I am fucking proud of the man I made of myself."

CHAPTER 3

RHODESIA

Two roads diverged in a wood, and I – I took the one less travelled by, and that has made the difference'– Robert Frost

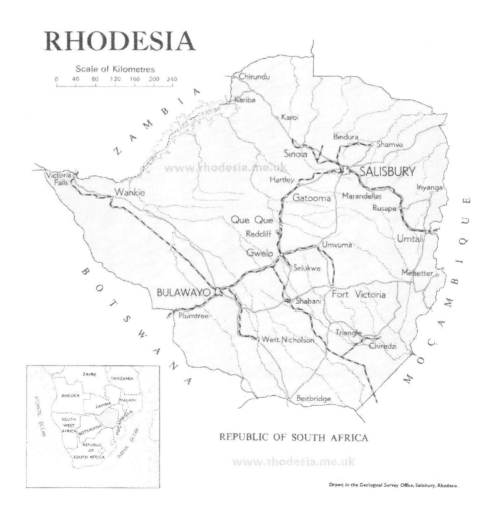

"I drove from Sasolburg to Salisbury, a distance of 1,200 kilometres, taking around 15 hours in my father's 1966 Peugeot station wagon. When I crossed the Limpopo River late in 1974 it was the first time I had been out of South Africa. I knew very little about the country but the moment I crossed that border into Rhodesia I felt excited and hopeful. My life, thus far, had not been a happy one, and I felt this was a second chance. At the time I came into the country, a ceasefire (in connection with the South African government-sponsored 'détente') was supposed to be in place but I imagined the terrorists hiding in every available bush.

"With the escalation in the war, a call had gone out for non-Rhodesian volunteers. Many soldiers responded, coming from Britain, Ireland, South Africa, Portugal, Hong Kong, Canada, Australia, New Zealand and the United States of America with the latter three being held in high regard for their recent Vietnam War experience.

"I went straight to the Recruitment Centre in Salisbury and duly completed the application form, including substantial mention of infantry experience and training at Voortrekker Hoogte Military Base which was of course, a load of crap. I'm still not sure if it was Fate that made them sign me up without references or a Deity I offended along the way, but I was pretty much immediately accepted. Arrangements were rapidly underway for my transfer from South Africa to Salisbury by train, so I would take the car back and then return at the expense of the Rhodesian army.

Grey's Scouts

"In less than a month after my return, I received my induction papers and off I went to Salisbury. I was met at the station by chaps in a military jeep, who drove me through to Inkomo Barracks outside the city, which was the Grey's Scout Base[8]. I knew little about horses and had never trained as a soldier and here I was joining a mounted infantry regiment. But I was desperate to get into action and I think they enjoyed my aggressive enthusiasm. So with no Matric, and with no basic military training, I was set for a serious adventure.

"There was a whole heap more learning to do, much of which was done without

---

8   The Grey's Scouts were only established by the Rhodesian Army as the Mounted Infantry
     Unit in July 1975. The unit was redesignated the Grey's Scouts in 1976.

formal instruction, just using common sense, intelligent guesses, calculated risks, trial and error and sometimes even just totally 'winging it'. There were a hundred small, and not so small, things that made the veterans more efficient, more comfortable and less likely to become casualties. You don't pick up all this stuff in a day, or even a couple of weeks but I paid close attention to everything they taught me.

"Again, it was either fate or the Deity, because along with the uniform and such, I was also issued a horse named Wetfoot. As a child, I had ridden the odd horse and donkey near the old mine compounds for a spot of bareback riding, so my only challenges were fitting the equipment – the bit, saddle and reins – because I had only ever seen those in movies. The Equestrian Centre at the barracks put us through the ropes, and off I went to war not even four weeks later.

"My first deployment was to Nyamapanda, a small border town in the north-east of Rhodesia on the road to Tete in Mozambique. We travelled with the horses in a well-armed military convoy.

"I was issued a 9mm pistol and a Belgian FN rifle. Fortunately, I had fired an FN once in my life in 1965 at the Prison Service College in Kroonstad. Back then, it was either that college or another home. I'm still glad the Welfare placed me there.

"I was all of 27 years old, an inexperienced troublemaker who couldn't sell salt in South Africa, now masquerading as a knowledgeable soldier. I was having the time of my life. Not even a child's first visit to *'Sweets from Heaven'* can equate to my happiness then. I had found myself among good guys who made me feel welcome and wanted, which was a big change for me.

"Lieutenant Cawood was the Base Commander at Nyamapanda with tented lodgings and endless bushveld around us stretching for miles into the distance. Soon we were called in for a briefing. An enemy group had been sighted and we were to deploy in the area via horseback, with the purpose of making contact and killing the enemy. I couldn't wait to 'John Wayne' into the fray.

"I was quite a solid lad, so Lieutenant Cawood figured I could handle an FN heavy-barrelled semi-automatic battle rifle. It was similar to the normal FN, with the same magazine capacity, but with the difference of a heavy barrel and bipods. I'd never seen anything like it in my life. It was also two kilograms heavier than an FN, but nothing could dampen my joy. Here I was on horse-back, saddle, stirrup and reins, carrying a heavy rifle, saddle bags filled with supplies, and 10-plus fully loaded magazines heading out for seven days into the wilderness in search of people to kill. It was the best day of my life. My Team Leader's name was Dave Sparkes. A Colour Sergeant, he later died quite suddenly, when he shot himself in February 1980 whilst playing Russian Roulette for drinks at the Monomotapa Hotel in Salisbury.

"Looking back now as a veteran of war, some observations:

- Horseback was certainly a good way to make yourself a moving target. We were fully exposed and it was a noisy deployment. You didn't need a tracker to find us and one good ambush would end us just like the ill-fated Indian fighter George Custer.

- Horse-flies were our greatest enemy.

- Imagine trying to find a safe lying up place (LUP), during the day, with 6 foot-stomping, farting horses being irritated by horseflies. You have to walk them at least 30 metres away, and tie them there. Then you have to remove your saddle and saddle bags. You have to walk back. At all times, a happy moving target, taking the long way round, attempting to look for terrs – all the while wondering if they were already watching you. Imagine trying to do this at night. You couldn't hear a duiker stampede, let alone approaching terrorists.

- Constantly worrying that we would wake up in the LUP the next morning, only to find our horses have been stolen (and probably by then becoming hamburgers) and we have a lengthy walk back to base to look forward to, carrying all our stuff ourselves. This is why we decided to rather sleep in the Guard Force Keeps[9] at night. These were present in all the Tribal Trustlands. They were surrounded by barbed wire, with defensive embankments on the inside for protection from outside fire. This way we could at least prevent the untimely demise of both ourselves and our horses.

"I did three seven-day deployments and It was frustrating; trying to find a terr whilst on horseback was like trying to hunt for rabbits on a motorcycle. We

---

9   The rural people were moved into protected villages or Keeps, designed to cut off the insurgents from supplies of food and comfort and to encourage the loyalty of the locals.

returned to Inkomo Barracks for RNR (Rest and Recuperation), after which it was back to Nyamapanda. Back to the horseflies. Back to being a moving target.

"I then did another deployment of seven days, and returned to the base camp again. Lieutenant Cawood was on his way to resupply some of our guys in a Rhodaf 45 truck. These 45s had water in the tyres, conveyor belting on the cab floor and sandbags. This was how the vehicles were made mine-proof, whilst travelling on gravel roads in operational areas. He ordered me to accompany him on the resupply. Just the two of us. By this time, I had discarded the heavy-barrelled FN, as it served no more purpose than its 2 kilogram lighter counterpart.

"You had to strap yourself in with the seatbelt, once in the '45'. This was to counter the damage experienced when meeting with a landmine. Lieutenant Cawood, myself, and 'Blue' (his Labrador) set off. We had barely driven five kilometres, when we were blown up by a landmine directly under the passenger side wheel, which is where I was. It turned out, after the Sappers came out to check, that it was a boosted Yugoslavian TMA-3 'Cheesecake' Landmine, known to us as a 'Double Cheesecake'.

"All I remember is blackness. We were heading in an easterly direction on detonation, it blew us off the road and when the vehicle settled we were facing south. When I came to, there was dust throughout the cabin. I was dazed and stone deaf as I had burst an eardrum. My seatbelt had snapped from the impact, and I had been slammed into the cab roof, rendering me unconscious. I will never forget the smell. I was still holding my FN, which I had been holding out the window when we departed in order to open fire if necessary. It had broken during the impact. The weapon was wrecked and still in my hands. How it never took my head off, when we both flew into the roof, I will never know. Both Lieutenant Cawood and I were looking at each other, stunned. The windscreen had disappeared – and Blue with it. Realising that we were sitting ducks, we knew we had to get out ASAP. Cawood warned me to be careful of where I step because AP (anti-personnel) mines were usually strategically placed near landmines, in order to eliminate survivors of the original blast.

"To our surprise, Blue came running up, jumping happily. He had survived the blast and the unexpected flight. Not a hair out of place. If only I had sat in the middle like the dog, maybe I would have been jumping happily, too. The power of the blast had sent the truck airborne and it had spun around in the air so we landed facing a different direction. How the help arrived so rapidly, I don't know. Military vehicles came out of nowhere, and they began sweeping for AP mines.

"The strangest part of this all was I felt incredibly elated. I had just survived the blast of a landmine that I couldn't identify in a line up if you paid me to. I had heard of landmines, but I had never seen one before – it didn't seem important at the time.

"Here I was, a raw recruit with no military experience other than I knew how to shoot a FN and I was so proud after we hit the landmine – I was a hero of sorts! The engineers on site, who analysed the blast sight and resultant crater, said that it could only be a Yugoslavian TMA 3 Cheesecake Landmine.

"The wreckage was towed back to base. You won't believe the reception that I got. The back slapping was great, but I didn't let on that my back felt broken and my left ankle was wonky. Still deaf, dazed, and grinning. I refused medical assistance. I had never felt better in a strange way. I later heard so many stories about deaths and limb loss due to landmines, and here I was, One life down, and eight more to go.

"The fact is, I had literally begun my war career with a big bang, and I was so proud of myself. The photos speak for themselves. But when this bush trip came to an end, and I returned to Inkomo Barracks, I had had my fill of horses, and hunting but not killing.

"All credit to the Grey's Scouts. They undoubtedly contributed their part to the war effort, and I will always hold them in high regard, grateful for my Fibber's Beginning, but this wasn't my cup of tea; I had had a taste but I wanted more.

"I had heard of the Rhodesian Light Infantry (RLI) Fireforce Operations. They jumped from Dakotas, into combat. Now this was the kind of action I was look-ing for; leaping from perfectly good airplanes, directly into enemy contact. I could now literally get at them. I completed the necessary documentation and was posted to the RLI. Off to join, 'The RLI, soldiers from the sky!'

The RLI

There is no hunting like the hunting of man, and those who have hunted armed men long enough and liked it, never care for anything else thereafter –Ernest Hemingway

"In a way, a dream became a reality when I joined 2 Commando RLI. I was 28 years old; it was 1976, and, unlike most of them, I was married and a father. So I was the biggest, ugliest and oldest of the lot, surrounded by youngsters. Their ages ranged from 18 to 21 years. I was in awe of the kids around me; they had seen more combat than I had in all my years. And these guys were commando-trained and I had fuck-all training at that level. I had lied my way into the Rhodesian Army. Ahead of me I would fight alongside some of the bravest young men anywhere who did not think twice about dying for the country they loved so dearly.

"There was a whole heap more learning to do, much of which was done without formal instruction, again just using common sense, intelligent guesses, calculated risks, trial and error and sometimes even just totally 'winging it'. There were a hundred small, and not so small, things that made you more efficient, more comfortable and less likely to become casualties.

"The Rhodesians were virtually all from schools with strict discipline, including corporal punishment and compulsory sport, and many had been boarders. These lads were easily trainable, had previously been exposed to the 'team ethic', and were already relatively fit and tough unlike many school-leavers in the UK and Europe.

"Steroids had not yet reached Rhodesia, so we did not have any of those heavily muscled freaks with such over-developed *latissimus dorsi* (back muscles) that they had to strut around like birds trying to take off. They were volunteers so there was a high level of competitive enthusiasm among the men.

"Soon after I signed up, I was sent on a parachute course at New Sarum Air Force Base outside Salisbury. My instructor was Andy Steen. For the Special Air Service (SAS) para-training is obviously a prerequisite, but the Rhodesian Army was getting more and more troops (RLI by end of 1976 and RAR by end of 1977) para-trained because we just did not have enough helicopters for the 'Fireforce' to deploy enough troops, so the para numbers had to be increased.

"Our trusty old 'Daks'[10] were way past their sell-by date – one even had a brass plaque above the door reminding us it had been used at Arnhem! The 'Blues' (Rhodesian Air Force) technicians were absolute genii keeping that whole force of aging aircraft battle-worthy. Word was they could fix most things with duct tape and 'No. 8' wire!

"Dispatches on operations were such rapid events, not exactly carefully choreographed, but somehow the instructors and dispatchers created order out of chaos. The RLI, with their light Fireforce equipment, were said to have the world record for the fastest dispatch of a full 'Dak' load.

"On completing the course, we, of course, were all immensely proud of our new para-wings on our shoulders. I was in my element jumping into combat; from the first time I jumped, I loved it.

Into the Fire

"My first Fireforce deployment was at Grand Reef, near Umtali. The air complement was three Alouette G-Cars each carrying four RLI combatants, each helicopter armed with twin Brownings, plus one K-Car with a 20mm cannon which carried the commander, and for ground-attack there was a Cessna 'Lynx' aircraft carrying Frantan (Napalm).

"My Team Leader was a 21 year-old corporal, already a seasoned veteran, with bigger balls than a T-Rex. My troop officer was Mike Rich. I was in 7 Troop and this is where I found my niche. This was a dream come true. I had found my proverbial Home. The way that you threw a child into the water in the 1960s, 70s and 80s, and yelled 'swim!' This is pretty much how my introduction to real war began. I parachuted out of a Dakota, as part of the 'Fireforce' team, which was 12-soldiers strong, and landed my arse smack in the middle of what appeared to be full-on war! The shit had already hit the fan and it was flying freely when I hit the dirt.

"These terrs had been spotted by the Selous Scouts, who had observation posts on kopjes and mountains throughout Rhodesia. Their job was to notify Fireforce of enemy activity on the ground so that it could be dealt with swiftly.

"I was, it seemed, the 'old man' of the team. Hell, our corporal was seven years

---

10   Dakota DC3.

younger than me – but the balls on these kids were huge! You had to witness it to believe it. Once we hit the ground, we formed an extended line, and swept towards the enemy. We were being guided by the Fireforce Commander in the K-Car chopper, running the operation from an eagle-eye point of view.

"Hot lead was flying, enemy were incoming, running in all directions, and taking shots at us. This was my baptism of fire, and I was getting the full treatment. Our young commander was calmly leading our line of attack through the battle. We moved fast and aggressively while eliminating everything in our path.

"Being the 'old man', and the largest of the bunch, I was bestowed with the honour of lugging the not-so-light MAG (light machine gun), which fires a 7.62 round, same as the FN. There was a 100-round belt fitted to this machine gun, plus I had another three belts of 100 rounds each in my small backpack. I had just loaded a fresh belt, and I was on the extreme left flank of the line.

"There, in the not so distant, sparse, undulating, rocky ground, were two terrs firing AK47s at one of the choppers, which seemed rather engaged with their fellow comrades, further along on the ground. It was near impossible for the gunships to spot them from the air as they were firing through the canopy of a thorn tree, but I could see them just fine from where I was on the ground. I turned and began firing on them with the MAG. By some luck, considering that it was over 100 metres I nailed one of them. The firing stopped as that particular individual exited the planet, and as the other one went to ground. I persisted in my firing, and successfully nailed the second guy, even though it cost me near on a whole belt to wipe out that 'leopard-crawler'.

"I was new at this, and pretty damn chuffed with myself. So were the kids. Not bad for a beginner – and an old one at that, in comparison. We reached an open area, where we were slightly elevated. What lay of ahead of us was denser bush than that which we'd already encountered.

"My young commander, still glowing for the way I handled a threat in the first few hours of my first day, requested that I not proceed forward with the rest of the team, but instead remain static on that high ground, in order to deliver covering fire, whilst they were sweeping through the enemy positions. Soon, when they were still in open ground, shots were fired from the area that they were sweeping towards. I released three bursts of my own, into likely cover.

"The Troop Officer halted the advance and had his men fire on the area as well. He signalled that I stop, and the rest of the assault proceeded rapidly without further resistance. Upon sweeping through, it was evident that the enemy had 'gapped it'. This combined effort had successfully eliminated the threat on the ground. We regrouped to be uplifted by chopper, and were flown back to Grand Reef Airforce Base, near Umtali.

"On reaching the base, our officer left to debrief the OC (Officer Commanding) on the day's work. The rest of us headed for our living quarters to clean our weapons, reload our magazines, and prepare for the next Fireforce callout.

"The next morning, the 'kids' and I were off to attend to our chores. We passed the OC's office. He addressed me firmly, but with mirth, as he commented on my 100 rounds to eliminate a total tally of two terrorists. I realised that my young commander had conveyed the events of my first day during the debriefing. The kids burst out laughing and slapped me on the back. It was great moment. It was a good day. Those youngsters called me 'Mike' even though I could have fathered some of them; we were pretty informal out there.

"The Fireforce was a 24/7 reaction force. All deployment was immediate. When the alarm sounded, we kitted up, ran with our gear to get 'chutes' fitted, jumped aboard the Dakota and off to war we went. It was the name of the game then and battle-hardened young men were routinely dropped at low altitude from these old Daks. Those chutes could not be steered so we went with the wind and on landing often crashed hard into trees, thorn bushes and rocks.

"On one occasion I jumped out of a Dakota in a Fireforce roll, carrying a MAG machine gun, and had a very hard landing thanks to the wind and snapped the butt off of the machine gun. There was no time to cut from the scene of the action, obtain a new one, and recommence battle. I released the bipods in front of the weapon, used them as a grip, and the other hand was working the machine gun like a pistol, because with no sling, and no butt, I now had a rather large, heavy handgun. Edward Lindsell, a gutsy youngster managed to slot a terrorist carrying a RPD machine gun. They gave me the RPD, I had never seen a weapon like that before but I knew where the safety catch and trigger was and that was enough for me. All I had to do was point it in the right direction and fire.

"They were pouring fire onto us and the cordite smelled strong in the air but we managed to get into a skirmish line and attack them with help from the choppers. Once we initiated fire, dropping plenty of them, the survivors went to ground and fired from hidden positions. However, we were too aggressive, they panicked, ran, and we nailed them.

"You can imagine the mirth and laughter, post winning the battle, before the RPD, because I had a loose sling and broken butt thrown over my shoulder, firing the MAG pistol-style. It must have looked hilarious. You usually see this kind of craziness in comedies and not the battlefield. I haven't heard about anyone else being this unfortunate.

"The one day I remember, we responded to two call-outs on the same day. We were airborne at the crack of dawn, and when the sun went down, we were still shooting the shit out of each other. Twice we had to jump out of a perfectly good airplane. Twice we got the shit shot out of us, shot the shit out of the terrs and killed all or most of them. Two times that we had to be uplifted. Two times that we had to clean up, reload and ready ourselves for the next *tête-à-tête*. Just so that we could do it all again in a few hours, all of tomorrow, next week and so it went on.

"My admiration for those youngsters and leadership is beyond words. I was in awe. They were the bravest of the brave. I have, since then, in my many years of combat experience thereafter, and in South Africa, seen men of greater age and stature, who could not perform in combat situations with these youngsters. These young RLI combatants were gutsy killing machines of note and showed no fear.

"As modern armies go we operated off a shoe-string. Nothing was wasted and everything was accounted for. There was a wonderful blend of discipline and informality in the battalion. They weren't petty, we had our jobs to do and it was just a matter of getting it done. It was in some ways a corporal's war; young leaders having to make life and death decisions on their own without officers calling all the moves.

"The Dakotas that we were in, when ready to jump, were often shot at and would usually be penetrated through the toilet area. This continuous practice meant continuous patching with masking tape.

"Back from the bush, time to take some time off in Salisbury, I was picked by Lt Mike Rich to be a model, of all things. A group of wealthy local businessmen were going to donate to the 'cause' and they needed an operator to impress him. Mike picked me for some reason that is still not clear to me. I felt like a complete prick arriving at the Five-Star Monomotapa Hotel that was full of slick civvies and there I was complete with webbing, parachute, weapon and uniform.

"I was bloody embarrassed but then my spirits soared when Sally Donaldson appeared. She was the 'Forces Favourite', a radio and TV personality who did a weekly radio show passing messages to the 'boys in the bush' from their loved ones at home. She was beautiful, charming and blessed with a silky, sexy voice.

"Then it got more interesting when they decided to make a film documentary and I had to jump out of a Dak for them. Out the aircraft I went with my pal Gary Quinn and he ended up breaking his leg but we managed to get the shoot done with me standing next to him with a big grin on my face. This was shown on National TV and I suddenly became a bit of a Rhodesian movie-star."

'Operation Dingo'
While Mike West was making movies the plan for the biggest attack of the Rhodesian war was a work in progress that had commenced in late 1976. As a result of intelligence gathered from RENAMO[11] operators, captures, aerial photographs and close-in field reconnaissance, along with information gleaned following the Selous Scout raid on Nyadzonya camp on 9th August 1976, the evidence was overwhelming and of great concern. It indicated the rapid growth of two very substantial enemy camps in central Mozambique.

---

11   Resistência Nacional Moçambicana; the Rhodesia-backed anti-Frelimo Resistance Army.

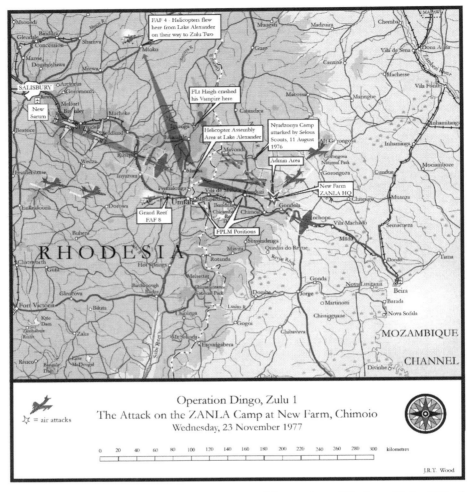

Operation Dingo, Zulu 1
The Attack on the ZANLA Camp at New Farm, Chimoio
Wednesday, 23 November 1977

Map courtesy of Professor Richard Wood

One was at a place known as 'New Farm', an abandoned Portuguese farm 17 kilometres north of Chimoio that constituted ZANLA's[12] main base of operations. Home to thousands of recruits and trained personnel it covered over 20 square kilometres and was a maze of trench lines bristling with dug-in anti-aircraft weapons. It was also an occasional place of work for the party hierarchy; Mugabe, Edgar Tekere and top military commanders, Josiah Tongogara, the military supremo, and his second in command Rex Nhongo. The other was at Tembue which served as Zanla's main base for operations into the northern

---

12   Zanla- Zimbabwe African National Liberation Army.

areas of Rhodesia. Being two hundred kilometres from the border it was a long shot that was going to stretch the Rhodesian offensive capability to the limit.

The experts from the photo-reconnaissance section studied the photos closely and concluded the facilities were large in area and contained thousands of potential combatants. One of the captures let it be known that the bulk of the terrorists were ready and merely awaiting the onset of the rains which would give them the cover to infiltrate Rhodesia. Going by rough estimates of the numbers inside the camps it was clear to the operational men that successful infiltration of the inmates into Rhodesia would be disastrous and, in all likelihood, mean the loss of the war leading to the sacking of the country. They had to be stopped; the problem was how. Adding to the problem was political pressure from South Africa not to escalate the war. South African Prime Minister John Vorster was still convinced he could find a way to use Rhodesia as a bargaining chip in his bid to find a way to release international pressure on his own country. The Rhodesians were between a rock and a hard place but as the numbers in the camps mounted the security threat from the east trumped the political pressure from the south. A year after planning and presentations began the politicians flashed the green light and the soldiers and airmen went to work with intent.

At 'New Farm' intelligence estimated there were between nine and eleven thousand potential combatants in the camp. Also within the facility was a FRELIMO[13] support-group armed with mortars and anti-aircraft weapons. Apart from the Frelimo garrison in nearby Chimoio there was a company of Tanzanian troops and over a hundred Soviet advisers equipped with armour and heavy artillery. At Tembue further north there were estimated another 5,000 of the enemy.

The target was situated on a farm abandoned by a fleeing Portuguese farmer and spanned approximately five square kilometres. Some of the buildings, consisting of the old homestead, offices, sheds and tobacco barns, had been converted into military facilities, turning the camp into what was effectively the administrative centre for Zanla. There were rooms and offices for Robert Mugabe, Josiah Tongogara, Rex Nhongo and the rest of the organisation's top

---

13   Frelimo – from the Portuguese Frente de Libertação de Moçambique, basically 'Liberation Front of Mozambique'.

echelon. The attackers hoped to catch them *in situ* and thereby decapitate the leadership element while also reducing their force levels.

A maze of trenches, revetments and defensive lines had been constructed, anti-aircraft weapons and other heavy weapons were dug in and an early warning system of sentries in towers (complete with whistles) was in place. Tethered baboons were strategically placed and watched by sentries. It was believed that their senses were better tuned and any restive behaviour on their part was to be considered a possible indication of an approaching attack.

Limited resources ruled out the possibility of simultaneous attacks on both targets. The plan produced by Major Brian Robinson (SAS) and Group Captain Norman Walsh (RhAF) called for a hit on the Chimoio base followed immediately by an attack on Tembue.

For the attack on Chimoio alone, virtually every aircraft in the air-force hangars would be required, leaving the country bereft of air cover and support for the duration of the operation. To initiate the assault they knew their only effective means would have to come from the air, so they turned to the Air Force to give them the maximum number of jet aircraft for the pre-emptive strike as well as the transport aircraft and helicopter support to deliver the ground forces. Virtually every soldier in the SAS and the RLI would also be required.

Walsh and Robinson looked forlornly at the odds. They would have to attack a target accommodating 10 000 people with 185 men. On the face of it, it was impossible but if the country were to survive, they had no option. Quite simply, it was a matter of do or die.

To guard against leaks the details of what was about to happen was kept to a select few while troops and airmen from around the country were quietly recalled to their bases and told to prepare for action without any knowledge of what was to be expected of them. When told what equipment and ammunition they were required to draw they knew something big was about to happen.

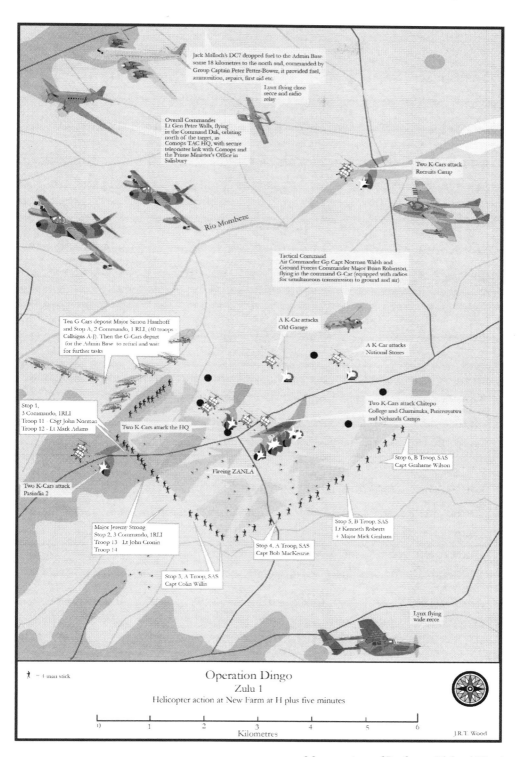

Jack Malloch's DC7 dropped fuel to the Admin Base some 18 kilometres to the north and, commanded by Group Captain Peter Petter-Bower, it provided fuel, ammunition, repairs, first aid etc.

Lynx flying close recce and radio relay

Overall Commander
Lt Gen Peter Walls, flying in the Command Dak, orbiting north of the target, as Comops TAC HQ, with secure teleprinter link with Comops and the Prime Minister's Office in Salisbury

Two K-Cars attack Recruits Camp

Rio Mombeze

Tactical Command
Air Commander Gp Capt Norman Walsh and Ground Forces Commander Major Brian Robinson, flying in the command G-Car (equipped with radios for simultaneous transmission to ground and air)

Ten G-Cars deposit Major Simon Haarhoff and Stop A, 2 Commando, 1 RLI (40 troops Callsigns A–J). Then the G-Cars depart for the Admin Base to refuel and wait for further tasks

A K-Car attacks Old Garage

A K-Car attacks National Stores

Stop 1,
3 Commando, 1RLI
Troop 11 - CSgt John Norman
Troop 12 - Lt Mark Adams

Two K-Cars attack the HQ

Two K-Cars attack Chitepo College and Chaminuka, Parirenyatwa and Nehanda Camps

Stop 6, B Troop, SAS
Capt Grahame Wilson

Two K-Cars attack Pasinda 2

Fleeing ZANLA

Major Jeremy Strong
Stop 2, 3 Commando, 1RLI
Troop 13 - Lt John Cronin
Troop 14

Stop 5, B Troop, SAS
Lt Kenneth Roberts
+ Major Mick Graham

Stop 4, A Troop, SAS
Capt Bob MacKenzie

Stop 3, A Troop, SAS
Capt Colin Willis

Lynx flying wide recce

ǂ = 4 man stick

Operation Dingo
Zulu 1
Helicopter action at New Farm at H plus five minutes

0   1   2   3   4   5   6
Kilometres

J.R.T. Wood

Map courtesy of Professor Richard Wood

Mike West continues the narrative:

"I just remember being told that we were going on a big operation, and we were to take as much ammo as we could carry. Carrying the MAG, I always did anyway so nobody needed to tell me to do it, but I loaded up with ten belts of 50 rounds. The riflemen carried 12 x 20-round magazines and we each had four M962 fragmentation grenades, four white phosphorous grenades, one bunker-bomb, smoke grenades, flares and each stick (of four) was carrying two claymores for ambushes. Prior to the attack we were based at Grand Reef FAF[14] and everyone was strictly confined; no movement in or out was allowed. We trained hard every day and practised our drills. Some guys sorted their wills out because we were warned casualties were going to be high but that didn't worry me too much. I must admit I didn't pay too much attention to the details; I was just pleased we were going off to kill terrs; I didn't really care where they were, how far away they were, or how many, I just wanted to kill them.

"Forty of us from Two Commando RLI were going to be choppered in and dropped at precise points as stop-groups on a ridge to the north of the camp to catch the enemy fleeing the air and ground assault. From Three Commando RLI, 48 guys under the command of Major Jerry Strong would parachute in along with 97 SAS guys. They would leave from New Sarum in Salisbury. We were told there would be women in the camp, but they were likely to be armed and therefore fair game; children were to be spared."

Unbeknown to most of the fighting soldiers, the movement orders preparatory to the raid were exhaustive, with a huge translocation of men and equipment to points around the country. Officers worked on the co-ordination of the administrative and signals side making sure everyone was familiar with the network, their codes, call-signs and radio procedure.

They also worked on the logistics of ensuring every one of the men arrived at his point of attack with all he would need to carry out his task. Because the Alouette helicopters were very sensitive to the weight they could carry a balance that had to be struck between necessity and weight and what a man could reasonably carry bearing in mind he also had to be very mobile if he was

---

14   FAF – Forward Air Field

to fight and survive. Every soldier's payload had to be accounted for down to the last grenade, round of ammunition and food and water. Boots, packs and webbing had to be checked and honed.

Because the helicopters had a limited range, a refuelling and re-supply facility had to be set up in Mozambique to enable the choppers to complete their tasks. This was known as the 'Admin Base' where fuel, ammunition, medics, first-line reserves and other back-up personnel were positioned. It would also serve as a medical half-way-house for the wounded where they would be attended to prior to being ferried home to hospital. Setting up an admin area to refuel and re-supply in enemy territory might have been a first in modern guerrilla warfare. The rear air-base was FAF 8[15] at Grand Reef just west of Umtali where a reserve force of 48 men from Support Commando RLI would be stationed.

Surprise was absolutely vital to the attackers, so the sound of approaching air-craft presented a major challenge. To confuse the defenders, Jack Malloch was tasked to fly his DC8 civilian airliner over the camp as a decoy on the morning of the attack and minutes before the arrival of the raiders. At this time it was expected the defenders were on parade, would see the commercial airliner in the sky and relax. This, it was hoped, would provide the vital moments required to mask the sound of the approaching armada of aircraft.

Hawker Hunters of No. 1 Squadron RhAF would then initiate the attack with bombs, rockets and cannon. They would be followed immediately by the Vampire jets and finally the Canberra bombers which would keep the ene-mies' heads down to cover the paratrooper deployment. Immediately after the Canberra strike the paratroopers would be dropped at the same time as the men from 2 Commando RLI were deployed by helicopter. The vertical envelopment would cover three sides of a 'box' and the fourth would be covered by K-Cars armed with 20mm cannons. Timings for the coordination of the air-strike and the para-drop had to be perfect. If the helicopters were too close to the target the noise would give the game away. If the Canberra strike was too early the 'paras' would be shot to pieces in the air. If the Canberra strike came in too late the 'paras' would land among exploding ordnance.

---

15   There were nine Forward Air Fields: FAF1 (Wankie); FAF2 (Kariba); FAF3 (Centenary); FAF4 (Mount Darwin); FAF5 (Mtoko); FAF6 (Chipinga); FAF7 (Buffalo Range); FAF8 (Grand Reef); and FAF9 (Rutenga).

"The night before the raid most of the guys went to bed early and at 3 o'clock in the morning we loaded up into the trucks and drove north to Lake Alexander[16]," recalled Mike. "Along with us was a mortar troop from Support Commando RLI. Most of the guys were quiet and dealing in their own ways with what lay ahead. Just as dawn was breaking after we arrived, the choppers flew in, and we prepared to board. We did not realise it then, but this was to be the biggest helicopter assault since the Vietnam War.

"On the 23rd November 1977 we attacked. The flight in was a fantastic sight with lines of aircraft. Initially we flew high but as soon as we entered Mozambique the helicopters went down to treetop level. When we flew over Chicamba Dam we knew the target was close. Then we saw the airstrikes going in and as we came over the camp we saw mayhem below us with thousands of people running in all directions. I could smell the cordite and explosives as we jumped out the chopper and dashed for cover. Although early morning it was already hot as hell. There was firing going in all directions and tracers lined the sky. Plenty of it was aimed at the aircraft and I believe virtually all the choppers took hits at some stage of the attack.

"We moved quickly into cover in the bush, were given our arcs of fire and then they were coming at us at speed and at close range. It was a machine-gunner's dream come true; I mowed them down in droves while the riflemen double-tapped their targets; the fire was lethal, and I don't think anyone escaped us. Some changed direction at the last second and went the other way but we either got them or they ran into other stop-groups. Lt. Mike Rich was one of our troop commanders and also involved in the thick of the fighting was his father Colonel Peter Rich.

"When it all quietened down, we started working through all the bodies gathering weapons and equipment. There were corpses everywhere; I don't know how many we killed but there must have been hundreds. Fighting continued all around us as the enemy was flushed from their hiding places and air-strikes were being called in. Most were dead or surrendered but some of the braver ones fought on. One of our call-signs was mistaken for the enemy and almost taken out by a Vampire. We swept through our sector of the camp cleaning out

---

16   Also known as Odzani Dam by the local residents

gullies and thickets. Amazingly, we heard, we had lost only one man in the whole operation: Jannie Nel from the SAS. There was lots of loot to be had but I was unable to get my hands on much of it.

"We spent the night there and some of the call-signs laid ambushes. The firing continued through the dark hours and by morning another 60 Zanla were dead. On our side I remember one of the SAS guys was stung by a scorpion. At the end of it, I think 1,200 enemy were killed and hospitals could not cope with all the wounded. Frelimo, based nearby in the town, with all their armour and big guns, never came near us, nor did the Mozambique Air Force. The world watched while the enemy received an organised and aggressive military assault involving some of the best soldiers and airmen in the world and I was damn proud to be part of that. Now I was a little famous from my short movie career and had experienced the most exciting six months of my life but I wanted more; I was addicted to war and wanted to aim for the top. I applied for the Special Air Service Selection."

CHAPTER 4

THE SAS

"You have never lived until you have nearly died and for those who have had to fight for it, life has a flavour the protected will never know."– Guy de Maupassant.

"To my knowledge, 'C Squadron' was the only member of the worldwide SAS family, at that time, to run their own recruit courses. This was a brilliant idea in our circumstances, because keen young men, free of entrenched bad (military) habits picked up elsewhere, could be moulded any which way the Squadron wanted. I had left a fantastic fighting unit to join an even better one. I thought I was tough, but that selection was pure torture, but I wanted that beret so badly I was ready to go to hell and back for it and I did."

Darrell Watt remembers: "Mike was rough and tough when he came to go on selection and the training and selection staff did not like the look of him, but he caught my eye. There was something I liked about him but coming from where he did, we wanted to know more. We were not too keen on guys with criminal pasts. Rob Johnson was the Training Officer and I asked him to make it as tough as possible and try and break him. I think I was unsure, and I was happy to see him fail and then he wouldn't be on my mind anymore. Brian Murphy, the Rhodesia rugby star was on the same selection, so we let these two loose on one another and it was a serious test of strength with neither getting the better of the other. Rob did as I asked and made life hell for Mike, but he refused to go down. When Rob came and told me he couldn't break him, I said, 'OK thanks for trying, let him in, and I'll take him on."

"It is very hard to describe the feeling when I received my SAS colours," remembered Mike. "I felt I had come a long way from being a thug on the streets of Pretoria and found my niche with men I liked and respected, who liked and respected me. Once the badge goes on, it never comes off, whether they can see it, or not! It fuses the soul through adversity, fear and adrenalin, and no one who has ever worn it with pride, integrity and guts can ever sleep through the 'call of the wild' that wafts through the bedroom windows in the deep of the night!

"In fact, I was a little proud of myself; a welfare case, juvenile delinquent, petty criminal, expelled from school, no academic qualifications, a misfit in society, no military training; and now a proud member of the finest fighting force in the fucking world. I was my own goddamn hero, but then came another blessing; I was destined to have the privilege of serving under the 'War God' himself, the man I came to know and love – Darrell Watt. I was to be led by the most lethal SAS soldier of them all, a tactical genius, bushmaster, fearless and a deadly marksman. He plucked me from the pack, made me a better person, and took me on the ride of my life. I soared to new heights, trying to follow in his footsteps. I was determined to be just like him. I will go to my grave with an unparalleled level of respect for this man. To me, he was God. I salute you, Darrell Watt."

First kill as a 'BlueBelter'

"Unlike some of the other officers I was seldom given the opportunity to choose the men I wanted to operate with," remembers Watt. "I just went with what I was given and most of the time they were good guys but when Mike appeared none of them wanted him. I liked him immediately; big, strong and brave, he made it clear to me the moment we hooked up that he was in a big hurry to be 'blooded' into the SAS by killing someone as soon as possible.

"My first operation with him was to do a recce (reconnaisance) near the village known as Kavalamanja in the Zambezi Valley in eastern Zambia. We went into Zambia from Kanyemba by Klepper canoe. It was late February 1978. We were looking for a big ZIPRA[17] camp there. Chris Schulenburg had been in before us with Martin Chikondo. Chris lived in an ant bear hole, right inside the perimeter for two weeks while watching the camp but ComOps (Combined Operations) had not cleared an attack and we were sent back in to see what was going on.

"I found lots of tracks but most of it was old. Three days later we were lying up in our position when we heard a shot. Mike asked me what was going on and I

---

17   Zimbabwe Peoples Revolutionary Army, the armed wing of ZAPU (Zimbabwe African Peoples Union) led by Joshua Nkomo.

told him that it was almost certainly a Zipra hunting party shooting for the pot. Being a little bored and fully aware we were there to recce and not engage the enemy, I thought this was as good a time as any to help Mike so I asked him if he wanted to go and take these guys out. He was like a dog on a leash when I suggested it so off we went. We left our packs and walked off with webbing, weapons and water only. Soon I found tracks and we started following them. They were on an elephant path cutting through thick bush and had no idea we were behind them so I put Mike in front and said off you go. I told him it was only a matter of time and we'll catch them."

"I was walking ahead with an RPD," remembers Mike. "Then suddenly there they were and I didn't have time to get the gun to my shoulder so I let rip from the hip and cut these guys to pieces. Fortunately the gunfire was far enough from the main enemy base and not heard. I was so excited I thought I was going to have a heart attack; Darrell was calm as always. He always seemed to be in control."

"A day later we moved position again to where I found fresh tracks and we went on to a hill to watch and wait," recalled Watt. "I knew the enemy were close but could not actually pinpoint their location. Then just before the sun went down and the angle of light changed I caught a glint of an AK magazine and there they were on a ridgeline about a kilometre away. That night we went right in to the camp and saw they had vehicles there. I radioed the information back and they decided to react immediately; the next day the attack went in."

"Just before the main attack came in, we were in an extended line approaching the camp when we encountered an early warning post," remembers Mike. "We leopard-crawled forward and one of the terrs was taking a 'dump' on an ant mound. He became suspicious and pulled up his pants and moved towards us, AK at the ready. We remained very still hoping he wouldn't see us and return to his original position as shooting him would alert his pals in the base and they would gap it. But he kept coming and Darrell dropped him with one shot and then we started running into them and there they were right in front of us, and we ripped into them.

"The airstrikes came in and there were shouts and screams and figures running in all directions, some of the enemy were firing blindly over their shoulders as they ran away. We were firing at such a rate it was crazy. Many of those that escaped our assault were cut down by stop groups. After the main attack we were left behind as a stay-behind party with Darrell. Then Darrell took us onto high ground to watch for movement coming out of the smouldering camp. It was common practice for a team to stay behind, after a camp attack, and eliminate any visiting looters or returning terrs. From there we were sent racing down in pairs to wipe groups out as we picked them up.

"Waiting and watching, we noticed two terrs carrying another wounded guy on a stretcher, headed in the direction of the camp. They were about a 100 metres from us. Darrell looked at me and said 'Go and get them'. The God of War had spoken and I went off to do his bidding. Myself and Frank Tunney dashed down, unseen, to eliminate them.

"What made this slightly amusing was that they saw us coming at about 30 metres. We took out the two carrying the stretcher thinking the injured guy was going nowhere. We were dead wrong, it was the fucker on the stretcher that got away. We still can't explain it. Was this man even injured? I think he just wanted the day off, because he disappeared in a flash.

"We stayed roughly seven days until Darrell had decided that the situation was under control, and no one else was returning or attempting to loot. They only returned in small groups, and these men were eliminated. Believe me when I say that some of these walk-ins engaged us aggressively with their AKs. But they didn't last long. Only 'Stretcher Terr' did.

'Many were killed and we picked up a lot of equipment including 14.5mm anti aircraft guns and heat-seeking missiles. In the base we found tents with medical supplies from Switzerland and other European countries which made us realise that our enemies were scattered worldwide. Unfortunately, the camp was very spread out so many of the enemy escaped."

Tembué

"One of the longest-range operations I did was up to northern Mozambique near the Malawi border. August 1978 we went to attack a camp that had been recced by the Selous Scouts. We flew from Salisbury in the dark and the flight seemed to go on forever. The guys were expecting a major punch-up and we were all wondering how the hell we would get back if we survived. We jumped into the camp at first light expecting some heavy fighting, but the enemy were not there in the numbers we expected. We killed some of them, but it was all a bit of a disappointment. Then out of the trees appeared this huge guy with a big beard looking like he had been living in a cave all his life. Darrell was in front and went up to greet him when fuck me, I couldn't believe my eyes, but it was Chris Schulenburg. I had no idea he had been there doing the reconnaissance, but I went straight up to him and he too got a bit of a fright when he saw who I was. The last time we had seen one another was years before in his pub in Pretoria when I was 'bouncing' people out of it. It was a very strange place and way to meet up with an old friend. Darrell was pissed off about the lack of enemy in the camp and he and Chris were trying to figure out what had gone wrong.

"We were then told to stay behind and watch the camp after all the other troops went home. We were issued rations for another seven days and followed Darrell back into the bush and up a hill to hide and wait. By day we watched for movement and by night we ambushed. But we kept moving positions, anti-tracking all the way. We were a very long way from home if we got into shit. For choppers to get to us they would have to make a refuelling stop and that had been abandoned after the attack, so we were pretty much on our own. This was the furthest I had ever been into Mozambique, but it didn't worry me too much because Darrell was running the show.

"We hitched up our kit and he marched us to the top of an inselberg[18] while anti-tracking the whole way. Every night thereafter we would ambush the paths and roads at night and watch them from the mountains by day. Incredibly, the enemy were always behind us and could never catch up because we kept moving and anti-tracking.

"Every night Darrell was on the TR48 radio to Salisbury, but I didn't really have a clue what was happening. Every day we picked up movement, there were terrs around but not in big numbers. Then a big group of Frelimo appeared. They seemed to know we were around but Darrell was always ahead of them. Our problem was food. After two weeks and no resupply we were bloody hungry. Then we heard vehicles in the night and Darrell was back on the radio to Salisbury to tell them what was going on and to let them know our position.

---

18   An isolated hill or mountain rising abruptly from a plain

"Fuck me, but in the morning in came the Hunters and they smacked the vehicle column. Those fuckers could not have known what had hit them but there were vehicles exploding and terrs running and screaming in all directions. We just lay low and listened to our stomachs grumbling about lack of food. Later that afternoon Darrell took us down to survey the carnage. One of the trucks was undamaged, thank God, and when we looked inside the container, I couldn't believe my eyes. It was stuffed with tins of imported food. It was like a gift from God and the boys got stuck in. I then stuffed my pack with tins of fish to keep me going and grabbed some other loot as well to take back home and sell for my kids.

"I thought we would be heading home, but Darrell wasn't finished. We booby-trapped the truck with the food and went off onto high ground to wait and watch. The next day, they must have been hungry because they started to creep out the bush and I saw Darrell smiling. Next thing, in came more vehicles to load food and stuff up. They were obviously very hungry. Then there was the most incredible explosion as our explosives detonated and stuff was flying everywhere. Mayhem again and then all quiet. Down we went again and the first thing I saw was a ribcage high in a tree. There were body-parts hanging everywhere.

"After this I thought we must surely be going home. But not a fuck; the War God was not finished with these fuckers. We started to mine the roads by night and then lie up during the day and wait for the blasts and then we would see smoke spiralling into the air. And there was Mr Watt sitting with a big grin on his face. Darrell would check paths during the day and decide where to ambush in the night.

"We hit them time and again; they must have been going nuts trying to figure out where we were hiding and where we were going to strike next. We stayed there in that wild, enemy infested country for a month and fucked the terrs around every day and every night and not one of us got hurt thanks to the War God.

"I had dumped water for tins of food and loot in my pack and this caught up with me so I ended up trading tins of fish for water with the other blokes. Eventually the choppers came to get us. We were in rags, and we stank. I had all my loot; water pumps and tools to take back and sell in town but the pilot told me it was too heavy. I pleaded with him, telling him it was for my kids, and he said okay so I chucked it all in and off we went. We were so far away from home we had to stop twice on the way to refuel. What a special time it was.

Gaza

"I think being part of a four-man team deployed to the Russian Front[19] was one of the toughest tasks of the war. We were in flat, featureless, sandalwood forests much of the time, sandy soil underfoot making it almost impossible to anti-track and water was almost always a problem. We were carrying a very heavy weight with extra water bottles, plenty of ammo, landmines and mortar bombs. On top of that the Frelimo patrols were mobile, aggressive, they knew the lay of the land, and they operated in strength. From the moment we hit the ground on the jump in, we were on high alert because we knew trouble was coming. But this is how Darrell liked it. If there was not enough trouble, he would go to the other side of the world to find it. The same thing in town when we went out boozing. He would get bored and make sure something exciting happened; a real action man.

"My first foray into the Front was after Chimoio and other targets in Mozambique had been hit hard so the 'Freds'[20] were fucking angry and looking for revenge. President Machel (of Mozambique) badly wanted one of us captured so as to humiliate us in the eyes of the world. We were going to fight to the death rather than be captured.

"The enemy coming into Rhodesia kept changing their entry routes and we were sent in to look for these, so bigger numbers could be deployed to hit them and stop them. Machel had ordered the 'Freds' to join the terrs in infiltrating and fighting in Rhodesia, so the insurgent numbers coming in was on the rise.

"Our team formation was for the RPD machine gunner to walk in the front, followed by Darrell, then the signaller and then the medic. I was the gunner. Each member of the team carried his own emergency medical kit, which held a drip, bandages and Sosegon (pain killers). Darrell had the morphine. Our medics were the best and he carried a well-kitted medical pack.

"Luckily for me Darrell knew the place well and had an uncanny feel for what

---

19   The South Eastern border area between Rhodesia and Mozambique

20   A nickname for the Frelimo solders

was going on around him. I didn't have a fucking clue; all I knew was I was going to fuck up anything that moved my way.

"We only moved very early in the morning and in the evenings because of the intense heat and also to avoid being seen. The best lying up place (LUP) was deep in the thick of the forests where it was cooler, but there was never any time when we could relax because they could hit us anytime. It was a non-stop game of hide and seek. They knew we were there, somewhere, and we knew they were there. We would walk on their tracks and they would walk on ours. But they were wary; the enemy knew we could punch way above our weight and when we used our weapons we normally hit someone. They were inclined to fire recklessly when engaged, whilst we were highly trained in the art of selective shooting; only firing when there was a chance of hitting someone and thereby conserving precious ammo.

"Where Darrell was in a league of this own was his ability to read their minds and anticipate what they were going to do next. On one occasion we were moving through the forest in a south-westerly direction just before dawn using the moon for visibility. To our north the 'Freds' had set up a 61mm mortar platoon to lay down a barrage, while stop-groups lined the thickets to the south to catch us when we tried to run from the mortars. We heard the distant pops as the bombs left the tubes in the distance and then the blasts as they rained down on us. Darrell knew where they would be waiting, and led us away at pace in a northerly direction to a position that we could defend and there we waited for them to find us but they never came. They knew we were ready for them and we were going to kill a lot of them before they killed us.

"Then we walked big distances at night to give them work to do in the morning. As they became more frustrated they brought in more and more troops to find us. I'm sure they had several hundred deployed in the search for the four of us and when Darrell decided there was no point in staying, he called for uplift and the choppers came and collected us.

"On one of the four-man recce patrols I went in with Darrell, John Corken and Rob Slingsby, we almost died of thirst. Before going in we planned on finding water near to where we were going to be dropped by helicopter, but the information turned out to be wrong and the river we walked to during the first two days was dry when we arrived there. It was late in the year, hot as hell and very dry. We kept going and I was pleased to have lip-ice with me to keep my mouth, lips and tongue from cracking. We found a place to rest after last light and Rob and I volunteered to go south to the Nuanetsi River to replenish our supplies while John and Darrell stayed behind.

"Without doubt, the hardest, longest night of my life; we walked virtually non-stop and about midnight made it to the river. My tongue was so swollen it filled my mouth, the lip-ice had turned to a sort of sludge and my vision had become impaired. When I looked up at the moon it was blurred by rings and I could not focus. When we made it to the water Rob and I lay in it for about 30 minutes looking up at the stars, just happy to be alive. It was amazing lying there, looking up at the moon coming back into focus as my body and eyes responded to the intake of water.

"Then the walk back carrying as much as we could, but the bags kept snagging on thorns which ripped through the plastic and we couldn't stop all the leaks, but we made it back with enough water to keep us going. All the way we walked on a compass-bearing from last light to first light, it was a very long trek.

"With enough water we prepared to continue the recce the following day when our plans were upset by a bee which stung John Corken. We had anti-histamine to suppress the reaction but it was not effective and Darrell feared the worst so a casevac (casualty evacuation) had to be called for. A chopper was dispatched immediately and I assumed we would all go home because we were effectively compromised. The chopper landed, John was in a bad way, Darrell spoke to the pilot and the next thing they were airborne and we were still on the ground.

"'We're carrying on,' said Darrell, 'three of us is enough and we still have some 'comrades' to kill.'

"I was reminded why I loved this man; a law unto himself, afraid of nothing. That night he changed direction; he knew they would have seen the chopper and would react but he was thinking ahead of them. I was pretty sure we were going to be tracked so decided to leave them a message. I tore a piece of paper out my notebook and wrote: *'God made the terrorists, he made them in night, he made them in a hurry and forgot to paint them white'*, which I stuck to a tree with a camelthorn.

"I thought that would really piss them off. We moved quickly then switched to due-north and moving to the edge of a wooded area we could see what looked like a riverbed with a reed bank in the middle. Just by looking at Darrell's face and eyes, I knew he had seen something but Rob and I were clueless; we just watched him. Then like a cat stalking its prey he lay down and raised his rifle; he was carrying his FN which he loved. I went down on one side of him and Rob on the other. Only then did I see what he saw – a group of enemy fighters came slowly out of the bush on the other side and started moving towards the riverbed. They were on high alert and moving carefully. As they approached, they bunched together to follow a point where they could cross, and as they did this Darrell double-tapped the guy in front and blew his head away. Instantly I let rip with my RPD and emptied 100 rounds into them. Rob also got stuck in with his AK47. Within 30 seconds there were seven stone-dead terrs. How he knew to find them there in this massive expanse of country I will never know but this was a genius at work. There was little point in staying on and Darrell called for uplift. I was happy to be back home but as usual, when working with Darrell, nobody said well done, thanks, or fuck all!

"But my best times with Darrell were when we were in the 12-man hunter-killer role. Each guy would carry an RPD and as many rounds as could be carried. This was a self-contained set-up with us pretty much doing our own thing without help from anyone else. Darrell would track and direct and we would engage and kill. Every one of our gunners was an expert in the use of his weapon and I don't know where else you would find 12 soldiers who could put down such heavy and effective fire-power as we could.

"The terrs just didn't know what the fuck had hit them when we arrived and the few that survived the original onslaught would run like fuck but we would still go after them, find them, and kill them; the pace was fast and unrelenting and the adrenaline was pumping. We roamed around in an extended line in terr-infested country and Darrell would leave messages with the chiefs to give to the enemy challenging them to come to battle us. He promised them we would only be 12 and no support and they must bring any number they wanted. The local civilians were terrified and word spread to the enemy groups to get out of the area fast because there were some mad white men on the loose.

"He had us aggressively pursue them, in extended line and on their tracks. Contact would break out, and anything in front of us would find out just how mighty was the fire power of 12 SAS Operators, each armed with a RPD machine gun. Very little could stand up to that. We were phenomenal gunners.

"He just seemed to know where the enemy was without actually seeing them and he was a tactical genius. He would look at the landscape and know almost immediately where they were, where they would run to, and how he wanted to attack them. Then the orders would fly fast and we would be told what the plan was. Often he would break us into three smaller groups so we advanced from different directions but the key was he always knew where they were hiding and sure enough we would launch ourselves and there they were. Some ran as far as they could and then swopped their uniforms for civvies and buried their weapons and equipment, but Darrell could smell a terr a mile away and he would nail them.

"Always very gentle and polite with those we captured, he would assure them he was not going to kill them but ask for help in eliminating the rest. Sometimes he let prisoners go telling them to go back to the comrades and tell them he was coming with his men to fuck them up properly. It was bloody funny watching some of these bastards sprint off into the distance in sheer terror."

Mkushi

On Sunday, September 3rd 1978 the Air Rhodesia Viscount *Hunyani* carrying 58 passengers from Kariba to Salisbury crashed after an explosion in one of the starboard engines caused, almost certainly by a shoulder-fired heat-seeking missile. The pilot, Captain John Hood, did the best he could in the course of a crash-landing but a ditch ripped the undercarriage off and the aircraft broke up. Only 18 of the passengers and crew survived. Ten of the survivors were then gunned down in cold blood by a group of terrorists. Rhodesian blood boiled and pressure to go on the attack grew.

On 20 September 'Operation Snoopy' commenced. This attack involved the SAS, RLI and South African Recces and led to an attack on a Zanla base near Chimoio in Mozambique. The target was far bigger than expected and heavy bombing by Canberras and Hunters followed. One Hunter strike went awry resulting in the accidental death of SAS Corporal Steve Donnelly. The enemy countered with tanks and armoured cars, some of which were destroyed. After three days of heavy fighting and the heaviest anti-aircraft fire Rhodesian pilots had ever encountered the Rhodesian and South African invaders left. Four white men who had been abducted previously in Rhodesia and held in the camp were not found having been recently moved but documents relating to them were discovered. These were then forwarded to the International Red Cross and they were subsequently released.

Focus of attention then switched to Zambia. 'Operation Gatling' commenced October 19th, 1978. Three targets were identified; Westlands Farm outside Lusaka was the location of what was named FC Camp and home to approximately 4,000 Zipra combatants. This would be attacked first. The second target was another Zipra camp near the farming town of Mkushi about 120 kilometres north of Lusaka. Because of FC's proximity to Lusaka and a large Zambian Army presence, the plan was to limit the raid on FC to an airborne one and then attack Mkushi with a combined air and ground assault using the SAS. Jumping out of the Daks would be 120 men while 45 would be helicopter-borne. The third target was CGT-2 camp roughly 100 kilometres east of Lusaka and estimated to be accommodating several thousand fighters. This too would be attacked from the air followed by the deployment of airborne RLI Commandos. In preparation, troops readied at New Sarum in Salisbury, Kariba and at a bush-strip in the Mana Pools National Park.

Of concern to the Rhodesian Air Force was the fact that the Zambian Army had taken delivery of British supplied Rapier anti-aircraft missiles plus the possibility of the Zambian Air Force scrambling their MiG-19 interceptors. To counter this, two Hunters were directed to fly straight to Mumbwa Air Base and ensure the MiGs were not able to get airborne while the bombers would approach the target at low level to avoid radar detection and limit the chances of them being hit by heat-seeking projectiles.

The well-planned attack was flawlessly executed, and the enemy taken completely by surprise. Once the bombers had dropped their loads, four K-Cars with 20mm cannons blazing came in to kill survivors. Lusaka was convulsed as combatants and civilians fled the fires raging in the aftermath and sought safety at hospitals in the city. To the surprise of many, locals cheered the sight of truck-borne dead and wounded Zipra fighters. Clearly, the 'Freedom-Fighters' had not endeared themselves to many Zambians who saw them as arrogant and ungrateful.

"We were briefed at Kabrit by Major Barrett two days before the attack on Mkushi," recalled Mike. "All the Squadrons were involved with some going in by chopper and some by Dakota. Because of the distance a staging base was to be set up in Zambia by the RLI and this would be a refuelling station for the choppers. We were going to jump in. He explained how half of us were being split into assault groups and the others into stopgroups. With them on the ground and the choppers watching from the air, the plan was to attack while cutting off all routes to escape. We were told no blackening up or wearing of any uniform other than Rhodesian camo so as to avoid 'friendly-fire' incidents.

"On D-Day Major Barrett and the heliborne troops flew to Mana Pools to refuel while we remained in Salisbury at New Sarum ready to board the Daks. As we were putting on our chutes and preparing to go, the Canberra bombers, led by Green Leader Chris Dixon, who had been bombing the big camp outside Lusaka, landed. The officers were already up in the control-tower listening to the radios while we waited and they told us the bombing had gone well. I was itching to get going. Eventually the order came to go, and off we went, 20 of us in each aircraft and there were seven Daks. But once we reached some altitude there was turbulence and we were thrown around inside the planes. It was also damn hot and some of the guys were sick. We couldn't wait to bail out and get some fresh air. Over the target there was a lot of smoke from the bushfires started by the bombing, and I think the pilots became unsure about the drop-zones. Some of the guys were dropped in the wrong places as a result.

"We were dropped right on top of the camp rather than on the perimeter so I could see them running and shooting below me. I was firing my 9mm pistol at them while I was still in the air as we were being fired at from below and at all angles. I heard a slapping sound, looked up and saw holes in my canopy. I couldn't get down fast enough. I hit the deck and had to move fucking quick to get my weapon ready as it was tied down to my shoulder with paracord, I had two terrs running towards me and I dropped them with my 9mm. They were running everywhere and there was chaos. It was a hell of an attack with plenty of targets but quite hard going because of all the smoke. Charred bodies were spread around from the air-strikes. There were foxholes everywhere that had to be cleared. The camp had been well designed by the Russians, with an underground HQ and weapons store. Above was a large administrative block, huge communal kitchen with tables and chairs, several parade grounds, a clinic and even a library bulging with communist propaganda.

"Serious firefights started almost as we hit the ground and tried to organise our sweep-lines. Much to our surprise most of the people we came up against were women in black uniforms. We landed between the female and male camps and the terrs were running all over the place. The gunners in the helicopters were picking off running targets. Luckily for us, the terr command element seemed to be absent and they did not have a defensive plan. We were heavily outnumbered so it's just as well.

"They were well dug in along the Mkushi River and as we charged forward our Medic Bruce Laing had his jaw shot away. Sweeping towards the defenders, Jeff Collett was hit by a woman with an SKS rifle and went down, blood pouring from a leg wound. His femoral artery had been severed and they couldn't save him. Bob McKenzie's guys came in by chopper and took up a position outside the camp. As we assaulted the camp the enemy fled and ran into Bob's guys who just mowed them down. Darrell was leading another sweep line. The terrs were running over dead bodies and being gunned down. It was complete fucking mayhem.

"I think I saved Colin Willis's life at Mkushi. He stepped around a large broken-off branch while we were moving through the base. I was about five metres behind him due to some broken ground. I spotted movement in a big bush still covered with leaves and approached carefully. I pulled the branch to one side and sure enough a female terr was positioning herself with an SKS aiming towards him. I jerked the weapon out her hands and shot her twice in the head with her own weapon. Colin at least had the decency to say thank you. At one point, what looked like an enemy officer came out of the bush in front of Bruce Fraser. Bruce told her to drop her weapon, or he would shoot. She said, 'Shoot me. I am a Comrade'. So Bruce blew her head off.

"Darrell was running our sweep line keeping us aligned as we moved forward at speed with RPDs blazing," remembers Rodger MacDonald. "In thick bush I saw movement nearby, fired into it and then I reached for a branch and pulled it to the side and there was a woman with an SKS pointing at my head. I slapped it away just as she fired, and it went off in her face as she fell back, and I was able to kill her. I think that gave me such a fright that aggression just kicked in and I launched myself into the ravine rather recklessly, emptying an entire belt into the enemy hiding in there.

"It all went quiet, and I remember Darrell coming over a minute or so later and surveying the carnage. There were about twenty dead and dying sprawled all over the place. He looked at me and said, 'What the fuck's going on here, Rog?' I wasn't sure what to say. I got a big fright that day and will go to my grave not knowing why that woman never pulled the trigger and sent me to meet my maker."

"When the heavy fighting died down," remembers Mike, "we moved north out of the camp to high gound where there was a slow flowing river running through a reed bed and in the distance we saw enemy troops approaching with a white guy with white hair who turned out to be a doctor. We were all smiles because we could see they had not seen us. They must have been coming in to help the wounded. We opened fire on them dropping many of them and the survivors took cover in the riverbed and amongst the reeds.

"I was then part of a section under the command of Colin Willis. We were ordered by Grahame Wilson to approach through the riverline, go around and hit them from the side with a flanking attack. When we suddenly appeared out of the reeds their eyes were popping out their heads; they could not believe what they were seeing. They did not have long to look at us because we slaughtered them. All except for the white doctor who we all wanted to kill more than any of the blacks. He disappeared into the reeds and we chucked grenades in the water where we thought he was hiding, but never found the bastard. One guy I hit with a burst from my RPD from three metres away and blew his head right off his shoulders. John Barry[21], buggering around, picked up a Zambian army helmet and put it on his head but it was full of brains and blood which ran down his face and neck. That wiped the smile off his face and he went head first into the river to wash all the crap off with us laughing like lunatics. I think we had all gone a little mad with all the adrenaline pumping through our bodies that day.

"Later in the day a Zambian Air Force MiG appeared above us, but I think the Hunters chased him away. We killed over 400 of the Zipra force, but a lot escaped because the stop groups had been dropped too far from the main camp. There were plenty of wounded and too many prisoners for us to deal with. One of our officers 'borrowed' an enemy troop carrier and went off to plant landmines on all the incoming roads. When all was quiet, they flew in the international press so that they could see we had not attacked a refugee camp as they kept reporting. But they probably did report it as a refugee camp anyway."

---

21   John's mother Cath was born in Glasgow, Scotland in 1928. An advertisement in a London newspaper caught her eye: 'Teachers needed in Umtali, Rhodesia' it read. She applied, was accepted, and not knowing anyone in Rhodesia, or indeed Africa, sailed for Beira in Mozambique. From there she travelled by train to the border town and commenced work at Umtali Junior School.

His father Bill was born in Swellendam, South Africa in 1933 and was schooled at Bishops in Cape Town. In 1948, Bill's brother Remo toured Rhodesia with the school rugby 1st XV and played one game in Umtali. After contact was made with Fred and Ben Barry, then farming at Odzi, Remo returned and went to work as an assistant to Ben at 'Orasi Farm'. Bill then followed and after working for Ben for a while, became a section manager on Transsau Estates, which was then owned by the Salisbury family.

John was born in Umtali on 16th August 1958 with a deformed foot. In calipers for three years the doctors insisted he would not be able to play sport.

He shrugged this opinion off and was selected for the Umtali Boys High 1st XV aged 15. In the same year he won the JB Clarke trophy for the best tackler. In 1975 and 1976 he was awarded colours and represented Rhodesia Schools as a loose forward in the Craven Week rugby competition. He also excelled as a swimmer and represented the school 1st Teams in water polo and basketball.

Ons leaving school with 3 'M Levels' in English, History and Geography, and one 'A Level' he joined the army early 1977 and quickly became a sergeant. He was posted to 5 Rhodesia Regiment based at Adams Barracks outside Umtali, before doing SAS selection and joining 'C Squadron' in January 1978. When not soldiering he played for the 1977 Rhodesian Under 20 Rugby side that was unbeaten in the regular season and again in 1978.

A talented painter, he worked quietly at this under the tutelage of Jock Forsyth who had taught him at school.

CHAPTER 5

Battling On

Colin Willis

"We were deployed in Mozambique, under the command of Colin Willis," remembers Mike. "Two of my best friends, Nick Barber (KIA 7th February 1979) and Barry Bricknell, were on the team. I think the gutsiest bastards out there were in our unit and these men added shine to that diamond.

"On this particular day, we had had a 'punch up' with the enemy, the firing was heavy but most of them turned and fled. Colin had us formed in extended line, with 45° angles of fire to ensure maximum coverage of the killing field while we pursued the trail of these people. I was on the extreme right flank, armed with my RPD when I suddenly had a clear view of a terr running that the other guys had not picked up and I immediately fired a burst in his direction. He was approximately 100 metres away, and the arrogant bastard wasn't even in camouflage. I could spot his white hat and faded shirt from that distance. Colin, unaware of the target, shouted 'Cease Fire!' I pointed and shouted 'Terr!'

"Nothing came of this, as no one had seen him, and so we continued our advance. We'd covered approximately another 50 metres of ground, when we encountered their sudden, sporadic, and fucking unfriendly fire and we could still not see anything through this vegetation.

"We were skilled at what we called 'The Deliberate Shoot', which is firing into likely enemy cover. Basically, we learned to guess where people, who really wanted to kill us, were hiding. We had to know our shit, because it was always tough to figure out where the bastards were hiding. Don't believe the bullshit you see in movies; this is not just something anyone can do. This is an 8th sense, so to speak, that is awoken in you by the SAS, through ardent, deliberate training and combat.

"Barry (who was directly to my left), was weaving through the vegetation when he spotted the bipods of an RPD behind the trunk of a tree. This gun was firing towards the centre of our extended line on my left flank.

"Barry yelled, 'RPD!' and pointed to the tree. I immediately identified the target, raised my weapon to my shoulder, and walked directly towards that tree, pumping short bursts at the hidden terr. His firing stopped.

"As I reached that tree, I saw that I'd not only hit the magazine drum of his RPD, but that his head (what was left of it) was distorted from the number of my rounds that had penetrated it. But then the shock. This was the first albino I had encountered in my brief time of fighting in the bush. This being my first, and last of his kind, it really stayed with me. When you spend this much time having to kill what's coming at you, you learn to appreciate the little things.

"Whilst all of this was underway, Colin kept our line in full motion, without faltering. We never took cover because if you lose momentum, you can lose the battle. We closed down on their position. Some jumped up and tried to 'gap it', but they were cut down by fire. Shortly after, 17 bodies (none of our own) were scattered in what seemed like their own broken, extended line. Sure as fuck, Mr 'White Hat' had been nailed, too. He lay sprawled, and very dead, between his comrades. Not once did we falter. Not once did we fall.

"There are few words in the English language that can effectively communicate the impressive way that Colin Willis led such a professional, effective and aggressive assault against a threat that could have caused us massive casualties. Simply put: Even with the bloody confusing bush working against us, we overran them."

My Best Friend Dies

"Provision was made within the Rhodesian Army for serving soldiers to receive incentives for fighting on during their leave periods but with the understanding they would be acting outside the formal logistical and support structures, so while they were quietly encouraged, they were also warned they could not expect any assistance if plans went awry. Being married, with children to support, I was always looking for some way to make more money. Another reason is that I was always on the hunt for loot whenever we attacked camps and other targets where there was stuff of value. I was also permanently greedy for action; somehow, I just couldn't get enough of it.

"Early December 1978, it was Mark from the SAS who came and told me that people from the Rhodesia Tobacco Association (RTA) had asked him if he knew of any SAS Operators who would be interested in hunting down resident terrs in the Mount Darwin area who were giving the farmers there a very hard time. They had got it down to an art, living as civilians during the day, then becoming terrorists at night and hitting the farmers and their labour. The potential for quick money was not something to which I could say no; $1000 a terr was a damn fortune then. I went to the offices of the RTA to get a full briefing on the situation and the deal was explained. I then spoke to my best chum, John Barry.

"At this stage John was out of the army and awaiting the start of university in the new year. He was godfather to my daughter and we had seen a lot of action together. He was playing good rugby then and on the verge of selection for the Rhodesian team as a flanker. A handsome bloke, blonde, blue-eyes and a brainy bastard to boot; the girls loved him. He was all action and not much talk. He came from a family that ranched in Manicaland; his father actually worked for the Marquess of Salisbury as the Cecil family owned a large cattle spread in the Eastern Districts.

"John was keen; he also wanted more action and the money was too tempting. Christmas was coming up and we needed money to buy presents, He understood the risks; we were going into terr-infested territory with very little in the way of weapons and equipment in the full knowledge that if we got into trouble, we were on our own. With Mark and John, we also found a fourth chap who came from an infantry battalion. None of us knew him but he was the only bloke we could find in the short space of time we had.

"I was living at Rosshire Heights in Salisbury at the time. On the day we left, John came around to the apartment to say good bye to my family and his god-daughter Michelle. It was a happy farewell, almost as if we were off on a fishing trip. Everyone was happy and smiling when we waved them goodbye and got on the road.

"The RTA people organised our transport out into the operational area and on arrival, we first checked into the local JOC (Joint Operation Command) in

Mount Darwin to get a briefing on what was going on in the area. They were quite amused at the sight of the four of us getting ready to go out, and hunt the enemy where some of the most experienced territorial soldiers had already tried and struggled.

"We soon learned the place was crawling with the damn terrs so we knew we were going to find them, but also knew there weren't many of us when the shit did hit the fan. At this time the country just did not have enough troops to cover all the trouble spots in the country and we gathered the enemy were talking about the area being a 'liberated zone'.

"After finishing at the JOC we were taken to a farm for the night to stay with Dennis Watson and his wife Jackie who farmed near the Kandeya TTL where all the trouble was coming from. They had been attacked twice and ambushed once. Those people were the unsung heroes of the Rhodesian war and I was so happy to be there to help them. They were very kind and hospitable and couldn't do enough for us. We ate and drank like kings and with a few beers under our belts John and I did some sparring on the verandah. At the time John was keen to get me into a fight with Raymond Mordt, then in the RLI, but playing wing for the Rhodesian rugby team (He subsequently played 18 tests as wing for the Springbok rugby team from 1980 until 1984). Raymond had never lost a fight and neither had I, so there was a lot of interest in us having a punch-up. The venue was to be the Prospectors Bar at the Monomotapa Hotel. The fight never happened… after all we had bigger battles to fight.

"We decided before going out there was no need for anyone of us to take command, the three of us from the SAS knew each other well, we had worked together on difficult operations and we felt we would manage as a team; the fourth guy would just have to tag along. We just wanted to get into action and make a lot of money. I had not been able to get an RPD so I took an MAG and the others had FNs plus we had some claymores for ambushing.

"Our deployment was delayed and we ended up spending a second night with the Watsons. On the second morning we left the farm early and headed on foot for the Mavuradonha Mountains where we had decided to set up our Observation Post (OP) on high ground and see what activity we could pick up. We had been told the terrs were getting food out of the PVs (Keeps or Protected Villages) which were guarded by Internal Affairs personnel but some of these people were believed to be colluding with the enemy. From our position, we had sight of one of the Keeps.

"We spent two days on that OP, keeping a very low profile while I made sure we all followed the correct procedures. Mid-morning on the third day I had my binos focused on the guard at the gate of the Keep. I watched closely as he opened the gate to allow a young male to leave carrying what looked like food wrapped in some sort of cover. The guard gave the guy a very fond farewell which made me suspicious. I then watched this guy for as long as I could until he disappeared into a forest in a small valley in the foothills of the mountains. I reported to the other guys and told them I was sure I knew where the terr camp was and suggested we go and investigate. It was decided Mark and I would go and check it out, leaving John and the other guy on the OP.

"We left mid-afternoon for a long walk down the mountain side through some rugged country over rocky ground. As soon as the terrain levelled out we came upon a rocky open area, the ground underfoot softened, the light faded, and and the air cooled as we walked carefully into it. Then suddenly the foliage opened up and there before us we could see their hiding places; all the sleeping positions, beautifully clean, nestled in amongst the rocks and trees but no movement and total silence. By the fesh spoor we could see they had been there recently and no doubt they would soon be back. Going to the perimeter I saw it was bordered by a stream and noticed a likely entry-point through some bush near the water. I decided this was a perfect position to place the three claymores we were carrying. We quickly unrolled the trip-wires across likely tracks and set the mines before moving back towards our OP at some speed.

"On the way back I questioned my judgement; would it not have been better to keep the mines with us and return with the other two to ambush and attack in the morning when we might take them by surprise? I did not have to second-guess myself for long because as we started to climb the mountain up to our position we heard the blasts of the mines being detonated; the terrs were back already and some were going to be full of shrapnel but we had lost the element of surprise.

"Knowing we had to react fast if we were going to get the kills we wanted, I got on the 'small means' (A63 radio) and told the other two guys in the LUP to hurry down to where we were so we could go back and hit them with all the firepower we had. By the time they arrived it was getting dark and it had started raining making the approach over rocky ground very difficult.

"Just outside the camp perimeter the first movement I saw, about 80m from me, were two terrs in raincoats carrying one of their wounded on a stretcher heading downhill and away from the camp. With that, heavy firing started and we opened up with everything we had towards where the firing was coming from.

"Then, all of a sudden, above the deafening gunfire I heard John screaming 'I'm hit ... I'm hit'! I ran towards the call for help while firing my MAG and there was John lying soaked in blood having been shot right through his torso from one side to the other. I could not drag him over the rocky ground and with fire pouring in so I knelt behind him, firing over his body to protect him and returned fire at likely targets. By this time the rain was pelting down and I could see no decent cover to drag him into. Making matters worse, John was our medic and he had left the medical pack behind on the LUP so all I had was my bandages and Sosegon around my neck for the pain. No drips! Still protecting him, I tried to stop the flow of blood with the bomb-bandages, but the blood kept pumping out. I injected two vials of Sosegons, his and mine, but he kept screaming with pain and this noise could draw more intense fire. He begged me to knock him out. It broke me to do it, but I had to punch him three times before he became more subdued but still making too much noise so I stuffed his mouth with a face-veil because I couldn't hit my friend anymore. This is where I realised that this mission had gone totally wrong, there was my friend, badly wounded and dying with blood pouring out of him, no help; no support; terrs all over and soaking wet. I reminded myself we were there for the money and look at the mess we were in; I just wanted to save my friend but I knew his life was disappearing in the little rivers of blood running through the grass where he lay and there was nothing else I could do.

"I stayed by him the whole night, holding him, talking to him. I remember the smell of his warm blood on my hands as the rain pelted down. The other two had taken cover amongst the rocks while I tried to keep his spirits up by telling him a chopper was coming when it wasn't. Nothing is more important in that moment, to a soldier leaving this world, than to know he has hope – even if you have to lie. For some reason he was more worried about his hand which had a bullet through it, now wrapped in a make shift tourniquet; he believed me when I assured him he was going to be fine and soon he would be happy at university.

"December 18th 1978, my daughter was turning four. My youngest son was only nine months old. It was so wet. So cold. As the life of my friend left his body, I still sat vigil over him. No help. No way out of this. As first light broke, the longest night of my life had finally ended. I looked at my dead friend, and cried.

"Mark left to climb a hill to find a radio signal and send in a SitRep to the JOC at Centenary. They told us to get an LZ (Landing Zone) ready and mark it with smoke once the chopper was in the vicinity. We had to mow trees down with the MAG in order to make enough space for a chopper to land. Quite a while later, we heard the chopper. Marked the area with white phosphorous and the chopper landed. They threw a body-bag out for us, for my dead friend. There was still so much blood. When the body bag tipped, whilst loading it on the chopper, I was at the back end. The blood flooded out of the bag, and over me. I pushed it away.

"You won't fucking believe how I was condemned for this later on. No – I was not repulsed by this. I was already soaked in his blood. I walked down to the stream and washed off most of the coagulated blood on my webbing and clothing. All that was left of him. Do you have any fucking idea what that does to a person?

"We were ordered to get out and report back to JOC. We walked back and told them what had happened before being taken back to Salisbury. We had to give a statement of what had transpired on the ground. This was sent through to the SAS. I took all the responsibility for what happened; I had broad shoulders, and I was smarting from the loss of my friend.

"Back at barracks, I was 'doubled' (fast marched) into a room by the RSM and there before me was just about the entire SAS officers corps waiting for me. This makeshift jury hit me from all angles. I was ripped apart. These were not 'Jamstealers'; these were combat-experienced officers. They were troubled by me hitting my friend, to knock him out, and accused me of hiding behind his body instead of understanding that I was literally fighting over him, still trying to save him. I took a lot of abuse, but then they did allow me a chance to tell them my story and to their credit they listened. Then they told me to fuck off and wait outside. The RSM told me to 'double' but I refused and marched out at normal pace. I believed that this was the end of my military career anyway; I was about to be kicked out the SAS family I had grown to love being part of, so they could all get fucked. Unfortunately, there was no denying that I had conducted an illegal operation, and not only lost a dear friend, but a fully qualified SAS Operator.

"I was only a Trooper then but I had a lot of experience. I was then recalled for a hearing before the team of senior officers who had listened to the facts, asked a few more questions and then found me not guilty. This came as a relief, and I then had a chance to sit amongst my fighting friends. I went over the story with them. They were sympathetic. They all could relate to what I had just been through.

"Regardless of the lawlessness, I had still executed our illegal mission with precision, and my decisions made on the ground were considered reasonable. I was promoted shortly afterwards to lance corporal. Not long after that I was sent on a course and was made a sergeant. From then on doors opened for me and I had a war-happy-filled life.

"I did not run away. I did not leave a man behind. I did not leave my friend behind. The loss and suffering Madeth the Man. We never found out how many we killed and we never got paid.

"Still to this day, I think of this; my best friend; a very brave operator, the bravest bastard I ever met, who loved life and loved to laugh. I now know we made the wrong decision by laying the claymores. It would have been better if we had attacked them in the early hours of the morning. Would he still be alive if we had simply gone back, reported the position, got our group of four together, and attacked them in the morning? I will never know.

Matibi Fighting Patrol

"In April 1979 I went with Darrell into the Matibi Tribal Trust Land in the south-east of the country. We were told that Zanla had basically 'liberated' the area' and were effectively in control of it with full support from the local people.

Twelve of us flew to Buffalo Range to commence the deployment.

"We were a fit bunch, and as fighting soldiers I think we were all on top of our games. We were looking forward to a good scrap. All of us had learned from Darrell but when it came to tracking and bushcraft we were not in the same league. We all had RPDs and carried lots of ammo. Graham van Zuydam was our signaller carrying the TR48, so he was probably carrying the most weight.

"Most of the time we operated without air-cover but with the bigger groups Darrell called for air-support and a Lynx came, normally with Kevin 'Cocky' Benecke flying, and he and Darrell had an amazing working relationship. Cocky was already a legend for being able to find and follow tracks from the air, so when he and Darrell got together, they made a formidable combination. We were moving so quickly through the area other troops were withdrawn to avoid friendly-fire incidents.

"On one occasion Darrell positioned Graham with the radio on top of a small hill so we would have comms then went back down the hill and we flushed a group who then let rip with mortars on the hill-top because they thought that was where we were positioned but again, they were mistaken and we hit them from an unexpected angle; they ran like hell with us in hot pursuit. We went to another OP position on a hill and Darrell saw they were butchering a cow in the distance. He knew they would be feeding the enemy so we raced off, grabbed the butcher and let him know he better show us where they were, or he would go the same way as the cow. He quickly agreed and off we went around a small hill where we took them completely by surprise and mowed them down with the RPDs. Our only problem was we were running out of ammo so in came a re-supply and off we went again.

"We were in gunfights virtually every day. Some of the guys took a little strain because it was non-stop walk-fight-walk-fight and Darrell never tired; he just kept going. Numbers were no worry to him; one time we ran down well over a hundred heavily armed terrs who did not know what had hit them despite the fact they outnumbered us by at least ten to 1. Darrell was a master of the art of anti-tracking, so he knew how to shake them off and confuse them. Then when he wanted to take them on, he would pick the spot that suited us and then lure them in. There were times when we watched them cross-graining as they searched for our spoor on hard ground; we could see they were angry, and we just kept hitting them from all angles and they were thrown into a state of complete confusions. They called in reinforcements from Mozambique, some of whom were actually Frelimo, but we were on their tracks almost as soon as they crossed the border, and we nailed them. If Darrell found spoor, we were never in any doubt we were in for a punch-up.

"From being a 'liberated area' suddenly the 'Comrades' were on the run and the locals completely changed their attitude when they saw we were on top of them. Darrell was going into the villages asking the Headmen to tell the 'comrades' to come and take us on, but they were running scared. The locals then started asking to be taken into the protected villages because they feared retaliation from their so-called 'Liberators'.

"We would hit them and then track them and hit them again and again no matter how far they ran; we were stronger and fitter than they were. Some escaped and some were wounded but we stayed on their spoor and hammered them again. We could see them running ahead of us, shouting for help and telling their comrades to get the fuck out of the area. There was panic and we just kept hitting them again and again. All the time the Air Force was on standby and reacted quickly to our calls, so they picked off a lot of terrs running in all directions.

"In one engagement we had over a hundred moving fast in front of us. The Fireforce came in and hit them on the run. We were so close to them one of our blokes was hit by shrapnel from the K Car in the ensuing battle. On another occasion it was midday and hot and I knew we were close to a group. Darrell spotted women carrying food and water and knew it was for the enemy, so we grabbed them and ordered them to tell us exactly where the enemy was. The women were terrified. They said they were right here and pointed over a rise nearby. We dropped our packs and attacked immediately. We hit them at almost point-blank range. They just ran. We shot them down, but some escaped so we followed them again until we caught them again and shot them.

"The bad time was when Rob Slingsby was killed. There were only six of us chasing about 70 of them. There was blood on the tracks, so we had most likely already tangled with these guys. Darrell stopped momentarily on the spoor and one of the guys saw the terrs in the grass ahead and opened up on them. Darrell ran straight at them charging forward into heavy fire and some of them ran up a hill to get the high ground. He called for air-support and then ordered us around the hill, but Rob just carried on charging up the hill after them and they were waiting for him. He took a round in the head and was dead on his feet. I know that Rob died in a team that he loved and respected, not that anyone wants to die, but dying in your team made a difference."

"The one day we were told on the radio that the Keep (protected village) in the area had been attacked. I think the enemy were trying to show the locals that they were still in control. Soon we were there and on fresh tracks. The terrs were moving quickly but not fast enough. We saw a village coming up and Darrell ordered us to circle around it while more troops were brought in to do a sweep through the hut complex. We moved quickly, anti-tracking all the way to get into position without any of the *mujibas*[22] picking up our tracks. Once we were in position Darrell called the Fireforce. The commander asked if we had the group visual and Darrell said no but come quickly, they're here. The pilots knew Darrell was never wrong and soon they were airborne. Right on target RLI paras jumped and landed on the other side of the huts. The terrs shat themselves and ran straight into us. We stood in a solid line and mowed them down and the ones that broke to the flanks got nailed by the RLI stop-groups. They were completely and utterly fucked. I think between the RLI and us we nailed all of them; nearly 50 hard-core terrs who had been strutting around the area like they owned it; bad luck for them that Darrell Watt was sent to teach them a lesson. We were in the area for about 12 absolutely action-packed days and some of the best days of my life; I had come to Rhodesia looking for war and I had come to the right place. By the end of our deployment, if there were any Zanla left in the area, they were keeping very quiet.

When we got back after a job well done, I think Darrell asked for a medal for Rob Slingsby but that was turned down. It didn't seem to matter what Darrell and his guys did, no recognitions would be coming our way."

---

22   Young non-combatant teenagers being used as the 'eyes and ears' of the terrorist gangs throughout the country

Bounty Hunting with Darrell

"After we returned from the Lowveld, Darrell assembled another team for another bounty hunt, in the Marymount area. He had got permission from Grahame Wilson and Garth Barrett. He went to speak to Andy Samuels, the Selous Scout Intelligence Officer to find out where in the country were the most terrs and was told to head for the area near Mukumbura in the north-east of the country.

"We were approximately ten this time and knew if we got into trouble we were pretty much on our own. And off we went; we were adrenaline junkies but there was also the chance of making some good money while we were on leave and I had a family to support.

"Darrell somehow got the chopper pilots to give us a ride in from Mount Darwin although they weren't supposed to. When we got into the area, we found a place to lie up during the day then walked hard through the night. When the sun came up, we were looking down on terr infested country and we could see what looked like a training area. We were lying low on this hilltop when a *mujiba* with cattle walked onto us and we had no option but to grab him. Now we knew it was just a matter of time when there would be a reaction to his non-return. Darrell told us to get ready for the fight of our lives and he was not wrong.

"They opened up on us with mortars, machine guns and rockets and we hunkered down in the rocks and crevices while holding our fire. Then the barrage went quiet, and the ground assault started with lines of terrs coming at us at speed, shouting and screaming. Darrell told us to hold fire until they were on us and that's what we did. At close range, I don't think they knew what had hit them, but our fire was accurate and intense, and they ran into hell. It was chaos as they lost their formations and bomb-shelled in all directions. Some jumping off rocks were hit in the air. There was lots of screaming as they gave up the attack and ran away. A few of us launched a downhill assault, I had my RPD on a sling over my shoulder, firing with one hand at the terrs while talking to the chopper which Darrell had summoned from Mount Darwin, on my A63 radio. The pilot was Terry McCormick and he did us a huge favour by coming to our aid because he was not, strictly speaking, authorised to do this.

"Maybe they thought a Fireforce was coming because after the chopper came they gapped it. The pilot who had full view of the combat scene later remarked that I looked like Audie Murphy, running down the hill firing a RPD with one hand and talking on the handset with the other. Soon after dark Darrell said we were moving out and we made it to a road where we were collected by police vehicles. Darrell warned us to be ready for an ambush and he was right.

"We had not gone far when we were hit by rockets and machine-guns. That ambush they caught us in was of epic proportions. The driver and a BSAP intelligence officer by the name of Hein were both killed in the ambush. Hein was sitting at the rear end of the vehicle, known as a 'Crocodile'. They had a Goryunov heavy machine gun lined up on us and shot the shit out of us. A real lucky escape. Darrell was behind in another vehicle and had us in full view. Thank God, because he saved us when he jumped to the ground and let fly with a 60mm mortar. They did not like the sound of that and took off. The dead driver was a mess: eyes blown out and both arms severed from taking a direct hit from a rocket. I had a guardian angel with me that day. I was sitting with my right shoulder against the driver's cab, the rocket entered the cab roughly half a meter from my head and the impact blew me and my RPD to the floor of the truck and perforated my eardrums. I got up off the floor firing my RPD into the ambush area. From the ambushed vehicle we moved towards Darrell's position. I was so bomb-shocked and dazed from the attack and complete hearing loss from the blown out eardrums that I nearly lost my head walking in front of the mortar tube which Darrell was firing. Luckily one of the operators shoved me out of the way. All I can remember is the smell of cordite, soldiers around me, my weapon in my hand and my feet feeling as heavy as lead.

"When the firefight ended, we regrouped and were taken back to a base near Marymount Mission. Only there and then I discovered that my RPD which I was holding in my hand, was pitted from shrapnel from the RPG7 that hit the cab which killed the driver. It immediately brought back memories of earlier years with Grey's Scouts when I was blown up by a landmine that totally destroyed my weapon. I can only believe that I had divine protection.

"At the same time, we also found out that the terrs had raided the mission and abducted all the nuns and staff and taken them across the border into Mozambique.

"When we arrived back in Salisbury, we were not popular; Darrell was hauled in by the CO, Garth Barrett, and shat on. Again, Mike West had not listened. And there I was, once more the cunt in question.

"I was actually literally told: 'You are such a cunt. Don't you ever listen?'"

'Operation Uric'

"We were told there was a massive build-up of enemy troops in the town of Mapai in Mozambique and with the rate of infiltration into Rhodesia rising the Top Brass had decided to launch a big attack aimed at killing as many of the enemy as possible while also blowing bridges and dams to try and force the Mozambique government to stop supporting the enemy.

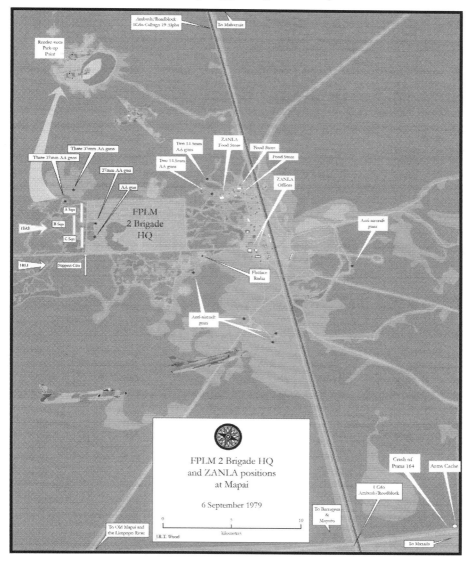

Map courtesy of Professor Richard Wood

77

"As far as I was concerned, I wasn't listening too closely to the details; we were getting the shit shot out of us every day anyway, so it was just going to be another day at the office and the more terrs to kill the merrier. Remember, I would be going in with the God of War, he did what dads are supposed to do with their sons; make them feel invincible. I knew there was always a way to win with this martial 'MacGyver'. They could bring the whole Russian army and we would fuck them up too. Also along for the punch-up was Henri Lepetit who had come from France to join the SAS. He too was scared of fuck-all.

"But hell I did get quite a shock when we landed smack in the middle of the shit show. The airforce Canberras and Hunters were bombing the crap out of the place but there was well-positioned heavy machine-gun nests, mortars and 122mm rockets raining very effective fire down on us. The bad news for us was that they were expecting to be attacked and they had prepared well for it. It's not like you have the time to look over to your neighbour and think about what we're going to do next; there's no checking in, just know you are with the best and fight for the rest; no margin for error in a crisis like this; raw professionalism and superior leadership are the factors that save lives and slot enemies.

"I know I sing his praises, and repeatedly so, throughout my retelling of events, but I will continue to do so because the calm confidence that Darrell brought to us men facing near certain death is impossible to describe, but he had a magical aura about him that almost enveloped us, he was in a league of his own.

"Deep into the trenches we went, sand blasting into our faces from rounds ripping it up, but Darrell kept us moving. Enemy heads kept popping up and it seemed the trench-lines would never end. Rick Norrad, the American Hillbilly, was on my immediate right. He had fought in Vietnam and received a Purple Heart after being wounded in action. We were both carrying RPDs. Then the sounds of firing to my right stopped sounding like a machine gun; it had slowed down to single shots and this got my attention. There was Rick, RPD slung over his shoulder having been rendered useless by a round that hit the breech-block, strolling nonchalantly forward taking aimed shots with .45 revolver. He didn't give a fuck, I was in awe.

"Then the firing stopped abruptly; anything could have happened to stop it, but I think they received an order to withdraw. All we cared about was that it bought us some time; we raced from the trench and dived into a shallow dip with a slight rise in front but then the booming of the big guns started again and back into the trenches we jumped. We too laid down heavy accurate fire; when quiet again we ran forward but we knew progress was too slow and this was a fight without end it seemed. Then Darrell called me over; he had instructions to carry out an emergency procedure, I did not understand the details and could barely hear him but I simply followed him; as I would have done into Hades.

"In no time we were running towards the outer perimeter of the camp; nice moving targets for terrs to take pot shots at and they let us have it. Short and stocky though Darrell may have been, I had to pump my much longer legs to keep up. The rounds certainly motivated us both.

"Darrell stopped abruptly, dropped his FN by me, and scaled up the tree like a monkey pursued. He had to place a remote radio-device in the tree that sent out a signal in order to bring in the bombers, to hone the strike. Please keep in mind that we were still under serious fire, and I was angled behind the tree, firing back. Two terrs easily spotted Darrell in the tree, waiting patiently for the radio-device to light up showing it had connected with the incoming aircraft. They were so busy trying to shoot him out the tree they forgot about me and I let them have it with my RPD using the base of the tree for support. I silenced both of them. I'm happy to tell you I was just typical; SAS gunners, armed with RPD machine guns were deadly up to 200 metres and these two were not that far away when I fired from my shoulder, like a rifle.

"We were trained to be accurate because our numbers were always few and sometimes ammo was scarce; every round had to count. Bullets kept whistling through the branches when Darrell connected the device, secured it and came scaling down the trunk. Then we ran like hell again.

"Reflecting on it all, later, I realised that had Darrell been hit, I would not have left him and we both would have died. Had I been hit, Darrell would not have left me, and we both would have died. Thank flying shrapnel we both made it.

"To this day, I cannot recall my feet touching the ground. That's how we were moving. Heavily laden with RPD belts, grinding heat, soft sand underfoot slowing us down, bullets cracking close to our heads; trying to keep up with Darrell, there's no dramatic movie moment where you stop to tell the other to go on without you. Who has that kind of fucking time? You run; quite simply for your life. While I was running I felt a thud on my backpack. Afterwards I saw that one of the straps was shredded; it may have been a bullet but I was not in the mood for finding out.

"This, dear reader, is precisely why the Rhodesian SAS Selection was equal to none; so goddamn tough. This is exactly why so few earned that beret. The physical torture and resultant strength of spirit evoked prepared you for this. We were mentally and physically aligned to survive.

We were uplifted by chopper, and as if we had not just survived enough shit… a round went through the chopper and hit the pilot's helmet, knocking him unconscious. Luckily the co-pilot was able to pull us out of a death-dive – but along came the second round and another strike sending us plummeting to the earth. I was backseat driver in that chopper, and I was aware of the first burst, not the second, but I knew we were tickets. I could feel the imminent fuck up. Bless him, the co-pilot somehow managed to keep control, steady the chopper and land amidst heavy bombing which shook the earth and blasted our senses. Taking stock of the fact I was still alive, the first thing I did, post bailing out the chopper, was take my first piss in many, many hours. And it was bliss – pumping with adrenaline the whole time. Stone deaf. Relieved to be alive. We were told to withdraw to a point for uplift.

"And still: I had no idea, that whole time, that we were losing. Never in a million years would I have believed that Darrell Watt would retreat. He had never before withdrawn, and it must have been a gut-wrenching blow to him. We were ordered to do so. Had we received orders to go back in, we all would have. Regardless of what we had just survived. Darrell wanted to go back in, but was ordered to stand down. Such was the discipline. Such was the trust.

"All having survived, we were totally drenched. 'Black is Beautiful'[23] rinsed off with the streaming sweat. It had been hot in more than one way with both heavy fire and excessive humidity. Cats are purported to have nine lives. Considering my survival rate, I would say that the SAS Operator has a few more.

"Bullshitting afterwards, one of the officers made a rather derisory remark about Rick Norrad's incredible bravado. 'Did you see that cunt, walking in the skirmish line, firing with a .45, thinking he's Audie Murphy.'

---

23   Black cream applied to darken the soldier's white skins.

Sir, that took fucking balls," I said angrily.

"Rick was no oil painting, he wore true-to-life coke-bottle glasses. I recall him losing them when we were hastily deployed by Alouette, amidst a firefight. He didn't drop to find his glasses, blind as he was without them – he instead stood his ground, without taking cover, growling out noises I could not translate, and laid down a fucking incredible rate of fire to where he could hear the fire coming from. I have never seen anything like this in my entire life. We sorted out the terrs, and thankfully nothing happened to Rick. I think Chuck Norris used him as inspiration for his war scenes.

"His lack of etiquette at a dining room table would even upset an Italian. Rick would push the chair back, stand up, fart and burp, growl and then depart. Most uncouth. Jaws lay on the floor, every time. As long as I live, I will never forget Rick Norrad, the Tennessee Hillbilly.

"Unparalled heroics were on display that day. Not a jot of recognition, especially for Mr Watt who should by now have been commanding his own battalion. Another day at the office. Such is the life of an SAS Operator."

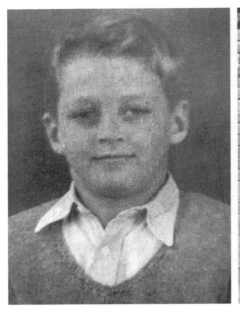 

Mike at five years of age   *In the South African Prison Service*

My grandparents: Dorothy West (neé Warren) 25 September 1899 - 29 May 1933
Joseph West 06 July 1888 - 24 December 1960

Lance Corporal
Michael West
1892-1918
Aged 26

Mike's uncle

*Rhodesian Military Supremo General,
Peter Walls*

With daughter, Michelle

Rhodesian PM Ian Smith at SAS Officer's Mess

RLI Fireforce about to get airborne

In Grey's Scouts

Mike after the landmine with broken FN

Mike 2nd from right with 2 Commando RLI men

During SAS selection Mike (left) wrestling with Rhodesian rugby star Brian Murphy

In Mozambique with Bob Jones-Davies and Roger MacDonald

With Rick Norrod

John Barry on extreme left. Mike's best friend, killled while 'Bounty Hunting'

Mentor and hero, Darrell Watt (on left), before raid into Mozambique

With the SAS team prior to Beira raid. Colin Willis front 2nd left

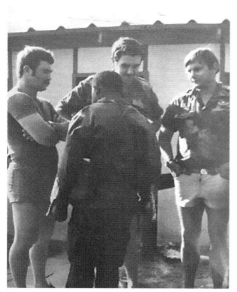

Captured Peugeot in Zambia

Darrell Watt, Andre Scheepers and Dave Berry quizzing Renamo man

Darrell Watt with Renamo commander, Luke Mhlanga

SAS team celebrating bridge destruction in Zambia

Renamo fighters raising their flag while on operations with the SAS

Dave Berry. One of the Rhodesian SAS's great NCO's

Henri Lepetit. Fine French soldier who fought for Rhodesia

Left: Bomb crater after attempt to kill Robert Mugabe at Fort Victoria in 1980

Former Rhodesian SAS operators in the South African Recces

Before Matola

*Left: Ready for Matola,
Mike on the right*

Rob Johnson (former SAS) prior to Matola. Exceptional officer; fearless and cool under fire

Dave Berry before Matola

Mike busy on the radio

Operation Katiso; on the way to Beira

Mike (extreme left) with Barend van Zyl,
Mike Smith and Colin Ott.
Before Op Katiso to Beira

Freefalling

93

With Teddy the Lion

Right: With Teddy

With Miss South Africa Andrea Steltzer

Aboard a Strike Craft.
Mike bottom left

Left: John Brokaar at Fort Rev.
The AK I am holding housed the
only 60-round AK magazine in
Special Forces

At sea on the way to Luanda. Op Kerslig. Gert Eksteen (back left) Frans Fourie,
Mike in the middle. Frank Tunney, middle right

CHAPTER 6

Fighting Till the End

'Operation Boxer'

"It was mid-September 1979 when we were at our barracks at Kabrit when called in by Captain Colin Willis and told that I and nine other operators had been picked to do a seaborne operation aimed at destroying targets in the city of Beira, in Mozambique. The main focus of the attack was the telephone exchange which was the communications relay-hub for message transmission from the capital Maputo to the enemy bases from which the attacks on Rhodesia were being launched. The plan also included an attack on a storage facility and the central prison to free inmates, many of whom were believed to be Renamo activists.

"We were informed we would be going up there in a South African Navy Strike-Craft, accompanied by the guys from 4 Recce who would take us on to the beach and then deploy divers to sink the dredgers that were in regular use to stop the harbour silting up.

"Captain Colin Willis was in charge, with Lt Pete Cole the second in command and Lt Mike Rich next in the chain of command. We had some good guys along, including Colin Ott, Mike Smith, Les van Blerk and Keith Cloete. Also along with us was a Renamo operator who knew his way around the city.

"We started training exercises, at Kabrit, and went to the telephone exchange in Salisbury to better understand how these worked and what we needed to be sure we destroyed the exchange. We saw a plan of the building which we planned to enter from the rear using boltcutters and then we would have to get up on to the first floor to do the damage. We would kill all the operators and then blow the place apart. Cubans were running the exchange and I was keen to kill a few of them.

"We departed from New Sarum in Jack Malloch's DC7 and landed at the South African Air Force Base at Langebaanweg, from where we went by road to the

4 Recce base in Langebaan. From there we went to their training facility on the island called 'Donkergat' where we conducted further training exercises.

"The weapons to be used for this operation were:

- 4 x Casull M290s. They were silenced .22 USA manufactured machine guns, and each one had a pan magazine of 100 rounds.

- 2 x RPDs

- 4 x AK47s

- Spare ammo for all the weapons

- Explosive devices necessary to destroy the communication centre.

"We were told Hunters from the Rhodesian Air Force were on standby to attack targets if we ended up in big trouble and were unable to extricate.

"Once we completed all the additional training, we were flown to Durban and from there to the Naval Base where we immediately boarded the Strike Craft for the journey to Beira. Sunday night 16th September was decided upon for the raid, as the city was expected to be quiet.

"Rough seas lasted a few days, and understandably many of us lost our lunch. If you know anything about ears, you will know that perforated eardrums from combat are in no way conducive to achieving sea legs. We fed many fish. Unfortunately, the rough water slowed us down and we were unable to launch on the Sunday night, so it was postponed to Monday.

"When we finally arrived off the coast and prepared to board the inflatable Zodiacs we were all pleased to be getting off that damn boat. We were just over the horizon, about 30 kilometres out to sea when we left the mothership. The first Zodiac that left had three attack-divers from 4 Recce aboard, who were to be dropped near the entrance of the harbour. They would get to work on the dredgers and the dry dock.

"It was rough going in but we hit the beach at about 21h00 without any problems. Our only difficulty was getting our balance back after all the rocking and rolling over the last couple of days. We then set off into the city in two lines of five in file as was done by Frelimo patrols. Colin Ott and I as the two RPD gunners walked in front. Our orders were to shoot the shit out of any serious threat the moment it happened but if the resistance could be dealt with more subtly then we were to step aside quietly and let the officers behind us, Willis and Cole, sort the problem out with their silenced weapons so as not to draw any further attention.

"Covered in our 'Black is Beautiful' face paint, and dressed in our Frelimo uniforms we all tried to look relaxed and we were pleased to hear warm greetings and some happy whistles and shouts which told me our disguise was working. But we had been told the city would be quiet and that, we soon realised, was not the case; the place was bustling with people, cars and buses. Our late arrival had had serious implications; Monday was a working day and the city was busy. We expected dimly lit streets but the lights were as bright as hell. Undeterred, we strode down the main street straight into the heart of the city. The bus stops we walked past were packed and waiting passengers shouted and waved at us; we tried to wave back looking as friendly as possible while knowing all this activity did not bode well for a surprise, sneak attack on the exchange.

"With some relief we reached an open patch of ground which lay between us and the target and while crossing it we were suddenly confronted by two Frelimo soldiers looking very alert. As planned, Colin and I stepped aside and Willis and Cole killed them quietly, but then it was as if the Gates of Hell opened and we came under fire from fuck-knows-where but we were in big shit. We were smack in the middle of it. Leaving the way we came wasn't an option, either, because there was fire coming in from that direction as well. I'll probably never know if they had been tipped off and were waiting for us but the element of surprise was well and truly gone, and we now had to get into escape and evade mode immediately. We well knew, Beira was home to an army brigade equipped with armour, and if we got bogged down, with or without the Hunters coming in to do air strikes, we would be in for the fight of our lives. Unfortunately Rambo, Chuck Norris and Jean-Claude Van Damme were filming at the time, and thus unable to save us with but a toothpick and a headband.

"It was total mayhem as we ran at high speed straight into the city centre but on the way came to a wide drainage canal with grey sludge, which we had to leap across weighed down with all our kit and weapons. Captain Willis was about five metres in front of me when he jumped and as he landed I saw his rear webbing belt break loose and with it went the pouch in which was the radio and our only means of calling for help. He was in such a rush he did not know what had happened, but luckily I saw it and picked it up before continuing the race into the city where we hoped to lose our pursuers in amongst the buildings. As we ran, some of the guys were chucking out Renamo propaganda leaflets which were supposed to show that we were local resistance fighters and not Rhodesian soldiers.

"In a narrow street, with less light, we paused and I caught up to Captain Willis and gave him back his radio, for which he thanked me. Once we checked and saw everyone was alive and intact, we then ducked and dived through the city to get back to the beach. It was whilst running down the streets of the city, we heard the heavy engine sound of something approaching us. I pictured Frelimo approaching in their armoured vehicles. I took cover behind a substation, and the rest of the team did the same behind whatever was available (and hiding space was sparse). Knowing that we were already deep in shit, I pointed my RPD machine gun in the direction of the approaching sound. This was, as I saw it: the end of the line.

"In reality, ten guys with handheld weapons, taking on armoured vehicles manned with troops and heavy machine guns, is nothing if not material for a one-way-ticket to Valhalla. We waited nervously and then to our massive relief, saw it was nothing more than a refuse removal truck, coming around the corner. We upped sticks and legged our way out of there, before a real threat could materialise, thanking our lucky stars the whole way.

"Arriving at the beach, Captain Willis radioed for a rapid extraction via the Zodiacs. All along the way, our escape had been witnessed by hundreds of city-dwellers who could easily have aided in our immediate capture but luckily they did not intervene. We learned later that the people of Beira were anti-Frelimo.

"Looking back, had I not recovered the radio, I suppose it could have been either capture, torture and a slow death, or a long swim back to South Africa, sharks permitting.

The relief we felt when we leapt aboard the Zodiacs manned by the Recce guys and headed out to the Strike Craft, can never be put into words. That was closer than anyone ever wanted to get with that many Frelimo trying to kill you.

"We were truly fucking fortunate to have survived this – all of us, for that matter – but to undertake this extremely dangerous mission, I'm not afraid to say, you have to be a next-level highly-trained, supremely efficient, Special Forces Operator, with balls of steel.

Think about it: You are walking into the heart of the enemy's territory, with but a smattering of men, civilians afoot, with you dressed like the enemy patrols that frequent the city. Your face is painted, and you are off to blow up their main source of communication – which was no doubt guarded.

"Had it not been for the locals at the bus stop, I think we would have made our target but the noise they made when we walked past them drew the full attention of the troops in the vicinity, and changed everything. Now, in retrospect, as I put this down on paper… it's funny. It wasn't funny at the time. Thank fuck I'm here to relay this story, as it happened on the ground.

"The mission was not a complete failure; the Recce guys did an amazing job, blew the dredgers and the dry-dock, putting the harbour out of action for a while."

'Operation Tepid'

"I'll never forget 'Operation Tepid' which happened late October 1979, soon before the war came to a sad end," remembers Mike West. "There were, undoubtedly, many great officers in the Rhodesian SAS. The Rhodesian SAS, as it was then, was a rite of passage for any man who wanted to count himself amongst the 'Soldier Elite'. However, to me, three men stood head and shoulders above the rest. Taller than their stories because of the guts, bravado and sheer lack of fear that they commanded and lead with.

"One of them was Major Rob Johnson. He was a squadron commander at both Cranborne and Kabrit Barracks. On 'Op Tepid', we were deployed in Zambia, outside a terr stronghold. It was late afternoon, heading for last light. During our infiltration, one of our operators connected with the tripwire of a booby trap. He was wounded in the upper leg and was evacuated.

"The terr stronghold had a mountain backdrop. We were on an elevated section of scattered dark, volcanic rock, roughly 500 to 800 metres away, separated by a valley. Our Hunter fighter jets were already engaged, strafing the enemy defences. The terrs were returning fire with Soviet-supplied 14.5mm anti-air-craft guns. These AA guns have a range of three kilometres horizontally, and two kilometres vertically. One very potent and lethal weapon.

"Obviously, they had been expecting company. This weapon was also rather effective at wiping out ground-level infantry. The terrs also had the B-10 recoilless rifle. This packs an 82mm round – the kind of weapon successfully utilized against vehicles and infantry.

"From our vantage point, we could see the repeat flash of the 14.5mm firing. It throws one helluva muzzle flash. The terrs also fired off rounds from their B-10. They were not aware of our presence because they didn't fire directly at us. It was more to our easterly direction, so I suspect that they had picked up the sounds of the chopper that performed the casevac. The noise from the battle underway was so intense that we felt the ground shake. Unfortunately, it was too damn dark, and way too fucking chaotic to launch an assault at that time on a position where the terrs were centralised so Rob decided that we would attack at dawn.

"In the fading light, there were four of us, huddled together on a hill under the overhang of a rock. Myself, Dave Berry, 'Chunky' Chesterman and Frank Tunney. We were watching the battle, making comments in a low tone. You don't talk loudly, nor stand up in a situation like this, because movement can be detected easily and you do your best to not draw attention to yourself. Why? Because you'll be one very dead fucking moron.

"In this moment, under this duress, Rob came strolling over to our position much like a chap on an afternoon stroll, completely unperturbed by the heavy battle just a hop, skip and a jump away from us. He stood there, smiling, and said: 'You cunts better keep your heads down. We don't want to bring that shit down on us. Move to my position in five minutes for a briefing.'

"Then he turned and sauntered off to wherever the fuck he'd come from, appar-ently in no hurry. You cannot imagine how funny a situation like this is, unless you're in it. We weren't the ones walking the fuck around. We were at first stunned, and then we chuckled quietly. This was one fearless fucking leader.

I was involved in numerous hellish base camp attacks with this crazy-calm goddamn fearless leader. Never once did I see him flustered or lose control. His composure was unnerving.

"Later, the four of us moved towards the position where Rob was, as instructed – but we sure as shit did not stroll, nor saunter, we fucked off at some speed! As we entered the location there was Andre Scheepers leaning casually against a rock, arms crossed, smiling at us. He and Dave Berry were good mates. Andre was also completely unperturbed by the 'fuck-fest' underway. He pointed in the direction of the cacophony, grinning and said: 'Ain't that something else...' Andre Scheepers. Another officer in the SAS. One very brave and daring leader.

"This brings me to my final lionization: That of my hero, mentor and leader; Captain Darrell Watt. Kids of today should be reading comics about these guys, not fictitious fuckers like 'Superman' and 'Spiderman'. Real, true-life heroes. Men who stood their ground where others feared to tread. Their heroics saved countless lives. Mine included. There are not enough words in the English vocabulary to canonize them as they truly deserve to be. Men who inspired such admiration and respect, that you would sacrifice your very life in order to save theirs. If you've never met anyone like that, nor walked in the footsteps of men worthy of such reverence, you truly have not tasted the flavour of life, itself.

Bridge Busting

By November 1979 with the Lancaster House Conference delicately poised a decision was taken in Salisbury at the highest level to bring maximum pressure to bear on the presidents of Mozambique and Zambia knowing that if successful they would in turn bring pressure on both Mugabe and Nkomo to moderate their demands and reach a political settlement.

In this endeavour a prime target given to the SAS was the bridge across the Zambezi river at Tete. This was the lone land link between the north and south of the country and if severed it would divide the country and cause enormous disruption to the flow of people and goods. At the last moment this operation was aborted, probably as a result of pressure coming from the British at Lancaster House. At the same time a big combined air and ground attack aimed at bridges, and strategic installations in Mozambique was also being planned.

Meanwhile Renamo was getting stronger with the help of the SAS and other support personnel who were training recruits back in Rhodesia. It appeared Machel was buckling under the pressure, so with him somewhat neutralised the main focus of attention turned to Zambia where Nkomo's Zipra conventional forces were becoming increasingly threatening.

At this point Nkomo and his generals were well aware of the fact that within Rhodesia they were outnumbered by Zanla in terms of the numbers of men on the ground. They needed to rectify the situation by infiltrating as many men as they could as fast as they could.

Adding to Rhodesian woes was the news that the Zipra invasion was to involve armour and Russian-supplied air cover. The number of trained troops prepared to move south was estimated in the region of some 20 000 personnel. The points of entry into the country were Victoria Falls and Kariba. The conflict was about to switch from being a guerrilla war to a conventional one.

In response it was decided to focus SAS attentions on hitting that country's infrastructure in a direct attack on its economic viability and in an effort to disrupt the enemy ability to move forces closer to the Rhodesian border. The earlier destruction of the Chambeshi bridge by the SAS had seriously disrupted Zambia's lifeline to the north and had alerted the authorities to the need for increased surveillance around strategic targets that might attract the attention of the Rhodesians. The stakes were extremely high and much of the country's hopes were pinned on the SAS.

With the concentration of Zipra troops in and around Lusaka, the plan called for the city to be cut off from all routes southwards and so 'Operation Dice' was triggered on 16th November 1979 with Bell helicopters flying in teams to hit the bridges on three different link-roads. The plan called for quick deployment, destruction of bridges, and and a rapid return to Rhodesia once the bridges were down. With the Zambian Army and Air Force on high alert, strong resistance was expected and support teams armed with mortars and 20mm guns were to be positioned to provide added protection for the men engaged in the blowing of the bridges.

Mike West was part of a 12-man group choppered in under Captain Colin Willis tasked to blow up the Chongwe River Bridge about 30kms from the city of Lusaka.

"Prior to our deployment," recalled Mike, "a 20mm cannon-crew was posted on a hill position overlooking where we would be busy to give us covering fire if we had a problem with the Zambian Army that had a base near the target. We were heavily laden with ammo and the explosives required.

"On hitting the ground I was sent with the Rhodesian rugby captain, Brian Murphy, to watch the road leading to the bridge from the eastern side with orders not to let anything through while the demolition team went to work. Brian and another guy went further up the road to stop traffic while I hunkered down. My 100-round RPD belts were loaded. Every fifth round was a tracer, which was standard practice. Two other RPD gunners had the same orders on the western side.

"There was little cover close to the road so I had to move to a concealed position about 50 metres away from it where I did not have a great view of the road which was undulating with a deep dip, but I had to hide. The vegetation was incredibly dense and green. Soon after we were in position, the demolition team went to work on the bridge. I heard Brian open up. As he approached the scene of the contact a Mercedes came speeding down the road and the driver must have lost control because they crashed in the bush but I think the occupants survived and gapped it into the bush. Moments after that a Toyota Land Cruiser came down the road at speed and warning shots were fired but he just kept on coming until Brian stepped into the road to stop him. Brian told him we were busy blowing a bridge and he should not go any further, but this guy was angry. 'Fuck you Rhodesians,' he shouted, slammed the car into gear and raced away from them.

"Next thing in the distance I picked up a glint, which I knew was coming off the windscreen of a vehicle approaching and prepared myself. I couldn't hear the engine, but from what I could see through glimpses of movement it was travelling at high speed downhill towards me and I had to react quickly. When it was about 200 metres from the bridge, I started picking up the sound of the engine. When I saw enough view of the vehicle through the trees I knew I had to act and I opened up, following the tracer onto the target. I kept careful aim and my finger on the trigger. The vehicle kept coming, then suddenly careened off the road, into the ditch, tumbling over and over, coming to a stop roughly

100 meters from the bridge in a massive cloud of dust. No explosion, just dead quiet. I moved from my position down through the ridges to the wreckage and met Willis. It was not a pretty sight. An elderly white man groaning, blood pumping out his body, was struggling for air. He told us he was a doctor in Lusaka and asked us why we had shot him. I did not feel happy about this, but he had been warned. The medic tried to keep him alive long enough to be taken back to Rhodesia but he passed away.

"My mood was not helped when Colin Willis glared at me. But what was I to do? I was following his orders and had done exactly what I was told to do. I had been placed in that role because I had a reputation as a good machine-gunner and had done my duty by stopping a racing oncoming vehicle before it got to the bridge, exactly what my orders were. In this business, the death of an innocent is called 'collateral damage'; it sounds so innocuous and informal but the reality is that innocents do die and being responsible as I was, did not please me at all.

"Some terrs were spotted coming out of some huts and Brian took them out. The bridge was completely destroyed before we moved westwards to prepare for uplift. Mike Rich and his guys were busy further south blowing a bridge and planting landmines on access roads.

"As we moved away, a Yugoslavian-manufactured Zambian Jastreb fighter jet came cruising over the bridge and our position. I could easily have taken it out with my machine gun, because it was so low, and slow-moving that I could see the pilot in the cockpit, but I was still smarting from what had happened with the poor man in the vehicle. The pilot was looking at the bridge. He couldn't see us, masked by the bush, and there was enough shit afoot. We were uplifted, and not a word was ever spoken about this again. I had only acted on instruction.

"Later, we went back to do another bridge and again I had to open fire on a fast approaching vehicle taking out the occupants. The operation was a complete success in that the SAS teams blew enough bridges to make an invasion almost impossible. The damage done to the country's infrastructure was huge and Zambia's President Kaunda increased the pressure on Joshua Nkomo to find a political settlement and end the war. On the 22nd November we were ordered to halt all offensive operations and we were all pulled back to Rhodesia, and basically told the war was over; I was gutted and so were most of the other guys."

Renamo

In Mozambique, soon after the advent of Marxist rule under Frelimo in 1975, reports had been reaching Rhodesian intelligence of growing resistance to increasingly autocratic and incompetent Frelimo rule. This had led to a decision to commence covert activity designed to facilitate further opposition and thereby take the fight to the enemy in their own territory.

As always, money was short and into the breach stepped Tim Landon, the 'White Sultan' of Oman who had family connections in Rhodesia. Using his direct link to a sympathetic Sultan Qaboos, he managed to siphon financial support to the Rhodesians CIO (Central Intelligence Organisation) to fund the covert operation.

A first step was the establishment of the 'Voice of Free Africa' radio station, broadcasting propaganda into enemy country urging the populace to rise against the government. The insertion of armed insurgents only became a realistic possibility with the arrival in Rhodesia of André Matsangaissa (also spelled Matsangaiza), a disaffected former Frelimo officer who had escaped from prison where he was doing time for making known his disgruntlement with the Samora Machel regime. He confirmed the Mozambique people were thoroughly disillusioned and ready for regime change. He explained the number of men at his disposal was limited, but with Rhodesian assistance he planned to attack and liberate prison camps holding similarly disillusioned former Frelimo fighters.

A plan was immediately set in motion and along with an SAS support group a prison camp was attacked and André arrived back in Rhodesia with over 300 men ready to fight. A new phase of the war was about to begin.

While Renamo's new recruits were being trained secretly at an abandoned farm in the Odzi farming area near the border town of Umtali, Gorongoza Mountain in central Mozambique was selected as one operational base. Well suited from a tactical point of view because it was easily defensible, it was also known the local populace was angry and would be supportive of the burgeoning resistance army. The other base would be to the south near the settlement known as Gugoi, near the Save River under the command of Darrell Watt who would be working alongside another former Frelimo Officer called Luke Mhlanga.

The Gorongoza group were soon in action and André immediately impressed the SAS men with his spirited aggression and natural leadership qualities. Frelimo garrisons were hit and soon the Mozambique army was reeling under the onslaught. All the while, a full-blown political campaign was on the go whipping up popular support for the overthrow of the Machel regime. It was not long before government soldiers, sensing they were on the losing side, started to defect and offer their services.

Meanwhile Watt started to send out SAS men to accompany Luke's men on night patrols into the populated areas to establish a presence. The SAS men were ordered to remain out of view while the resistance fighters went in and explained their presence while asking for recruits. The response was over-whelmingly positive and the ranks quickly swelled. Little support for Samora Machel was encountered.

"It was late 1979 when I volunteered to join Darrell in Mozambique", remembers Mike. "I didn't know much about what was going on, I just wanted to go where Darrell was going because I knew there would be action. When I jumped in Darrell was already there. It was a night jump and I was first out the plane followed by Dick Stent who had just come accross to the SAS from the RLI. The blokes were waiting for us and we had a warm reception. Darrell was well established operating from his pole and dagga HQ complex where he had his TR48 radio and signaller. The next morning there were hundreds of rebel fighters on parade in a forest clearing with Luke in command. It was a new adventure for me in a beautiful wilderness area.

"We walked hard during the day but we all had bearers to help us so they carried all the heavy stuff. Dick and I gave our helpers vitamin pills and they became rocket-men, running rather than walking. They were really nice youngsters and couldn't do enough for us. There were hundreds of rebels with us so we did not try to hide and we had time to bathe in the cool streams and rivers flowing out of the mountains. They would cook for us if we wanted and they gathered delicious wild mushrooms for us to fry. On one occasion I broke a small branch off a tree to stir my tea and one of them came running over and pulled it out the mug; unbeknown to me it contained a poison.

"As we passed through villages we were generally welcomed while the young men were recruited and our numbers grew steadily. On the march our medic would attend to the sick and wounded and there were plenty of them standing in line every morning to be attended to with all sorts of growths and sores. Lots of them had malaria and on the march they just fell over to be left to die.

"On the one day a man who appeared to be armed was called on to halt but he ran and I wanted to shoot but the Renamo guys ran him down and brought him back. He was a poacher carrying a huge longbow and arrows with massive steel tips on them. This guy must have been made of steel because Dick and I, both strong men, damn near bust a gut trying to draw that bowstring. Some of the black people there were absolutely terrified of us because they had never seen white men before.

"I actually didn't know what was going on as we marched on, but Luke and Darrell had a enemy camp attack in mind and that was where we were heading. At one point Luke gave us all Mauser hunting rifles in very good condition which would be useful for long range shooting.

"It was not long before we were told the camp had been sighted and the attack was going in. We were told that Renamo would do the assault while we remained on the perimenter to take down people fleeing the attack. We were well positioned on a rise looking down on the enemy position which was across a dry river bed. There were hundreds of fighters that went in with rockets and machine guns; plenty of noise and then smoke but I'm not sure how accurate the firing was. But then we saw the 'Freds' running away, the Mausers were perfect for the task and we nailed them. There was great excitement after the attack but a hell of a lot of ammo had been used and a resupply was asked for. The next night a Dakota flew over us and dropped a resupply. I did not realise it at the time but we were moving closer to the port city of Beira, and Darrell was planning to drop bridges that would cut the city off and create a major problem. We were on a roll and it looked like nothing could stop us.

"Then suddenly we were told to stop the advance and there was quite a lot of confusion amidst the disappointment. Some tense moments followed because Luke was pissed off as we were going home, and some harsh words were exchanged but orders were orders. A Canberra bomber flew over to give us air cover when the choppers arrived to take us home. I had no idea but when we were ordered home there were negotiations going on in London with the

British and this was a political decision.

"On our arrival back at Grand Reef, Major Rob Johnson, a great soldier, had just done a photo shoot. Meanwhile, Frank Tunney had got involved in an engagement in Mozambique. Frelimo had brought T34 Russian tanks and were getting involved. Johnson said we have to get reinforcements there. I said I would go , but he told me to shut up, I was going home. I was told that I was so over-confident that I was fucking obnoxious."

Last Throw of the Dice

On December 21st 1979 a ceasefire was signed by all the warring parties. An uneasy peace prevailed as thousands of terrorists crossed into the country to be accommodated at designated assembly points around Rhodesia. A Commonwealth monitoring force was deployed countrywide to supervise the peace and help prepare the country for elections. The word that was put out from on high was that there was no chance of Mugabe winning the election and if necessary military force would be used to ensure that Mugabe was denied power, but notwithstanding this optimistic view, people in the military and intelligence services decided to assassinate him.

"The plan that came together was in two parts," Mike West recalled, " 'Operation Hectic' and 'Operation Quartz'. The SAS role in 'Hectic' was handed to A Squadron, under the command of Darrell, and we were tasked with the covert elimination of select members of the ZANU[1] hierarchy, including Mugabe.

" 'Operation Quartz' involved the elimination of major Zanu targets in Salisbury and elsewhere. Meanwhile, the assembly points around the country were filling fast, however, but in violation of the Lancaster House agreement many terrorists remained in the bush, to force the outcome of the voting through intimidation. There were other plans in place for the RLI and the Air Force to attack these camps.

"One plan to kill Mugabe involved placing an explosive device in a microphone prior to him addressing a press conference, while another involved poisoning him on a flight from Salisbury to Bulawayo, but these were foiled, almost certainly as a result of tip-offs. An SAS team armed with a Strela heat-seeking

---

1   Zimbabwe African National Union.

missile was deployed to Salisbury airport and tasked with shooting down an airliner carrying Mugabe and his entourage back from a meeting in Maputo. At the last minute this was aborted because of concerns regarding the certain deaths of the flight crew. With the clock ticking, within the SAS there was no doubt, urgent and decisive action was now required and Darrell and I were summoned early February to kill the cunt.

"On the 10th February we were told he was to address a rally in Fort Victoria and we planned to get him on his way out at the end of the event. Darrell wanted to lay an ambush to ensure success, but ComOps did not want our involvement to be that obvious. So we placed an explosive device under a culvert on the road which would be detonated following the end of the rally as Mugabe's entourage returned. Another officer was airborne monitoring events from the air, and he was to give us advantageous warning of the convoy's approach. But I think they were tipped off, because the convoy returned early and at a very high speed. The charge detonated, but too early and they stopped the convoy and we missed the target. Mugabe's car stopped right on the crater. He came very close to dying.

"This was only the beginning of our problems, because the Fireforce at Fort Victoria was activated and Darrell and I were now on the run from our own soldiers and airmen. We just ran like hell through the bush trying to stay under tree-cover to avoid being spotted from above. We were very fit, lightly dressed and carrying pistols only so we moved fast. When we saw the K-Car go into an orbit, we stood stiff against a tree and held our breath. As soon as they were gone from above, we ran again as fast as we could. Eventually we made it to the road and were picked up by a pre-arranged getaway car which included two girls as passengers to make us look more ordinary. We changed into civvies quickly, washed the grime off us, changed number plates, dumped all the evidence, then took off.

"Just when it looked like we were safely out of there we came to a road-block manned by BSAP and Commonwealth Monitoring Force people. Darrell and I had our pistols ready. There were a few personnel milling around the car, then finally a big BSAP man put his head through the window to see who was inside. He looked at the driver, and then he looked in the back seat where Darrell was sitting. He recognised Darrell immediately and knew what was going on. We waited anxiously to see what he would do, then saw him smile, then with an eyewink, he waved us on with a cheery 'Carry on, Sir'.

"We were disappointed but covert operations continued under Darrell's command. Our usual camouflage uniforms were traded in for civilian clothing, and we were relocated from Kabrit to flats and houses at various locations around Salisbury. Military vehicles were replaced with civilian Kombis (VW station wagons) purchased in South Africa from a special 'slush' fund. We rehearsed setting roadblocks; house clearing drills; battle preparations; intelligence gathering; drive-pasts; and laying of clandestine ambushes on road-sides. Every possible contingency was practiced. We exchanged automatic rifles and machine guns for semi-automatic Star and Browning 9mm hand-guns. "Many weeks were spent in detailed surveillance and reconnaissance, and as a result several road blocks were hastily set up and terrorist leaders captured and bundled into the waiting Kombis. They were handed to BSAP Special Branch and not heard from again.

"One evening Darrell, I and two other guys in our Kombi gave chase to a known terrorist civilian vehicle and its single occupant down the Borrowdale road, waving pistols at him to try and pull him over. However the terrorist thought better than to stop so Darrell raced ahead and set up a hasty roadblock. We stopped him, and he was hauled off for further interrogation!

"Then we were tasked to lay an ambush near Gwelo, on the Salisbury side. Mugabe would be returning from another election rally. Darrell selected two teams in two Kombis; the first team of six men would comprise four members of the ambush group plus a driver and companion; the second team would be a drive-past and early warning for the approach of Mugabe, this team comprising a driver and companion. I was in the ambush group with Darrell.

"The idea was that the observation Kombi would go a mile or so ahead and give the all-clear for the ambush group Kombi to pull over and deposit the team. This would need to be quick and clean to remain clandestine. We wore latex gloves so no fingerprints could be lifted, in the hope that the hit on Mugabe would be blamed on Zipra or his own men. Our weapons were AKs and PKMs. We were all so pumped up and ready for this, when once again, we were to be disappointed when we were told Mugabe had changed plans and flown back to Salisbury.

"As the run-up to the election drew closer, Mugabe remained at his house in Quorn Avenue, Mt Pleasant, Salisbury. I went with Darrell and one other guy to hide and watch the house. We lay there for two nights in a bushy patch behind a telephone exchange, using infrared binoculars to monitor the comings and goings. On one occasion Mugabe showed up, briefly exiting a car and exchanging a few words with his cadres, before hastily entering the house.

"Mugabe was exposed sufficiently long for Darrell to put in a lethal shot, but he was under strict instruction to only observe as it had now entered the 'Op Quartz' phase. This operation was based on the assumption that if Mugabe survived 'Op Hectic' and Zanu were defeated in the elections it would be necessary to carry out a strike against Zanu to prevent its forces from attempting a coup. In this phase of the operation, following initiation of a particular codeword, A Squadron would take care of Mugabe and his lieutenants at his home in Quorn Avenue, as well as supporters at various locations in the capital; B Squadron would take care of Vice President Simon Muzenda and the 100-strong contingent of Zanla based in the Medical Arts Centre. C Squadron was tasked to take out the 200 Zipra and Zanla men with their commanders (Rex Nhongo, Dumiso Dabengwa and Lookout Masuku) based at the Audio Visual Arts building of the University of Rhodesia.

"The night the election results were announced we were certain we were going to be given the orders to strike, but it never happened and that was the saddest moment of my life.

General Peter Walls decided to give Mugabe a chance. We were all gutted and very angry; we had all tried so hard and it suddenly became clear, we had lost the war and all we had fought for."

Break for the Border

"Following the military decision to accept Mugabe's election win, the South African Defence Force liaison officer in Salisbury, Commandant Andre Bestbier, reported back to Pretoria the deep resentment on the part of some senior Rhodesian officers who had decided to serve the new government and were very unhappy with the South Africans who were trying to recruit some of their best soldiers.

"Mugabe had been making conciliatory speeches and some believed him; that all would be well but I certainly did not agree with them. They were also unhappy seeing so much equipment being taken out of the country because it was effectively on loan from South Africa, and they did not want it falling into 'enemy' hands. As it turned out, these optimists in the army would soon see for themselves that they had been conned and would soon be chucked out.

"Recruiters from the SADF has been visiting Rhodesia on recruiting drives for a while, enquiring whether SAS and other specialist soldiers would be interested in joining South African Special Forces on attractive terms. The idea was to form an equivalent Rhodesian SAS unit as part of the SADF which would become 1 Recce.

"When we realised that it was well and truly over in Rhodesia there was quite a lot of confusion; some of the guys wanted to go to South Africa and others wanted to stay in Rhodesia and hope for the best. For me I had no interest in a life under Mugabe and my mind was made up to head back to South Africa.

"There was again confusion within the ranks of the SAS and the Rhodesian Security Forces in general, when a South African Air Force C130 arrived and it was loaded with weapons and equipment to be taken back to South Africa. I remember Bob McKenzie wanting to put his boat on the plane but the South Africans refused permission. I know there was an ivory stash somewhere from tusks that had been collected in raids over the years but I had no idea what happened to that.

"There was also quite a bit of money in a Squadron fund, about $40 000, which was a lot in those days and I was asked to help organise getting it changed into South African Rand. In those days there were very strict currency controls in Rhodesia so changing the money without Reserve Bank approval was a criminal offense. The money was given to a lady by the name of Betty who was dating my friend JJ. She said she knew a trustworthy individual and she would organise the transaction. On the given day the guy came for the money with a pistol and took off with the cash. There were a lot of angry SAS officers when I told them the deal had been botched and I was not very popular at all. JJ tracked this guy down and killed him. Next thing I knew there was a murder investigation on the go and I, as a suspect, was arrested. Luckily for me Detective Superintendant

Dave Anderton was in charge of the case and he knew I was not responsible, so he had me released but then his orders were clear: 'Get the fuck out of this country as soon as you can!'

"I gathered my belongings and hitch-hiked to Beitbridge but as a fugitive, I could not take the risk of going through passport control so I waited until nightfall and spent the last night in the country I had grown to love, hiding in the bush near the Limpopo River. Then under cover of darkness I grabbed a dugout and crossed the river back into the country of my birth. My Rhodesian adventure was over."

* * * * *

Background to Conflict

South Africa's counter-insurgency war started in the mid-1960s with most of the fighting taking place on the northern border of South West Africa. The seeds of conflict were sown in 1919 when the then League of Nations mandated South Africa to administer the former German South West Africa (SWA) as a protectorate. In 1949 six seats in the House of Assembly, and four in the Senate, were reserved for representatives from the territory. All of those elected quickly fell under the National Party umbrella and shared the view that a form of apartheid should be implemented.

In 1962, the South West Africa People's Organisation (SWAPO) formed their armed wing PLAN[2], with material assistance from the Soviet Union, China, and sympathetic African states. In 1966 the General Assembly of the United Nations, (successor to the League of Nations) declared Pretoria's suzerainty to have been terminated, and in 1968 SWA became internationally and legally known as Namibia but the change then was largely one of semantics as indirect rule from Pretoria continued. South Africa continued to call it South West Africa. For South Africa it was important to hold onto the territory because of its value and as a buffer against the growing military threat from the north as more African countries became independent.

The South African military presence in the disputed territory grew with the establishment of numerous military bases from 1975 onwards. In the late 1980s

---

2   People's Liberation Army of Namibia

the SADF staged massive conventional raids into Angola to eliminate Plan's forward operating bases. Other offensives were also conducted in Tanzania and Zambia.

During this period the South African Special Forces came to the fore, working out of their own bases under command of a Special Forces general who reported directly to the commander of the South African Defence Force. 5 Recce maintained a fulltime base in Ondangwa (a town of 23,000 inhabitants about 60 kilometres from the Angolan border). From here continuous deployments against Swapo took place. Some seven bases were eventually set up during the hostilities for Recce battalions. These included Fort Doppies in the Caprivi Strip, Fort Foot from where long-range deployments with UNITA[3] were conducted, and Fort Rev in Ondangwa.

The Recces' work was very much that of a light and effective ground-based strike force. As the conflict intensified the workload increased and diversified. In addition to being a mobile, rapid deployment force that could perform high-powered raids, the units were also tasked to do maximum impact operations and limit the overall capacity of the enemy. This required strikes against selected national key-points aimed at inflicting maximum damage. In the execution of these tasks, the soldiers would deploy deep into Angola to destroy and neutralise the harbours, bridges, tunnels, and railway lines, along with disrupting power and fuel supplies. Attacks were also mounted aimed at limiting enemy air capability.

Following the Portuguese exit from Angola, civil war immediately erupted between rival political factions vying to seize control. This focused on the ascendant MPLA[4] and their armed wing EPLA[5], led by Agostino Neto and the anti-communist Unita led by the charismatic Jonas Savimbi.

By 1975 Cuba had dispatched nearly five hundred combat personnel to Angola, along with sophisticated weaponry and supplies. The persistent build-up of Cuban and Soviet military aid allowed the Mpla to drive its opponents from the

---

3   National Union for the Total Independence of Angola/União Nacional para a Independência Total de Angola

4   *Movimento Popular de Libertação de Angola* /People's Movement for the Liberation of Angola

5   *Exército Popular de Libertação de Angola*/People's Army for the Liberation of Angola

capital Luanda and blunt an abortive intervention by Zairean and South African troops which had deployed in a belated attempt to assist Holden Roberto's FNLA and Savimbi's Unita.

Independence was achieved on November 11, 1975. Epla became Angola's official armed forces, but was then replaced by the more effective FAPLA.[6]

Prior to this, during January 1969, the South African liberation movement, the ANC (African National Congress), along with its military wing, Umkhonto we Sizwe (MK) and the Mpla entered into a formal military alliance together with SWAPO, led by Sam Nujoma and the Zimbabwe African People's Union (Zapu), led by Joshua Nkomo. With Angola's independence, MK were granted permission to establish training facilities in Angola.

Following the 1976 Soweto uprising large numbers of young black South Africans fled the country and joined the ANC and MK, seeking the opportunity to join the struggle to end white rule in SWA and South Africa.

In late 1978 Defence Minister PW Botha took over the South African presidency from John Vorster. Botha's approach to the conflict was an aggressive one and this pleased the generals who had voiced concerns about Vorster's indecisiveness. Botha made it clear that if the Western democracies were not prepared to confront communism, South Africa would go it alone. Regular South African incursions into southern Angola, coupled with Unita's northward expansion from bases in the east, forced the Angolan government to increase expenditures on its military, sourcing most of the required materiel from the Soviet Union. Dependence also increased on imported military personnel from the Soviet Union, East Germany, and Cuba.

In March 1979 Botha ordered a wave of strikes against targets in Zambia and Angola. While enemy casualties were light a strong signal was sent to the host governments and in Lusaka President Kaunda, under pressure from the affected citizenry in the south-west of the country, ordered the closure of the Plan bases.

Aimed at ending 'apartheid rule', the 'Total Strategy' was activated involving MK, Plan, and Azanian People's Liberation Army (Apla) guerrilla raids into South Africa or against South African targets in SWA. The response from South Africa was to launch frequent reprisal attacks on these movements' external

---

6   Forças Armadas Populares de Libertação de Angola.

bases in Angola, Zambia, Mozambique, Lesotho, Zimbabwe, Botswana, and elsewhere, often involving collateral damage to foreign infrastructure and civilian populations.

USA-South African relations improved almost immediately, following the election victory of Ronald Reagan in the USA in 1980. His tough anti-communist message was music in Pretoria's ears. Mr. Chester Crocker was appointed Assistant Secretary of State for African Affairs and he formulated a policy of 'constructive engagement' which involved a strengthening of ties between SA and the USA. Crocker believed that overt pressure on South Africa would be contrary to USA's strategical goals, namely countering Soviet expansionist goals around the world. To this end the Americans made it clear they did not welcome the possibility of Namibia going the same way as Angola and falling within the Soviet orbit. Tacit support from Washington encouraged Botha and his commanders to go onto a more aggressive footing and between 1980 and 1982 SA troops launched three separate large-scale incursions into the country in an effort to destroy Plan facilities.

The SADF made use of extra-territorial operations to eliminate its military and political opponents, arguing that neighbouring states, including their civilian populations, which hosted, tolerated on their soil, or otherwise sheltered anti-apartheid insurgent groups could not evade responsibility for provoking retaliatory strikes. These operations effectively undermined the insurgents' external sanctuary areas. It also sent a clear message to the host governments that collaborating with insurgent forces involved potentially high costs.

Intensive conventional warfare of this nature carried the risk of severe casualties among white South African soldiers, which had to be kept to a minimum for political reasons. The South African government and military, through a variety of mechanisms, including outright censorship and management of the news process ensured that the South African public was kept ignorant of the scale and intensity of the warfare on the Namibian border.

CHAPTER 7

War for My Homeland

To win you need four commandments: consolidate, dominate, subjugate, and annihilate. – South African rugby legend Dr. Danie Craven.

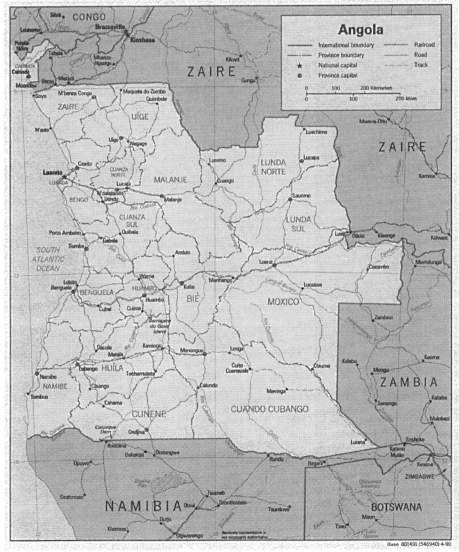

Here I am.

Still Mike West.

Still man of extremes you remember. One country, to the next.

Still not fucking listening

"I can't say I was welcomed home with open arms. After a night in the bush, early morning, having dried my clothes, I then brushed myself off and stood on the road with my thumb out. I hitched a lift into Pretoria, to Speskop and made my way to the Special Forces HQ offices. They wasted little time in sending me off to 1 Recce, based on the Bluff outside Durban. This was already the new home for the ex-Rhodesian SAS guys who had agreed to join the SADF so it was good to see some friendly faces again. My next war, this one for my homeland, was about to begin.

"Coming from the Rhodesian Special Air Service (SAS) we were not expected to do the Recce selection. We were paid R300 per month on the contract, but we had free accommodation in Amanzimtoti for me and my family. Recce military salary was more than the normal SADF soldier because of our specialised qualifications and Operator's allowance (Special Forces).

"Unfortunately, for the blokes from Rhodesia, the initial warm welcome quickly cooled when a whole different military culture emerged. The fact was the core guys in the Recces had really learned the special forces ropes by spending time in Rhodesia with the SAS and Selous Scouts and they had got along well, but now it was a different time and place and the Rhodesians were in their neck of the woods and under their command.

"The hierarchy was impressed with what they had heard from Rhodesia and they were very pleased to have some of the best trained, most experienced Special Force (SF) soldiers on the planet in their ranks, but at a lower level there were entrenched differences which almost immediately caused problems.

"This was not like the SAS where recruits were worked hard, but treated with respect and not fucked around with unnecessarily. The SAS was a well trained brotherhood. You fought firstly for your brother on your left and right, who both covered your back, and then for the SAS and Rhodesia. There was terrific camaraderie which just seemed to happen.

Here, the atmosphere was different. We were not a team pulling together. There were those in charge, the 'rockspiders', the Afrikaners (named by the English during the Boer War as the Boers (Afrikaners) appeared to climb over the rocks), and then the 'soutpiels', the English, because the Afrikaners said they had one foot in England and one foot in South Africa and their cocks hung in the sea which salted their foreskins. The Afrikaner instructors were in total control of all training in the PF (Permanent Force) and all commands were in Afrikaans. The fact was, if you were not Afrikaans, life was going to be tougher and this certainly applied to the Rhodesians.

"The army was also the first time many of the South African Afrikaans and English youngsters actually met and mixed, as they had pursued their own form of apartheid growing up insofar as where they lived, schools attended, and sport played. Now they had to assimilate, but always along the lines of the Afrikaner line of thought. There was no room for any discussion.

"This dogmatic approach had political roots. In 1980, despite international opposition, the Afrikaners wielded total political control over the country. This process began in 1948 when the National Party of Dr Daniël F Malan ousted Field Marshal Jan Smuts and his more moderate United Party. At last the Boers, defeated in 1902 by the British in the Anglo-Boer War 1899-1902, took back control of a country they felt was rightly theirs. There was also considerable, residual, anti-English bitterness as a result of the scorched earth policy of the British forces that had led to a heavy proportion of the Boer women, old men, and especially children dying in the British concentration camps. It's probably no surprise there was an anti-British mindset among the Afrikaners in the military. The same should not be said of the Navy and the Air Force where English speaking personnel were more welcome.

"Two-year automatic conscription was in place, and all South African white boys, after leaving school, which was usually when they were still 17 years of age, had to report for duty in the armed forces. Many of these conscripts were unwilling and hated the army. Blacks played a minimal part in these armed forces, and many left the country to be trained abroad in Cuba, China, and Russia to confront their white countrymen.

"I had mixed feelings about being in the SADF. Fresh in my mind was how they rudely rejected me in 1974 because I was too 'thick', I had been expelled from school, had no Matric, I was a free-thinker, and I was not a church-goer. Now, suddenly I was needed for the war effort; this time there was none of the religious shit and talk about Matric; now I belonged!

"Us new arrivals from Rhodesia were initially accommodated in an apartment block outside Durban. There were about 50 of us under the command of Garth Barrett. We did not enjoy swapping our Rhodesian camo for brown fatigues and being back on the drill-square being screamed at by an RSM. We were looking for a fight, not to be fucked around. The SAS was disciplined but in a more relaxed way. What came as a big shock to us all was the power of the damn Dominee in the unit. He seemed to have more power than anyone.

"The blokes were unhappy and then became restless and fights started breaking out. There were fights in town and the police were called. I think we were all angry and frustrated and so we lashed out. One of the guys was going through a bad time and opened up with an AK47 at the gym in the city. The gym was next to the police station, so he was soon arrested but they managed to get the charges dropped. The fact is our blokes were bored and unsettled and hungry for action. It was not a moment too soon when we were told we going to Maputo in Mozambique."

'Operation Beanbag'

This was a military operation conducted by the SADF Special Forces against the ANC headquarters on 30 January 1981. The target was three houses in the suburb of Matola which lay 16 kilometres from the centre of Maputo, Mozambique.

South African intelligence believed this was the ANC nerve-centre where the planning and control of enemy operations into the Transvaal province was taking place. It was also believed to be home to senior ANC leaders.

The first target was a double storey building believed to be a transit facility and occasional home to senior personnel including Joe Slovo. The second house, a spacious bungalow, was used by MK's 'Police Machinery' and served as a planning centre for attacks on police stations and other installations in South Africa.

The third, another double storey, was known as Matola Castle and was thought to be the most important. It was used by MK's 'Sabotage Machinery', run by Joe Slovo, and it was here that the planning and organisation for many major sabotage attacks within South Africa had taken place, including the attack on the SASOL[7] refinery (There were MK attacks on Sasol I, Natref and Sasol II on the night of 31 May/1 June 1980).

The SADF team was made up of members from 1 and 6 Reconnaissance Regiments, the latter also being made up of mainly old Rhodesian SAS personnel.

The mission was to eliminate the MK headquarters, gather as much documentation as they could for intelligence purposes, capture as many personnel as possible, and kill the rest, whilst taking all possible precautions to prevent civilian casualties.

These Special Forces were under the direct command of the Joint Operations Division of the SADF, and unlike other similar forces worldwide, were not a part of the Army or the Navy. The raid was planned by 'Section A' of the security police, headed by Colonel (later General) Jac Buchner and assisted by Major (later Brigadier) Callie Steyn of Military Intelligence (MI). Lt-Colonel Garth Barrett would take operational command assisted by Major John Pearson of 6 Recce.

Mike West recalled: "Surprise was essential, we were going into a big metropolitan area with plenty of possible defenders so we had to reach our targets without detection. The assault groups were trained intensively for two weeks, in fighting in built-up areas (FIBUA) and clearing houses. We went through drills from morning to night, rehearsing everything, and perfecting convoy procedures.

"The plan was for us to drive from the border in vehicles that resembled those used by the Mozambican army. In this disguise we planned to get in quickly, achieve the maximum surprise and damage, and get out with the minimum of casualties.

---

7   SASOL – South Africa Synthetic Oil Liquid company producing petrol and diesel from coal and natural gas.

There were three targets:

Target 'Alpha': A double storey house where we were told Joe Slovo, MK Chief of Staff, was occasionally housed. This was known as the 'Transit Facility' and this was for Bob MacKenzie's group with Rich Stannard as second in command.

Target 'Bravo': A house used by an MK unit tasked with attacking installations in South Africa. This facility was known as 'Sabotage Machinery'. This team was led by Major Steynberg with Corrie Meerholz as the second in command.

Target 'Charlie': Another house which was the planning HQ for most of the ANC attacks in South Africa. This group were known as 'Police Machinery'.

Our team was comprised of:

- The Commander, Lt Mike Rich with Lt Phil Cooke his second in command.
- The Vehicle Gunner, Don Kenny.
- The Assault Team: Dave Berry, Frank Tunney and myself.
- Driver: Cannot recall.

"To our dismay, just before deploying, the Dominee (Chaplain) appeared to deliver a sermon. He preached and prayed for 25-35 minutes, asking God in Afrikaans, to give the soldiers the power he gave them at Blood River. This was when the Voortrekkers defeated the Zulus on 16 December 1838, and emphasised that it was still *ons wit mense* – we whites – pitted against *die swart mense* – those blacks – and to slaughter the blacks. It was a tirade against blacks, but he never took into account that we had blacks fighting with us. It was very awkward for us.

"We ex-Rhodesian SAS, listened in embarrassment as he made a thorough fool of himself, and unfortunately, by association, the rest of the whites, by confidently predicting that with prayers, the bullets of the black enemies would turn to water. These guys were as bad as the witchdoctors that blacks believed in and we found so amusing. What a fool, we knew there were men out there who wanted to kill us, and the only thing that would stop them is if we killed them first. My loathing of organised religion had just increased. Lt-Colonel Barrett was furious because he had not included time for this sermon in his plan and we would now be leaving behind schedule.

"Eventually, now that we had been blessed, off we went in disguised vehicles under the battle command of Garth Barrett. The vehicle, a Russian Gaz, was armed with a 20mm Hispano Suiza. Three Gazs went to three different targets.

"We knew there was a powerful battalion-strength force of Frelimo's motorised infantry, supported by Soviet T34 tanks, based at Moamba outside the city. They were a standby reaction force, but intelligence indicated their organisation was chaotic and their reaction time likely to be slow. Nevertheless, it was decided to lessen their chances of reacting swiftly by dropping off two operators on bicycles with balloon type tyres to negotiate the soft sand, and cut the telephone wires from Moamba.

"Unfortunately, on our bundu-bashing way in – and before splitting up – we got horribly lost and drove right to the boom of a Frelimo Military Base. Thankfully we had a *mulatto* whose name was Quiroz, who was dressed as a Frelimo officer, and spoke the native tongue. He addressed the armed guard at the boom with authoritive severity, who saluted him, and then gave him the directions that we needed. Our entire convoy made a U-turn right in front of said boom, and headed off in the right direction. We arrived at our respective targets a little behind schedule.

"At our target the pathway from the gate to the front door was roughly 30 metres. As our team arrived, Don opened up with the 20mm cannon, let rip from the gate, and he had to keep to the left of a protruding wall hammering the shit into two large windows facing the gate to allow our team to reach the target. Dave, Frank and myself dashed for the building, carrying the explosives between us – a good weight of the stuff, too. We arrived at the door, and placed a 'Knock Knock' explosive device on the door, which destroyed the locking system in totality. Don was still firing at the building. He was supposed to be shooting at the left side of the building – the building corner being his arc – because we were entering on the right hand side, but something went wrong and he overshot, hitting the right side and sending shrapnel flying our way. It literally skimmed past me – between my body and the wall – and took out Dave's leg, hitting him on the side of the right knee.

"Frank stayed by the open door as I grabbed and carried Dave, and ran 30 metres back to the vehicle. Don, seeing this, thought we were being shot at, and really opened up as we were very exposed, given that there was a bedroom window directly above the front door which the gunner could not engage due to our team being by the door.

"Dave wasn't exactly a small lad, so I'm glad I got out with my back intact. I shoved him into the vehicle, and ran back to Frank. We entered the house, with torches on the front of our weapons. There was so much dust that you couldn't see further than 30cm in front of you. While setting up the charges, there was a helluva scuffling noise from the front, and towards me. I could only assume that someone was trying to get out of the house because everything in front of me was thick brown dust and blurred. I pumped a fair amount of lead into that direction, and it went quiet. Silence, in the thick dust.

"By our reckoning there were four or five MK cadres sleeping inside who were killed by gunfire. Ronnie Kasrils later said the house was used by MK's Natal operatives and confirmed that six, including their commander, Mduduzi Guma, were surprised and died in their beds. We left the house, jumped on the vehicle, and hastened out of there. We were supposed to search the house for information and documentation, but you couldn't even see a living being never mind a piece of paper – and with a 20mm still pumping lead into the place, plus one man down…"

Richard Stannard, who was in Alpha group under the command of Bob MacKenzie remembers: "We had no problem finding the house we were to attack and it all looked very quiet on arrival. Adjacent to the house was an orchard which two of the teams crept through while I prepared to launch the actual frontal assault with Frank Vivier and Mike Smith. Frank was a top operator from a farming family in Manicaland who I had worked with in the SAS and I was happy to have him along. Attacking from the rear of the house was another group that included Sergeant Rob Hutchinson, Ian Suttill, Jim Park and Wayne Ross Smith.

"As the attack went in with the other guys tossing grenades through the windows, we blew down the front door with a charge, lobbed a few grenades and a bunch of ANC guys immediately surrendered, pleading with us not to kill them. This came as a bit of a surprise, but as we were trying to get the prisoners cuffed and out the way there was a huge blast which almost knocked me off my feet followed by more blasts. To my horror, I could see some of my blokes were burning. Our medic Andy Johnston was trying to put out flames covering Ian Suttill, and Jim Park was also on fire. I could not see Rob Hutchinson as a grenade had bounced back and exploded at his feet killing him. I broke off the actual assault to go to their aid. Some of the captives seized the opportunity, jumped through windows and ran for it but went straight into deadly fire from Keith Cloete and Mario Vidal who took most, if not all, of them down.

"Just what happened to Ian, Rob and Jim remains unclear, but it seems grenades bounced back at them off the gauze windows or maybe they were fired on from the upper level of the building. It was white phosphorous that was burning on Jim and Ian. With Mike Smith and Andy Johnston helping me I tried my best to strip Ian's webbing, dislodge the grenade and douse the flames but to no avail; a grenade in one of his pouches exploded and one arm and a leg were blown off as I held him. I carried him to the vehicle, and he spoke his last on the way. 'Did we get them sir?' he whispered. 'Yes Ian, we did,' I replied. Then he died. Mike Smith and I were lucky to survive but we both took some shrapnel, with one piece going into my eye. Jim Parks, although badly wounded, staggered back to where Bob MacKenzie was with the HQ group. Wayne Ross Smith was also seriously injured with phosphorous burns and shrapnel wounds.

"It was chaotic, and we were still taking fire from some spirited resistance, having lost the initiative. The order came to end the assault and load up before I and my guys had had a chance to go in and clear the house out. Rob Riddell laid a charge to blow the house down and we boarded the vehicles. Looking back, maybe Bob MacKenzie and his guys should have gone to the aid of the wounded guys when they ran into trouble and allowed me to carry on with my assault but very easy for me to say that now I suppose. We boarded the vehicles and moved to Barrett's HQ to meet up with the other teams and exit from Mozambique. It was pandemonium and sitting in the truck beside Jim, he kept bursting into flames as pieces of phosphorous ignited. While there was a cursory check on bodies, on who was wounded and who was alive, it was not done thoroughly enough and only when we were about half an hour away from the target did we realise Rob Hutchinson was missing. In all the years of the Rhodesian war we had never left anyone behind, and some of the guys became very angry when we realised he was not with us. They demanded we return no matter what the consequences were, but this request was denied, and this triggered an almost mutinous feeling amongst some of the men. One of the drivers, Tom Oldridge, became hysterical, screaming and shouting while throwing weapons out the vehicle. He had to be sedated by the medic. Poor Jim died on the road home.

"Bravo Group', meanwhile went after the 'Sabotage Machinery'. Corrie Meerholz and his guys were expecting stiff resistance from a well defended facility, but they were pleasantly surprised to meet no such problem. They snuck up to the house and placed a 'Hulk' charge which was expected to blow a hole in the wall but damn near blew the whole wall down. Then they tossed grenades and went in firing at the lower level while support fire was directed at the upper storey. Corrie and his guys cleared the bottom of the building and then, after signalling to the support group to cease fire, went upstairs to clear that but most of the occupants were already dead. They killed quite a few people and made a few captures but there was not much of an enemy presence there and as I remember, not much of intelligence value was found and certainly no Joe Slovo. Later we heard he had been giving a briefing and left only hours before. One of the other vehicles had a 106mm Recoilless Rifle on it. They just blew the house off the map. No documentation. No more location.

"At Major Rob Johnson's roadblock, a Portuguese engineer, Jose Ramos, working for the state-owned energy company Electricidade de Moçambique, was 'mistakenly identified' by our guys as Joe Slovo. They tried to capture him but when he tried to jump the road block in his car, ignoring a warning flare, he was shot. Other motorists had halted at the road blocks, obediently turning around when ordered to, accepting that the soldiers there were Frelimo. We then regrouped at Komatipoort still in darkness, aware that Maputo would scramble MiGs at first light to search for the column."

The question on everyone's lips was how did the invaders manage to get to Matola undetected, and how did they manage to hit three separate targets and then get away to South Africa overland without being stopped. President Machel was enraged.

The next day, *The Star* newspaper headlines shouted: '**Matola: A paradox of lies and bloody death**'. Frelimo claimed it was an attack by a fascist government on innocent and unarmed refugees. Reference was made to the Nazis having resurrected themselves and mutilated bodies were presented to the press. The CIA was accused of involvement and American diplomats were expelled. Some senior Frelimo officers were accused of treachery and arrested.

"After the raid the English-Afrikaner divide did not narrow, it probably widened", remembers Mike. "This was 6 Recce's first and last external operation. The Rhodesians soon started to leave and it was not long before there were not many of of us left out of the 60 who came down. Because of religion and an entrenched dislike of people of English descent the SADF lost some brilliant soldiers. I was very sorry to see my 'blood-brothers' go. I then transferred to 1 Recce."

TWO South African soldiers died in the audacious SADF commando attack on African National Congress hideouts near Maputo.

The scene of the attack was littered today with unexploded grenades, blood-stained webbing and a South African helmet marked "Follow me to hell".

Among the shattered buildings where more than 50 ANC exiles were killed and a Portuguese technician died in crossfire, a sole ANC survivor wandered, stunned and bloodied clutching a pistol.

"I want to shoot somebody, I want to shoot somebody," he mumbled as the first party of British and American journalists arrived from Johannesburg to inspect the site of Friday's pre-dawn attack.

In Pretoria last night the SADF released the names of the South African soldiers who were killed. They are:

● Sergeant Robert Lewis Hutchinson, 24, son of Mr M L H Hutchinson, of 9 Levin Close, Lakes Estate, Bletchley, Milton Keyns, Buckinghamshire, England.

● Sergeant Ian Suttill, 32, who is survived by his wife, Mrs J Suttill, of 26 Camelot, Coronation Road, Malvern, Queenborough, Natal.

The foreign journalists who visited the village of Matola yesterday saw signs that thousands of rounds of small-arms fire and at least a dozen rockets were fired into the three houses occu-

By RAY SMUTS and GERHARD PIETERSE

pied by the ANC.

In a garage stood an expensive Mercedes-Benz car completely burnt out.

Outside another 350SE model with Bloemfontein number plates was pockmarked with bullet holes.

On walls inside the houses — which served as ANC logistics and planning facilities — there were cuttings from South African newspapers with pictures of the blaze from last year's limpet mine attack on Sasol — the ANC's most spectacular attack inside South Africa.

"It was certainly not a clean surgical-type strike," one observer told us last night.

"The South Africans obviously opened up with everything they had and placed their rounds at random rather than aiming at specific targets.

It appeared as if one soldier took a direct hit from a rocket round, the observer said.

"His webbing was blown clean off his body and was covered in blood. It was

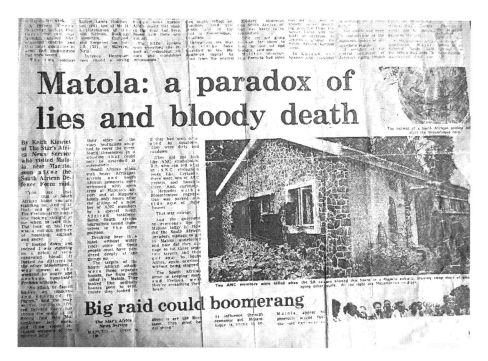

Matola: a paradox of lies and bloody death

Big raid could boomerang

'Operation Kerslig'

As it became clearer to the South Africans that the Angolan government, in concert with the Soviets, was stepping up support for Swapo, a high-level decision was taken to launch a strike that would remind them that these actions were not without consequences. The selected target was the Petrangol Refinery within the confines of Luanda harbour. It produced all the country's basic fuel requirements. Destroying it would instantly increase Angola's dependence on imported products and thereby give South Africa more leverage.

In mid 1981 a reconnaissance was done revealing the size of the facility and details of the seaborne approaches. The refinery was flanked by shanties and was in an industrial area. It was noted that an anti-aircraft battery was positioned to the north with a police station to the south.

Two Strike Craft, the SAS *Oswald Pirow*, commanded by Commander Arné Söderlund, and the SAS *Jim Fouche* commanded by Fanie Uys, would bring the teams in, while Barracudas from 4 Recce would secure the landing area. The SAS *Protea* would provide additional support including surgical facilities to deal with the wounded. A C130 TelStar was supplied by the Air Force to act as a communications hub. Captain Lambert Jackson (Woody) Woodburne was the Operation Commander and Commandant Andre Bestbier the Mission Commander. Malcolm Kinghorn from 4 Recce was the Boat Group Commander and Captain Douw Steyn the Raid Commander. Cdr Söderlund was the Naval Commander.

With personnel from both 1 and 4 Recce involved, training commenced at The Bluff in Durban with emphasis on all the raiders knowing everything about everyones' tasks. All the rehearsals were done at night. Close attention was paid to minimising the loads because the mines weighed 20 kilograms and would be carried in custom-made bags. Everything carried by the raiders was checked for traceability and all the weapons issued had been captured on previous raids. Carefully chosen RV points were established for the withdrawal which would commence after midnight.

Preparations complete, the men gathered at Donkergat in Langebaan where a full intelligence briefing was provided. Training aboard the Strike Craft for boarding the Barracudas was intensified.

There would be five raiding teams:

The HQ Team under Douw Steyn would manage the operation, provide fire support and secure the RV point for emergency withdrawal.

Team 1 would lead the raiders in, cut the wires and lay charges at the distillation towers.

Team 2 was tasked to destroy the jet-fuel tanks.

Team 3 was to destroy the LPG (Liquified Petroleum Gas) tanks.

Team 4 would destroy the large tanks holding crude oil.

Team 5 was to establish and protect the withdrawal route.

On 20 November the Strike Craft sailed out of Saldanha Harbour carrying the boats and men and headed for Walvis Bay where they refuelled under cover of darkness. The SAS *Protea* left from Simonstown, ostensibly to conduct a hydrographic survey. On the 25th the Strike Craft neared Luanda and the SAS *Oswald Pirow*, with decoy fishing lights on, launched the two Barracudas some six kilometres from the shore. The presence of a Soviet Destroyer in the harbour, equipped with a state of the art electronic warfare capability, was cause for concern. This concern turned to alarm when radar indicated a vessel closing in at speed which appeared to be a warship. To the relief of all the ship identified turned out to be the SAS *Jim Fouche*.

Sergeant Jack Greef and Corporal Sam Fourie made their way off the beach into an area where heavy trucks were operating. From there they moved into a bushy area only to discover they were inside a military facility. The pair found a thicket in which to hide and awaited the dawn. In the morning light they were surprised to see lines of military vehicles including tanks. The problems mounted when they were approached by two Cuban soldiers walking directly towards their position. Hearts pounding, they held their breath, while one of the men urinated close to their feet. Realising they were too vulnerable they decided to move to what they hoped would be a more secure position much closer to the cliffs. That night they went to check the anti-aircraft battery which appeared to be unmanned, then they went to the perimeter fence of the refinery to take photographs, and assess the best points of entry. It was not going to be easy with approximately 100 metres of well-lit open ground covered by guard-towers to be traversed before being able to breach the inner fence and begin the attack. Then they went back to their hide, signalled the conclusion of the recce and hunkered down for the rest of the night and the following day. That night, after checking entry points again, they were recovered and safely returned to the SAS *Oswald Pirow*.

On the night of 29 November the four boats carrying the sabotage teams left the mothership and headed for the targets. They were over 1000kms behind enemy lines and this was the most audacious seaborne attack ever conducted by the South Africans.

Mike West recalled: "We left the Strike Craft in four Zodiacs manned by the guys from 4 Recce. We could soon see the lights of Luanda and the sea was smooth and calm. Close to the shore the divers went into the sea and swam to clear the beaches for our landing. When we heard the coast was clear we glided in and jumped onto the beach and took up our formations.

"With Jack Greef in the lead we climbed the cliff-face and set up a command station on the edge with Bestbier in charge, where he would control events in conjunction with the TAC HQ aboard the SAS *Oswald Pirow*. We could all see the flame from the refinery burning at the top of the tower. Passing through some rough terrain, past the anti-aircraft battery, we made it to the northern perimeter where Captain Steyn supervised the breach. By midnight we were all though the fence.

"Frank Tunney, my old chum from Rhodesia, and I, took up a position at the point of the breach to cover the withdrawal. My eyes were on the guard towers. If they had had anyone in those we were toast but I could see no movement. We then waited while the teams went to lay their charges.

"But then the shit hit the fan when we heard an explosion. It turned out it was Team 4, Captain Abraham JP (Kokkie) de Kock, Japie Kloppers and Piet van Zyl. There was a premature detonation when Captain de Kock tried to arm one charge to make sure all the others blew, but something went wrong and he was blown to pieces. There were other explosions and fires broke out. Soon sirens were blaring, people were shouting and vehicle engines were fired up. The bad guys were coming for us in a big way.

"When Kloppers stumbled towards us we damn near shot him because we didn't recognise him. When we heard his mate Piet van Zyl had been left behind we immediately started organising ourselves to go to his rescue. Kloppies told us he had dragged his mate to safety. Lieutenant Franz Fourie, Corporal Sam Fourie, and Jack set off with Kloppies only to find Piet was not where Kloppies had last left him. It was chaos with people running all over the place as they worked the area looking for our lost operator. Eventually Franz saw someone crawling towards a group of soldiers and Kloppies said that it was Piet. He was completely disorientated and badly hurt.

"We were all back at our entry point in the fence, Douw Steyn said 'What the fuck now?' I moved out from the fence, knelt and pointed my M79 Grenade launcher at the tower. I made myself the obvious target if there was anyone in the guardtower overlooking the complex. I was ready to blow anyone out of that tower but nobody appeared. I was just a guy doing my job, not a hero. But instead of some form of acknowledgement, I was told later I was stupid for taking such a risk. Why did I do it I was asked? I did it because men were trapped! Then Frank Tunney and I helped carry Piet back to the beach. We decided to bolt back through the brightly lit area, made it back to the beach and to the boats and back to the Strike Craft. Piet was blinded and Kloppies was deaf and we lost Kokkie.

"We left an inferno behind us. The attack was only a partial success but we had given them a fright. We heard later that they had to introduce petrol rationing for a few weeks."

Both Unita and Fnla claimed responsibility but one of Captain de Kock's feet was recovered and shown on TV so the Angolans knew there was European involvement but then the story spread was that it was mercenaries employed by Unita. To Pretoria's relief neither the Angolan government nor their Soviet allies realised the South African Navy had been involved. This was a credit to the professionalism of their officers and sailors. Although the attack did not go off as planned, it shocked the Angolans and their allies and compelled them to pull in troops deployed farther afield and use them to protect the city and vital installations.

"Sam, Franz, Kloppies and Jack Greef were all awarded the Honoris Crux but not Mike West, the philistine," recalls Mike. "All I got was a reprimand for being stupid. This should not have surprised me. Our OC was a Parabat given command of 1 Recce in Durban. He was not an operator nor did he participate in, nor pass the Special Forces selection. In the SAS in Rhodesia our commanding officers were qualified operators who served in combat and had our respect as they had undergone what we operators were engaged in, meaning selection and physical combat. Our Rhodesian commanders were men of war and not glorified basecamp commanders.

"Bestbier specifically hated me. I only got a South African Medal some six months later and not on the first medal parade after Kerslig. I felt I was fighting two wars; one against my own seniors who disliked me, and one against the enemy. The nature of the story is that nothing balances. Bestbier and later Verwey went out of their way to make my life hell and I believe they would have been quite relieved to have seen me killed. They hated me. I was the rebel who had no religion, so they later had me reposted. I would not suck up to these assholes, so they treated me like shit. There were brilliant soldiers up to staff sergeant level, as well as a few officers, but many officers like Bestbier were not combatants on the ground. We got the impression that some of us rebels were considered expendable.

* * * * *

"After Kerslig we were based at Ruacana, we called our camp Fort Nomad and in May 1982 'Operation Boomslang' was initiated aimed at covert operations into Angola. Major Douw Steyn was the base commander. I remember the heat was intense and we could only really operate in the mornings and evenings. On the one occasion Douw tasked one of the officers, also a major, to carry out a mission. This officer stated that he thought it was way too risky.

"Douw called me over, and instructed me to carry out the mission. I was happy to comply, being an actual hands-on Team Leader. I assembled my team, gave orders, and off we went on our happy hunting trip. It was a success, as expected. Not a word was spoken about this again."

A Star is Not Born

"During 1982 Captain 'Oupa' van Dyk and I were approached to do the parachute jumping for the movie 'Crazy Jungle'. They were shooting the final part of the film at the Lion Park at Pietermaritzburg. I had to play the role of James Mitchum, the son of Robert Mitchum. Oupa had to play the role of a little black guy, Baldwin Dakili, so he had to blacken his face.

"The story was about a sleazy airline owner who forces a drunkard former airline pilot, 'Butch' (James Mitchum) to climb into the cockpit by threatening to kill his son if he did not comply. Butch was not aware the plane was rigged to crash as part of an insurance scam. They manage to crash on a remote island in a jungle where all sorts of other problems arise.

"So for Butch to save the day in the movie, we jumped out of a Sikorski helicopter, and landed near the lions. I didn't get a stand-up landing, but Oupa did. We were each paid R1,000. This was arranged by Major Peter Scofield, formerly of Rhodesia.

"Once we had done the jump, I was approached by the camera crew to come for an interview in the 'Camel Man' competition, and I was also given the opportunity to become a professional stuntman which Major Scofield offered to sponsor.

"The real Camel Guy was an actor named Bob Beck. The job enabled him to travel around the world, get rich and famous. Not sure if I was the perfect fit.

I might have looked the part but I was just a soldier who wanted to kill 'bad guys' and that might have given their brand a few problems. Their smokes killed with lung cancer, I wanted to enjoy a lot more of the sweet smell of cordite before I went down. My brush with movie stardom was over, however later on I did get close, not as close as I would have liked, but close to Andrea Steltzer who was then the reigning Miss South Africa.

"A bunch of us from the Recces were tasked to do a freefall descent at a dam near Lydenburg. Wearing her crown, she was seated on a throne below us close to the water's edge and we were told to land as close to her as possible. We leaped out of a Puma and not sure why but most of the guys landed with a splash in the water. I, I'm pleased to report, pulled off a perfect landing hitting the ground only a few feet in front of her and firmly on my feet. I stood to attention, removed my helmet and gave her a wink. Later we took her for a flip on the Puma and she absolutely enjoyed the flight."

CHAPTER 8

By Land and Sea

Helicopter Downed

"I was back to work and war when we left our HQ in Durban, and flew with the C130 (Flossie) to our forward base Rundu, east of Ondangwa. This camp was known as Fort Foot. Once there, we were briefed that we were going on a mission to shoot down Russian aircraft in the southern part of Angola, in order to cut off supply routes. This was a joint mission between the Special Forces and Unita. This type of mission had to be very carefully planned due to the fact that Russian MiGs escorted the aircraft transporting the supplies. After gaining all necessary intelligence, detailed orders were issued to us to commence with this task. My team comprised of eight guys: Me, Sean Mullen, Abel Erasmus, Sam van der Merwe, Johan Roets, Rassie Erasmus, Steyntjie and Anton Benadie.

"September 1982, from Rundu, we were taken by two Puma helicopters to a designated area in Southern Angola, between Cuito Cuanavale and Baixa do Longa, which was controlled by Unita. From there, we were transported by Russian GAZ vehicles to a Unita base camp deeper within the bush. The Unita Commander of the area, and some of his top-ranking officials, sat down with myself and Johan Roets to discuss the whole *modus operandi*. Once we reached an agreement, they moved my team and I, with a Unita support group, and our five SAM 7 surface-to-air missiles, to an area between Menongue and Baixa do Longa, where Russian aircraft were frequently seen.

"We had to move around quite a bit in this area, as the aircraft on these flight routes were out of range. We carried the SAM 7s, a light-weight, shoulder-fired, surface-to-air missile system designed to target aircraft at low altitudes, with passive infrared homing guidance and then destroy them with a high explosive warhead. The missile had a range of 25 000 feet.

"Roughly seven days into this operation we had moved to a new temporary base when I heard the sound of aircraft to the north. I couldn't be sure if it was an aircraft or helicopter. The sound was coming closer and I told Sean Mullen, who was our SAM 7 operator, to get ready for action. Sean ran, grabbed a missile and launcher, and we moved into a nice opening amongst the trees that had a clear view of the sky. By this stage, we could discern that it was a helicopter approaching, and although we had been told that this system was largely ineffective against choppers, (due to the rotors that disperse the heat), we decided to give it a go.

"When we could hear that it was extremely close, though we were still not able to see it, I activated the battery to energise the system. Sean then pointed the tube in the direction of the incoming sound. Through the clearing of trees we saw an Mil Mi-8 Helicopter (which, in addition to having the ability to carry 24 troops, was armed with rockets and anti-tank guided missiles) coming directly towards our position. He must have been about 50 metres above the trees.

"The SAM 7 sang into action, screaming as the gyro flew into full swing. When the chopper was directly over our position, Sean fired. The missile went straight up, right into the exhaust system of the Mi-8, which is situated directly below the rotor blades. There was one helluva explosion and, as the chopper moved past the clearing, it began to careen out of control. We watched the stricken aircraft as the nose went up into the sky, and the tail rotor pointed downwards, then it plummeted and crashed into Mother Earth, roughly a kilometre from the firing position.

"It all happened so fast. We heard a massive explosion, and black smoke billowed into the air above the tree line. I moved my guys, and the Unita support team rapidly towards the downed chopper hoping that there were survivors to apprehend. When we got close to the wreck, we realised that the only thing that we would be apprehending was ashes from the inferno once it had subsided. There was the odd Cuban helmet, magazines, and pieces of AK47s strewn around the wreckage site. All the bodies were trapped inside the blazing wreck. We did not realise it at the time but the Cuban co-pilot, although injured, had managed to escape and hide. We did a quick appreciation of the situation, recovered the scattered remnants, and got the hell out of the area, as there were bound to be unfriendlies moving rapidly towards that area. This kind of smoke would definitely attract all kinds.

"I thought to myself, 'time to go'. We moved due west at a rapid pace for at least four hours nonstop, covering roughly 16 kilometres. We rested for a while and tried to pick up the sound of vehicle engines and/or other dodgy noises from that general direction. We heard nothing. It was already getting dark and there was a moon in the sky. We kept walking right into the night to get well clear of the area which we knew would be a beehive of activity by morning.

"Come morning, we were already approximately 25 kilometres away from the site. Puma choppers came in to pick up our team and Unita were uplifted by their Russian GAZ vehicles, hightailing it to one of their strongholds. We were taken back to Rundu, where we were immediately met by Top Brass for a briefing. A communiqué was intercepted from Menongue, in Angola, stating that 18 Cuban soldiers died in the downed helicopter.

"During the briefing, we realised that we had made history as this was the first time that an Mi-8 Russian Helicopter had been taken down by a supposedly ineffective surface-to-air missile, namely the SAM 7, which had already been rendered virtually obsolete by the American Stinger surface-to-air missile.

"Needless to say, this incident struck fear into the hearts and minds of the South African Air Force who were now concerned that they, too, were vulnerable to this supposedly outdated weapon. These weapons were abundantly available to the enemy at the time.

I was then escorted by Captain Daan van Zyl to the Forward Operational Airbases where I had to explain how in the hell we'd managed to drop an Mi-8 with this near-toothless dinosaur. "How we did it: The chopper was dead overhead. The exhaust was exposed. The missile went home. The chance of this happening again: highly unlikely. This put the pilot's minds at ease to some degree, but this had them on high alert to the possibility.

Job done. We were uplifted and flown back to our Durban base.

"Unsurprisingly, because I was involved and not liked, nothing was mentioned about this event in the army or outside of it – not ever. Not even a simple 'well done'. Fuck all. We dropped a fucking chopper, dear reader. With an obsolete weapon. We brought a goddamn chisel to a fucking knife fight – AND WE WON, but this was swept under the carpet. Screw them all. We made history.

We remember.

"Years later I was in touch with Tinus de Klerk who was helping a Cuban fighter pilot with a book he was doing on Angola. I asked him if he could find out via the pilot if they knew about the Cubans who died when we shot down the Mi-8. We were told there were 19 Cubans onboard. Eighteen died and one managed to escape from the wreck. Lots of burn wounds. He was a co-pilot. Teniente (Lieutenant) Hernando Martinez."

"...he remained in the bush for weeks... twenty-five days after the crash when he finally made it back to his own troops he was nearly 20 kgs lighter and worms had taken up residence in the burn wounds of his head and ears."[8]

Bridges Blown

"This was another combined operation between 1 Recce, 5 Recce and 4 Recce, with the assistance of the SA Navy and the SA Air Force. The aim was to destroy the road and rail bridges over the Giraul River leading from the port of Moçâmedes to Lubango which was the provincial capital and from where Fapla and Swapo received the bulk of their supplies. The railway was also to be used for the export of minerals from a mine near Cassinga.

"From the SA Navy, we were to go in with two Strike Craft, the SAS *Oswald Pirow* under command of Bob Harrison, and the SAS *Jim Fouche* commanded by Fanie Uys. Taking the guys from 4 Recce in to do the initial reconnaissance of the target was the submarine SAS *Maria van Riebeeck* commanded by Captain Howell. The overall commander was Captain Viljoen and the Mission Commander was Commandant Hannes Venter. A SAAF C130 was to be the TelStar for communications and the Air Force was also on standby to strike if we got into big trouble and couldn't get out. Supporting the flotilla was the SAS *Tafelberg*. 4 Recce was tasked to do the initial reconnaissance the day before and they would do the attack along with 23 guys from 1 Recce and five from 5 Recce. We were sent to Donkergat near Langebaan to train and prepare for the mission and this is where my problems started.

"This preparation phase went off smoothly until a few nights before the deployment when a few of us visited the Tropicana Restaurant in Langebaan. Shock and

---

8   'The MiG Diaries': Lt. Col. Eduardo Gonzalez Sarria and Lionel Reid.

horror – we ended up in a punch-up with civilians. It was brief. Outside of the restaurant, I planted a civvie in a flowerbed for making a derogatory comment.

"Unfortunately for me, his teeth had embedded themselves in my right hand, between my ring finger and pinkie finger, right to the bone. The idiot didn't even have the decency to close his mouth when I punched him, and I now had an unnecessary injury. I bet he didn't make fucking comments like that again, for the rest of his life.

"Adding insult to injury, the commander of the base banned us from going out at night and I had to report to Sick Bay because my hand had started stiffening up from the idiot's clearly rotten teeth. Antibiotics and Tetanus were prescribed and administered.

Oh – and now all our pre-training involved rope ladders and climbing. Painful, but I pulled my own cliffhanger stunts, hooking my wrist and using my left hand, mostly. Remember this part about my hand. It's going to be very relevant shortly.

"We did our final rehearsal on 28 October and we were on the sea by 1st November. A few delightful days at sea, with many of us feeding fish at random, we anchored roughly 50 kilometres from the harbour. Those ships sure rolled a lot in rough seas and even hardened sailors got sick at times. I have eardrums perforated many times from bangs and boxing that screws with my balance, so the rocking of the ocean is the best goddamn diet for me, because I can't even retain water. Something to laugh about now, but not so much at the time.

"While we waited at anchor the sub went in with both two-man recce teams. They would go from the sub to the coast in inflatables. This was all happening later than planned because the sub had developed engine problems, but she made it there. Unfortunately, this reconnaissance did not go well and a shot was fired by someone near the target so there was talk of cancelling because they might have been compromised. Through the persiscope the submarine captain had also seen a Russian warship docked in the harbour so this was additional cause for concern. A decision was made to do another recce a day later and this went better. This time they saw no sign of the enemy and reported they had found a better way to the bridges. D-Day was set for 7 November.

"The teams were the Command Team led by Commandant Venter, two demolition teams and four small early-warning teams to watch the approaches while we went to work on the bridges. My team was under the command of Major van Niekerk, the other under command of Captain Jenkinson.

"We were ferried from the motherships by Barracuda MKII operational boats around midnight. Four teams dropped off in the shallows and waded in. Once we beached the Command Team and the early-warning guys went ahead to secure the area, and once they gave us the 'go', we started moving to the target under our heavy loads. The charges were made up in 15 kilogram satchels. At this point I got even angrier with the civvy who fucked my hand up. With us having to climb rope ladders and pass explosives to our Demolition Team, I took serious strain and pain with my stiff, swollen right hand, which I couldn't even close. I pushed through – or, should I say, I pulled through, and did my part, regardless, using my hatred for the stupid infectious civvy as fuel to fire me up.

"I think I was carrying 80kgs. We were all carrying weapons, webbing, rope ladders and lots of explosives. The rope ladders would allow us to scale the rocky cliff faces to get to the target. The layout of the land made it difficult to reach the bridges and we were behind schedule in getting there. The deadline for completion of the task was extended to 03h00 but we were still under a lot of pressure.

"At the river we split into two teams, one going to the rail bridge, the other to the road bridge. Our briefing had not really prepared us for this; it proved to be way more involved and arduous to lay these explosives than anticipated. The explosives were in satchels that were suspended close to the pillars using a special type of gunk super-glue. We also had timers, which were set for 06h00 in the morning, and there was no way to hurry it up other than get it fucking done.

"Without the explosives, the return journey to the beach was easier and quicker. We went ahead followed by the HQ group and the early-warning teams. By the time we got back to the beach, it was nearly Kaboom Time and the sun was coming up. But it was late and we were in deep shit. The Barracudas were coming in to uplift us, with the sun shining so we were out in the open if anyone was interested. Then, to add to our woes, there was a Russian Kirov-class battlecruiser in the harbour, heavily armed with missiles and cannons, it was a menacing sight. If this thing had got busy we were not going anywhere near home.

"It got worse because the tide was now coming in with the approaching boats, and we were supposed to exfiltrate as the tide was going out. We waited and watched the huge waves crashing before us and knew this was not going to be a problem-free extraction.

"Teams 1 and 2 managed without incident on the other side of the tide-break but Team 3 were not so fortunate. As they were throwing kit and weapons on to the boat the waves were too much and one caught the Barrracuda and flipped it; the boat became history and had to be abandoned. One of the officers was trapped underneath the capsized hull but rescued. The operators got on board one of the other boats with the waves crashing down. At the same time we, as Team 4, were treading water and dodging sharks trying to get to our boat but the sea was too rough and they couldn't get to us.

"Riptides, killer currents, sharks, full battle gear, weapons aloft, Russian warship lurking and in my case a fucked hand; we were drowning more than swimming.

We battled on and coxswain and crew were great. We were all very fortunate, and very grateful, to make it to the boat and get in but some of the Team 3 boys were thrashing around in the water, and I could see some of them were not going to make it if we did not help them. We raced over to save them. We were in amongst them hanging over the sides of the Barracuda, grabbing soldiers and pulling them to safety, from a violent sea. At one stage I just saw a hand disappearing and lunged at it and pulled with all my might. Up it came, a head appeared, it was Captain Chris Greyling. I grabbed him by his webbing unknowingly with my damaged right hand and hauled him up and over the side, how I did it remains a mystery, since my hand was completely immobile. He had given up and thought he was a goner; a second later I would not have been able to grab and save him. Just in time. He told me that all he remembered was a powerful hand grabbing him and yanking him out. He knew he was off to feed the sharks. Amidst all this chaos and crashing of waves we heard the blasts as the bridges blew. We were so deep in shit now that it was way past the eyeballs.

"And there, on the beach, stood Herman van Niekerk as the bridges blew and the sky exploded. Much like the captain going down with a ship, he had to first stay and ensure that everyone was safe. Once we were all aboard he had to dive in and swim – not something you can do in these rough seas. We also managed to get to him before he drowned. A very brave man, I salute you Sir.

"All this time, the lost Barracuda was being flung against the beach by the ferocious ocean. Two teams were on one Barracuda – which surpasses an overloaded taxi – with the transom low in the the water from the weight.

"Just when we thought we would soon be clear we all held our breath as all went suddenly quiet as the motor spluttered and died. The other two boats had disappeared. We were helpless, floating, in full view, broad daylight, no engine, no oars, no hope. And a Russian warship on the loose nearby.

"Now I thought there were two possibilities; we drown at sea because we were taking in water, or the Russians kill or capture us? I was not sure which option I preferred. It was an eerie time. Then the silence was broken when the Afrikaans-speaking soldiers started singing. There was nothing else to do. We accepted our fate, we were going to try and die happy.

"And then, just like true fucking heroes, the Navy came racing in with the Strike Craft to uplift our sorry arses. I don't believe in invisible friends, deities or flapping angels, but I believe in Captain Woodburne. He really saved us. We all owe our lives to his bravery and skill. Bless him!

"We were thrilled to be back on the Strike Craft, headed home aboard this Cotch Bucket, with a flapjack stiff hand, but many a grateful operator. We had survived one helluva hair-raising ordeal. Everyone had survived. No casualties. Truly remarkable.

"And what of the Russian Kirov? How did we give them the slip in full day-light, flapping around and making a racket on the ocean having blasted the bridges so close to them. Well thank God for Vodka; their Special Forces crew had apparently been given shore leave the night before. They had obviously disembarked, and had one helluva party and piss-up. So much so, that by the time they had gathered themselves and dragged their hungover arses back to the ship, we were long gone.

"The raid was a success, both bridges were dropped and the Angolans had a lot to think about. Troops that should have been guarding the bridges were arrested. Unita claimed responsibility, explaining that one of their special sabotage teams had carried out the raid but unfortunately there was the boat we left behind to discredit that claim. The fact that the Russians, despite a naval presence in the port had not spotted us, was a potential embarrassment to them so they discounted the suggestion that the SA Navy had been involved. There was talk from the Russians that the landing took place with the help of a Japanese fishing vessel, which they said was a violation of maritime law.

"But we got the job done and we all made it home safely. This, Dear Reader, is what you call Luck. Today, 38 years later, Chris Greyling and I still talk about that moment at sea. The bastard still owes me a beer."

'Operation Katiso'

The reason behind this operation was to increase pressure on Zimbabwe. With Mugabe taking an increasingly aggressive stance against South Africa, Pretoria sought to gain leverage by making the country dependent on fuel imports via South Africa. With the repair of the pipeline from Beira in Mozambique to Mutare in Zimbabwe, Mugabe was busy getting himself into a better position to distance himself and this needed to be addressed. As a result the decision was taken to blow the oil storage tanks in Beira that held fuel destined for Zimbabwe. The Renamo resistance movement would claim responsibility.

The plan was for 1 Recce to do the attack with marine support provided by 4 Recce. Barracudas launched from Strike Craft would get the men to the beaches. Prior to the raid a reconnaissance would be conducted under the command of Wynand du Toit.

Final approval was given on 19 November and the day set for the attack was 9th December. The SAS *Oswald Pirow* under command of Bob Harrison and SAS *Jim Fouche* commanded by Fanie Uys were the designated Strike Craft. The SAS *Tafelberg*, docked in Simonstown would provide medical and logistical support.

Commandant Ewald Olckers, Officer Commanding 1 Recce, was Operation Commander, Harrison the Naval Commander, Andre Bestbier the Mission Commander, and the OC 4 Recce, Hannes Venter, would run their boat and diving operations from SAS *Oswald Pirow*.

The Strike Craft would depart from Durban on 3rd December and arrive in the area after dark on 5th December. The recce team would then land that night on an island near the coast and then kayak in to the mainland. Their instructions; to establish the best points for deployment and recovery, and to observe movement in the vicinity of the target. They would be withdrawn on the morning of the 7th December.

The raiding group consisted of the Mission Commander and his protection party which would secure the landing area, a forward HQ element under Captain John Taylor, four demolition teams and a team in reserve. The raiding group would only land after the reconnaissance team confirmed that the landing area was clear. The teams would then proceed to the target.

At the depot the first team would enter to check for an enemy presence and withdraw if need be. Once in they were to place limpet mines on the pumps and on the pipeline to Mutare. Teams Two and Three were to place mines on all the 18 storage tanks. Charges laid, they would then return to the beach for evacuation.

"I was second in command to Lt. Fourie, tasked to blow the pump-station which pushed the oil through the pipeline to Mutare. I had already been to Beira with the Rhodesian SAS so I was not a stranger to this part of the world. The pump-station and fuel-line to Zimbabwe had been out of action for over ten years through the Rhodesian war, and after expensive repairs it was just about to reopen so there was quite a lot of excitement. Zimbabwe was trying to lessen its dependence on importing fuel from South Africa because they were calling for international sanctions against us and yet at the same time they needed to keep importing and trading with us. There was a lot of fuel in those tanks and we were told we would put the whole Zimbabwe economy out of action for a couple of months. The strangeness of war – the country I had fought so hard for, I was now fighting to destroy.

"The boat trip in went smoothly, we beached quietly and approached the target. The other groups went their different ways. We quietly approached the control room, which was brightly lit. There were goats making a noise and some movement but we were well hidden.

We then received the order from Frans Fourie to withdraw as he apparently had seen a vehicle arrive with Frelimo troops on it. None of the other team members saw the vehicle.

The other guys were also agitated to get the job done. I was pissed off when we withdrew reluctantly as were the guys behind me. I believe I could have taken over and got the job done, but I would like to clarify a point. Had I disobeyed the order and the situation went wrong and somebody died, I would have been court-martialled. Secondly had I taken over command against his orders and succeeded he would have got the praise. Prior to this operation while we were still in Durban, I jokingly asked if I could not lead the operation. I was told that Lt Fourie was the team leader and that was that. Personally I had no time or respect for this officer, but I could not voice my opinion. I felt that I had way more combat experience than he had, hence my request. This officer had apparently made a statement on a previous occasion that we Rhodesians were Philistines who ran away from our country and we should go back to where we came from.

"Team Two under Captain Van Zyl got their job done and laid charges on nine storage tanks before moving out with us. Team Three also successfully laid their charges, before Team Four came in and mined another six tanks before chucking out Renamo leaflets. An alarm then went off but nobody seemed to react to it.

"Everyone made it safely back to the beach and on to the boats. Not long after we hit the water and were well on our way back to the Strike Craft, the explosions started and the sky lit up. It was a big success but I was upset about the fact we had not done our job. It was a sort of no-win-no-win situation. Looking back I think I let myself and the other guys down; I should have taken the chance, grabbed Sean Mullen and Albie Heigers, and I could've taken over the op and done it, but I left it. Let me put it this way, If Darrell gave the order to withdraw, I didn't question him, but I did question this guy.

"Back in Durban, Albie reported that the operation could have been carried out and the wrong decision had been made. Following this report, an officer came to me and told me that a complaint was lodged against the decision that Frans had made to withdraw, but me as the 2nd in command, should support the decision. He told me that "I must remember I was in their army now" which I did, but I was and remain regretful because I believe we could have completed the task. To Albie and Shaun, we did not see what Frans Fourie saw. Frans was a highly decorated team leader and we were not in any space to question his decision. In basics we were taught, "Ours is not to reason why, ours is but to do or die" We obeyed our orders.

"The day after the attack, with fires still burning, Renamo, through their office in Lisbon, issued a statement claiming they were responsible for the attack. This was planned by our people who did not want South Africa to be blamed. I'm not sure how many people believed it was Renamo but I think we did a good job of hitting them and getting out without leaving our fingerprints on anything that they could use as proof it was us. Renamo had been blowing the pipeline but this had brought Zimbabwe troops into the country to guard it, making these attacks more difficult. This attack made them look a lot more effective than they were and they used this as a pretext to warn Mugabe that he should get his troops out of Mozambique or risk attacks on Zimbabwe itself. Some reports stated this was heaviest economic blow landed against Zimbabwe at that time. There was an immediate fuel shortage in Zimbabwe and big embarrassment for Mugabe and Machel. Mugabe had to shut his big mouth for a while because he had to start getting his fuel from South Africa again. I don't think that storage installation was ever rebuilt."

Teddy the Lion

"Virtually every SA Special Forces soldier spent time at Fort Doppies in the Caprivi Strip. We were in and out of there all the time throughout my time in the Recces doing training. Named after the camp's pet monkey it was also used as a hunting lodge by senior National Party politicians. Surrounded by wild natural beauty, situated near the Cuito River and the border with Angola, it was also used for operations into nearby Zambia. The facilities were rudimentary but it was functional and well organised. There was separate accommodation for the VIPs when they visited. It was also lion country, and this is where Teddy the Lion comes into the story.

"Born in captivity at a zoo in Windhoek, Teddy was adopted as a cub by the Recces, and went as their mascot to Fort Doppies. Our guys reared him and made him part of our family. Some of the guys lived with Teddy for weeks at a time and he would train with us. He would join us on our morning runs, swim in the river with us and even join us on the soccer field. I felt he had a really strong connection with me because when I was there he went everywhere with me and he liked my bed which was a problem because we both couldn't fit. I wasn't brave enough to tell him to find somewhere else to sleep so I had to make other arrangements some nights. When we left to go on operations and the camp was quiet he would wander off into the bush and live the life of a wild lion. But he knew when we were back and wasted no time in coming home. Teddy had a sister we named Lisa but she was badly mauled in a fight with a wild lion and sadly had to be put down.

"Teddy, however, being a big, powerful male, could look after himself when up against the wild lions in the area and adapted well to his double life. For us, dealing with the stresses and strains that come with a demanding and dangerous life, Teddy the ever-friendly and fun-loving lion was a massive morale boost.

"We showed our appreciation by making sure he was very well fed. If camp rations did not suffice, then someone would head into the bush and shoot something for him. If we had a braai, Teddy was always invited to join the fun.

"He enjoyed outings to the 'Survival Camp' where blokes went to train on tracking and bushcraft, but he was not interested in sleeping under the stars so one of the guys would have to surrender his 'bivvie' (small polystyrene shelter) to Teddy and sleep outside. Only problem was he liked to play in the morning, and if nothing else was going on he liked to shred the bivvie before coming out for the day.

"On one occasion one of the guys, tasked with feeding Teddy that day, was tired and not in the mood for doing it. He wanted his free time to himself but duty called so he went and found the food, a big slab of meat, but Teddy was not in the camp. So he wandered out the gate and there was the lion. He called Teddy but he growled, flicked his tail and scratched the dirt with his paws. This was unusually aggressive behaviour coming from Teddy and this guy was pissed off. Rather than going closer to deliver the meal, he shouted at Teddy, amid more growling, and then chucked the meat on the road and stormed off. He walked into the pub and his bad mood changed instantly when he walked in to find Teddy relaxing on the floor there. He had just fed a wild lion and realised he was damn lucky to be where he was.

"When the base became busier and more people started visiting, Teddy became a problem because people shat themselves when he suddenly appeared, so barriers had to be erected around the housing for visitors to keep him out. It was also done to let the men get some sleep. Coming back from a long deployment, tired and needing rest, having Teddy jump on to you in the middle of the night and sand-papering your face with his tongue, was not ideal."

An Operator remembers: "Early during 1980 our 5 Recce selection group moved to the base camp at Fort Doppies after completing our Tracking and Survival course, and were allocated to our different bungalows for the first time in our Recce career.

"We were aware of the existence and presence of Teddy the Lion but had not seen him at all during the day of our arrival at the camp. The late Basie Riekert was sleeping together with me in the same bungalow, and at some point during the middle of the night I was woken by a blood curdling scream from the direction of Basie's bed where he was sleeping.

"I instinctively went into action as I thought we were being attacked, and to my consternation I witnessed an incredible sight in the half darkness of the low moonlight that was shining through the open side of the bungalow. What I saw was a huge lion on top of Basie's bed, licking him in the face and his full weight pinning Basie down. It was a terrifying sight and momentarily I hesitated as to what to do till it dawned on me that it had to be Teddy the Lion who had decided to lie down a bit with Basie. At that point everyone in the camp was awake and roars of laughter emanated from the direction of some of the permanent staff's bungalows in the camp. It took Basie and the rest of us 'new looks' a while to settle down, and to get Teddy off Basie's bed, and out of the bungalow, and to barricade the entrance to prevent Teddy from returning.

"We learned later on that one of our instructors, namely Captain Jakes (Jakkerbos) Jakobs had a pathological fear of Teddy and did not trust this tame lion as far as he could see him. With this valuable knowledge in mind, us 'new looks' decided to pull a prank on Jakkerbos and late one night opened the entrance to the bungalow where Jakkie was sleeping so that Teddy could do a repeat performance on him, as he did on Basie. Miraculously it worked like clockwork and again at some ungodly hour of the night we were woken by screams and shouts and the most obscene swear words from the direction of Jakkie's bungalow. We knew that Teddy had revenged some of the hammerings that Jakkie had dished out to us on Survival Course.

"Teddy was a great source of amusement to visitors and residents of Fort

Doppies alike. During early 1981 a selection course had just finished and was moved to Fort Doppies camp where they were going to progress to their Minor Tactics Course. Among these students was the infamous, or later to become famous, Civvie Burger, a former Pretoria Municipality bus driver, with a reputation for driving skills never heard of before. Among his many talents was gymnastics, the trampoline being his favourite.

"As tradition would have it, all the facilities at Fort Doppies were thrown wide open for the successful candidates and the free beer was flowing till every aspiring Recce had more than his fill. Then Dewaldt De Beer declared the pub closed, and hustled the prospective Recces out of the pub.

"Civvie Burger, who was in very high spirits at that stage, strolled past the trampoline outside the mess with his hands in his trouser pockets, a cigarette dangling from his lips and a cap fitted backwards on his head, followed by his aspiring partners. This was when one of his fellow students cried out: 'Civvie, give us a demo on the trampoline man, we all know you can do it.'

"Civvie, never a man to miss a challenge, bounced effortlessly onto the trampoline without taking off his cap, removing his cigarette, or taking his hands out of his pockets. He commenced doing front saltos9, back saltos, double forward and backward saltos, twists and other mind-boggling manoeuvres. Needless to say the audience was standing agape. Never before in their entire lives had they seen an inebriated man carrying out feats like Civvie. But, as fate had would have it, Teddy the Lion decided to stroll past the trampoline, and Civvie immediately noticed him, and bounced from the trampoline and grabbed Teddy by his tail with one hand and his testicles with the other and started twisting.

"The result was even more stunning than Civvie's trampoline acrobatics. Teddy let out a thundering roar and took off at full speed through the low bush with Civvie hanging on for dear life. Needless to say, a better or more spectacular introduction to Fort Doppies could never be asked for by this aspiring group.

"At one stage, a group of cabinet ministers arrived for a visit to Fort Doppies. The politicians were not wildly popular with the Recce guys so I dont know if it was deliberate or not but they were not told about the lion we lived with. One cabinet minister needed to go to the toilet during the day and this facility

---

9   A gymnastic flip, somersault, or similar manoeuvre

was not protected by the barriers. He made it inside but when he tried to come out there was Teddy standing in all his majesty. He nearly shat himself again and started shouting for help. The nearest operators were in the signals tent and the radios were blaring; they thought they heard someone shouting but above the radio nosie they were not sure, so they did nothing while this poor minister was doing his nut in the toilet. Hours later the cabinet minister was nowhere to be found and somebody decided they better look for him. Strangely, the search began on the opposite side of the base to the toilet facilities and the last place to be searched were the facilities. Here, the Operators found Teddy sleeping outside a cubicle that was closed and bolted firmly. This was the only visit the cabinet ministers ever made to Fort Doppies."

CHAPTER 9

Death in the Desert

Mike West: "We were based at Epupa Falls on the Cunene River when Tony Vieira and I were tasked to go and find the 'Soviet Group' thought to be operating from somewhere on the fringes of the Namib desert. Tony was from Mozambique and one of the Small Teams operators. They wanted this group found and dealt with because there was concern they were carrying Strela Surface to Air Missiles (SAMs) and were therefore a threat to aircraft, civilian and military, in that region.

"Going in we flew a long way over the Namib Desert. It was going to be quite a challenge looking at how little cover there was. We saw some game along the way. When we were in the general area the pilot did a few wide-area dummy drops beforehand, as well as afterwards, in order to confuse the enemy as to where we were actually dropped but it did occur to me that going in during broad daylight like this was dangerous. I did point this out but nobody was listening. I would still like to know what exactly was going on in their minds dropping two people in broad daylight amongst 300 reported terrorists. It's suicidal. They might not know our exact location but they would have known immediately that there was something afoot and come looking. In retrospect we should have been dropped at least 20 kilometres from the target area and then made a clandestine entry. We knew the enemy were operating with the Himbas, who knew the desert well and were superb trackers. I was pretty sure from the outset we were heading for big shit, since we were only two operators up against an estimated enemy strength of at least 300. Even though daylight deployment was a big mistake, we were ordered to do so.

"We were dropped off east of the Namib desert proper, in a very rocky and arid regional area. Water here was but a fairy-tale, so we had no choice but to carry a massive amount of it. A 100 kilogram pack on my back, loaded with water, and the walking on rocky, uneven ground was difficult.

"We scoured the area for five days straight. By day, a high point, with as much shade as possible, to pick up movement or shine. During this time I found the caves where the Hyraxes (Rock Rabbits) lived to be the coolest places to lie up. Flying in we flew over the edges of the desert where I saw some antelope and were dropped off in an area filled with large volcanic rock as far as the eye could see. A few days after drop-off and thirsting for water, I spotted a black-eyed bulbul sitting on a dead tree. I knew they never moved far from water. I immediately started scouting the area looking for water in amongst the rocks. To my utter amazement I found several shaft-like, narrow holes in the rock full of water. I used the drainage pipe from the drip I was carrying to suck them dry. I slaked my thirst, filled my bottle and then felt a sense of guilt for drinking all his water. To this day it remains a mystery how those holes got there.

"This was a time to use all my hard learned skills. When making any movement on the high ground, I had to ensure that my weapon was on the shadow side of my body, so that the enemy could not pick up any shine from my side. Once on high ground, I would scout the ground closest to me, then middle ground, then far ground. Watching for any movement, ensuring that there was no danger nearby.

"Although there were none in this desert area a great bird to watch on my past deployments was the Grey Lourie, colloquially known as the 'Go Away' bird. This bird would sit at the top of the highest tree, and would not be perturbed by the movement of any local wildlife. However, should a human approach, this bird would take off suddenly and fly away so rapidly that you knew it was feeling threatened. They were not liked by the enemy. If they took off gently, and flitted from one tree to the next, you knew there was no danger.

"I knew by this time to use the water only for tea. Cold liquid is not suitable in that sort of heat because your body expels it too rapidly, hot liquids are retained better by the body. Lip ice was essential to stop the lips cracking.

"The problem during the day was that we couldn't see much through the heat-haze. The landscape was full of mirages and it played tricks on my mind in trying to figure out what I was actually seeing. By night we used our night-vision equipment and scanned the area for fires.

"On the fifth day, approximately midday, all was quiet, and I was sitting among some rocks preparing a hot brew. I had an opening of about 20 metres in front of me when suddenly I heard what I thought was voices. Initially very soft, but then a lot closer and I knew they were coming but I couldn't see anything because of the rocks. I had my weapon at the ready, waiting, when a terr came around the rock, walking with his AK at the ready. We saw each other simultaneously. He tried to lift his weapon, but I sent him off to the Happy Hunting Grounds. Sadly for him, if he had known who he was tracking that day, maybe he would have booked off sick and stayed home and saved himself the trouble. I filled him up with lead and then ran firing directly towards the threat that was still behind the rocks; they must have shat themselves and fucked off at speed. Tony let fly with his M79 rifle grenade but cocked up his aim and it exploded nearby sending pieces of rock in all directions, narrowly missing my head. We then moved a short distance after them, but saw nothing. From the tracks that I found in the sand, there must have been about three of them; a scouting party. But once the shooting was over I knew there was no time to hang around because reinforcements in big numbers would soon be on their way. Hunting these people in the rocks is a quick way to die; they can be hiding anywhere. I had been through this several times in Rhodesia and good men had been killed by shots to the head while doing it.

"I radioed Epupa to inform them that we had had a contact and requested an emergency uplift. I was informed that the area was considered too hot for uplift, and it was suggested that we move in a south-easterly direction, for 30 kilometres, in order to be uplifted. That was a fucking long way in the heat of the day, but off we went. Through the day and right through the night with our heavy loads we walked to the rendezvous point.

"To my joy, I was given a roasting back at our Epupa base. I had apparently compromised the operation by killing a man who was seconds away from killing me. After this officer had finished dressing me down I asked: 'With all respect Sir, did you expect me to stand there and let the cunt kill me?' This had him threatening me with insubordination. The fact is the operation was badly planned; they knew we were there, because they had seen or heard the chopper. They had investigated the dummy drops, and it wouldn't have been too hard to find us if they had been paying attention to the drop locations. We should have infiltrated at night. And this wonderfully flat, no cover, rocky region is the kind of area where Spiderman cannot hide. To boot, they also had Himba trackers, who were true experts. HQ's fucked up plan compromised the operation and nearly got me killed. But I was blamed for it later on."

Four Recces Missing

"Late October 1983, I was back in Durban when we heard from Captain Robbie Blake that four black 5 Recce guys, on 'Operation Slyk' in Angola, had gone missing. It was believed that they had been killed or captured but the army needed confirmation.[10] I was told to get a team together immediately and pre-pare to fly to Ondangwa. It all happened very quickly as the next day I briefed 26 guys on the task and then we were deployed in two Pumas and positioned close to where the missing soldiers were last heard from.

"Once on the ground I ordered the men into extended line and we commenced the search. Anton Benadie on the extreme right flank found the body of one of missing men. He had been stripped of all webbing, weapons and equipment. A little further on we came to a tree that had been hit by a rocket or rifle grenade and we found pieces of a broken AK47. We searched the area thoroughly but found no more signs of the other missing men. To this day I am not sure if anyone knows the exact circumstances of their disappearance. Were they killed or taken prisoner since we found no other bodies."

'Charlie Five' 1983/84

End of 1983 saw a build-up of South African armour and artillery on the Angolan border as 'Operation Askari' began to unfold. However, Soviet spies were aware of this and through the offices of the United Nations a message was passed to the South Africans warning them to desist from any further incur-sions. In a show of force, a powerful naval force including a carrier docked at Luanda harbour before sailing around the Cape. But the South Africans were undaunted and on the 9th December the battle-group crossed the border aiming to hit Plan training camps close to a heavily defended brigade HQ. In the face of the assault Russian commanders expressed confidence in the ability of the

---

10   There is information available on various Roll of Honours about these men. Names vary.

defenders to repel any SADF attack. After the assault commenced however, conflicting commands triggered confusion in the ranks and the enemy suffered heavy casualties.

But despite winning on the battlefield, 'Operation Askari' had made the South Africans very aware that they were in for a long fight as sophisticated military equipment continued to pour into Angola. Of major concern was the realisation they were losing control of the skies. And from Washington came the news the Americans wanted to help facilitate a compromise. On 13 February 1984 South African and Angolan officials met for the first time in Lusaka. Three days later, South Africa announced that it would withdraw its forces from southern Angola provided the Angolans agreed to put a stop to Plan incursions.

As part of what became known as the Lusaka Accords, it was agreed that a Joint Monitoring Commission would be established to supervise the disengagement. However the agreement did not receive the support of the Cubans and Fidel Castro was reportedly livid. Savimbi also rejected the new dispensation and issued his own conditions under which he would accept the terms of a ceasefire. One demand was for a government of national unity with the Mpla in which his party was granted a prominent role. He threatened to begin attacking major cities if he was ignored.

In October 1984, Angolan President dos Santos blamed South Africa for stalling the implementation of the Lusaka Accords and called for the USA to resolve the impasse by exerting pressure on Pretoria.

On 17 November, dos Santos proposed a five-point peace plan on the following terms: a complete SADF withdrawal from Angola; a renewed ceasefire agreement; a formal pledge by the South African government to begin implementing Namibian independence under the terms of UN Security Council Resolution 435; a formal pledge by the Angolan government to begin implementing a three year phased withdrawal of all but 5,000 Cuban troops; and recognition of Swapo and Cuba as an equal party in negotiations. In response, President Botha wanted all the Cuban military personnel to be withdrawn, and over a period of twelve months rather than three years. He also countered that the Namibian independence process could only take place once the Cuban withdrawal was initiated. A stalemate ensued.

While politicians bickered Fapla went on the offensive in a bid to destroy Unita. While they succeeded in pushing Savimbi's people eastwards they were unable to land a knockout blow. That June, Unita sabotaged the oil pipeline in Cabinda, kidnapping 16 British expatriate workers and a Portuguese technician. Six months later they raided Cafunfo, killing 100 Fapla personnel.

Most of these attacks were planned and executed from Jamba, a town in Cuando Cubango Province, which Savimbi had proclaimed Unita's new national head-quarters. The town had no prior strategic significance, with limited infrastructure, but it was located as far away from Fapla bases as possible and within easy reach of SADF bases in Ovamboland and the Caprivi Strip.

Charismatic and media-savvy Jonas Savimbi used Jamba to burnish the Unita brand and opened his HQ up to the media to try and make his case for support better known to the world.

Frustrated, the Soviets decided to increase their support in the provision of men and material in an effort to bolster the resources needed to defeat the Unita resistance and consolidate their hold on the conflict area. Given the size of the country and the poor communications infrastructure, attention had to be paid to airfields and roads so as to overcome the logistical problems hindering the movement of forces. To the Americans and the South Africans, it was clear that Unita would not survive alone.

Through the CIA and affiliates the Reagan administration in the USA stepped up covert support and the decision to supply Unita with state-of-the-art Stinger anti-aircraft missiles was a crucial tactical development, but it was also clear that boots on the ground were needed and only the South Africans were capable of filling that requirement.

Deployment of increased number of Special Forces troops took place in the contested area to keep an eye on enemy movements and to provide support where possible to other Unita and South African Defence Force units. It was also decided to boost resources needed to improve the fighting skills of Unita personnel. Mike West was one of those selected to help train Unita troops.

"Instructing came easy to me. I was totally fascinated by war. Despite my lack of academic credentials I think I had read enough, listened enough and experienced enough to become something of an expert, so felt I was well placed when removed from combat operations to be used in a training role. At this stage my star was rising and I was assured I would soon be made a warrant officer but then I blotted my copybook, but more about that later.

"A very memorable time was when we were sent to 'Charlie-Five' in eastern Angola on the Kwando River. This was an important Unita base and it was here I came to know their leader Jonas Savimbi. A big man with plenty of charisma, always very smartly kitted out, I liked him immediately because he looked you straight in the eyes. He was worshipped by his men.

"We were flown into the base by Pumas and I just remember it was a long time in the air. Jack Greeff was in charge of us guys and I was with Paddy Giblin, Sam van der Merwe and Johnny (Joao) de Gouveia. We lived under grass shelters but we were well looked after. No women in the camp. The LO (liaison officer) in the camp was an SADF guy who had lost both his arms when they were blown off in an explosion. He was beautifully looked after by his Unita nurses who washed him and dressed him.

"From my studies, particularly of the Vietnam war, I had learned a lot and this was a great opportunity to pass on some of that knowledge. One tactic I introduced was the 'fire blanket' for men on the ground dealing with air-strikes. It called for everyone to get on their knees, aim skyward, weapons on fully automatic, with one tracer every fifth round, and fill the sky with lead. Even for fast flying Migs, at low altitude, this was a formidable defence against them. I also taught them 'pop up ambushes', which was developed in dry, desert conditions where cover is scarce. The men have to dig below ground, hide below the surface waiting, then rise and fire when enemy is in the killing zone. I also showed them how to put a sniper with a Dragunov in a tree where one was available to pick off the officers in the vehicles once the ambush had been initiated. In training I sprung one of these on Hennie Blaauw and he got a hell of a fright.

"The Unita guys came to really enjoy and respect us. I was very much appreciated when I saved the eyes of one of them. We were doing a mock attack on a position when a spitting cobra stuck his head up and nailed one of them right in the eyes. There was general panic, but I calmed him and his comrades down and went to work washing this guys eyes out. Luckily we moved quickly and he got his eyesight back so after a few days I was a bit of a hero. It wasn't all work; being on the Kwando River as there was good fishing and we caught good tiger and bream on time off."

'Operation Electrode'

"In late 1984 close attention was being paid to the oil storage facility in the Cabinda enclave in northern Angola. Oil pumped from here was the main source of revenue for the country and if it was destroyed it would have hammered the country's economy. The problem was the Americans were involved in the refinery and South Africa had to avoid pissing them off so it was a delicate situation. At the same time Captain Wynand du Toit and his guys were looking at blowing it up, I was involved in another recce which was to look closely at destroying the bridge over the Cuanza River 30 kilometres south of Luanda. This was the road bridge that connected the capital to Lobito and Lubango. If that bridge went down it would have provided the government with some serious logistical problems.

"We went in close on the submarine SAS *Emily Hobhouse*. I took my hat off to those sailors who operated inside those stinking subs. When I was inside one all I wanted to do was get the hell out of the thing.

"On the night of the 2nd December 1984 we surfaced close to the Cuanza river mouth and were taken in on inflatables. There were four of us in two two-man teams. Me and Francois Bekker with Toby Tablai are the only ones I remember. The beach landing was rough coming in on the breakers but we made it and the coast looked clear so we quickly assembled our Kleppers (kayaks) near the river and prepared to head upstream.

"We paddled for about an hour before the bridge was visual in the moonlight and we were able to get close to the pillars by coming in under overhanging trees and bushes. Near one of the pillars we saw an amphibious vehicle and a couple of tents. Listening out we could hear voices so it seemed there were sentries posted. Then we saw movement on the other side of the bridge so there was definitely a presence that had to be taken into account. Wanting to get a better look we crossed over to the north bank and then we could see sentries armed with AKs. There was also a tent on the road and below the bridge on the shoulder. Taking this bridge down was not going to be without risk. Having seen as much as we could we made our way back down the river to the sea and we were picked up by the inflatables with no problems.

"The other team had problems getting on to the beach and then ran into people when approaching on land. It was close but they managed to avoid a firefight. They saw vehicles moving and another fence running up towards the bridge. They were collected and brought back to the sub after our upliftment and we immediately headed back out to sea for transfer to the Strike Craft for the trip back to Langebaan.

"The upshot of it all was it looked too difficult a task to complete without having to take out the protection element and as a result the plan was shelved."

But years of war were taking a severe financial toll on the Angolans and oil revenues were providing a financial lifeline. American owned Gulf Oil was a big player in this critical sector of the economy. By 1984 it was estimated the Gulf facility in Cabindas was generating 90% of Angola's foreign exchange. This statistic had not escaped the attention of the South Africans, but they had to find a way of disrupting this revenue flow without incurring American wrath. Pretoria decided a covert sabotage operation was possible, as long as the destruction was not attributable to South Africa and a credible cover story could be used to link the attack to a domestic Angolan movement such as Unita or FLEC (Front for the Liberation of Cabinda). A comprehensive attack on the entire facility was ruled out, as this was beyond the capabilities of either Unita or Flec, so the SADF opted to infiltrate the refinery's oil storage facilities and mine the fuel tanks. It was hoped the damage incurred would reduce Angola's ability to finance the war and make them less demanding at the negotiating table.

The sabotage mission, 'Operation Argon', involved 15 South African Recces under the command of Captain Wynand du Toit. They were deployed by sea in May 1985, but the operation went awry when they were discovered by a Fapla patrol during the infiltration attempt. Two of the raiders were shot dead and Captain du Toit was captured. Under interrogation, he disclosed the details and although the SA government tried to deny responsibility their protestations fell on deaf ears and further peace talks were abandoned.

Disgrace

That's the thing about pedestals.

People don't belong on them.

I never asked to be put on one.

So when I was told that I had fallen from one, I took it as an insult.

"They had been waiting. Looking for cracks. Sometimes, unexpectedly, setting a whole new standard can cost you everything," recalls Mike. "As an English-speaker in a predominantly Afrikaans outfit, namely 1 Recce based at the Bluff in Durban, I was doing well, I had more than proven myself, and I was told I would soon be promoted. I felt I deserved it. I was personally nominated by Captain Daan van Zyl of 1 Recce as a Team Leader, when I wasn't even an officer. You had to be an officer in order to fill this position, unlike the Rhodesian SAS, where, if an officer was lacking in experience, he would sometimes defer to an NCO. When SAS Lieutenant Dick Stent joined us in Mozambique when I was working with Darrell Watt, he was happy to let me take charge while he got to know what was going on. This did not happen in the SADF.

"Captain van Zyl dubbed my team 'The English Contingent'. Needless to say, this was viewed as favouritism by the Afrikaans NCOs, and the negativity was communicated to me indirectly.

"In late 1985 I was working with Jan Breytenbach and Hennie Blaauw at one of the bases where we were training a special forces group for Savimbi's Unita. I was enjoying it until Wayne Ross-Smith arrived. He was a good guy and and a good friend but he had disturbing news. He told me there was a lot of talk back at the Bluff about my wife. This hurt. I know I'm no angel but it's tough when you are out there, being shot the shit out of, you think you're doing this for your wife and family. That is who you are fighting for. That is who you are defending. They are your strength. They are your reason for being out there.

"When I got back to Durban, I started making inquiries and discovered it was all true. I lost control of myself, I was humiliated; I knew lots of people who had it in for me were finding this all very amusing. I confronted her. I completely lost my temper. I was angry and embarrassed becuse it seems everyone knew except me and I felt let down by my fellow soldiers. I still believe the RSM and offficers should have taken steps to protect us when we were deployed.

There was a lot of partying going on but they should have told the wives they had to stay on the base rather than going to town and playing around. When we were out on operations we needed peace of mind so we could concentrate on our tasks. They did not watch our backs; maybe some of them were having fun while we were away?

"After the incident, the first person that I confronted was one of the admin personnel ('Jam Stealer' as we called them), who worked with my wife. He had been quite loose tongued about my marriage, and talked a lot about me behind my back, so I handled him pretty roughly. The RSM, who lived right next door to this 'Jam Stealer', screamed at me from his yard, having witnessed this. I was ordered to report to his office at HQ. Although the RSM had been aware of everything that had transpired in my absence, he wilfully withheld this and instead told me that although he would not charge me for my actions, the 'Jam Stealer' would probably lodge a civil case. No case was ever made.

"Wanting to know more about all the rumours afloat, I visited the night clubs that they alleged my wife had frequented. At one particular club, there was an entrance fee, and I wasn't prepared to pay this, wanting only to look around. The bouncer challenged me, and I dropped him like a fucking log. It was important for me to get the lay of the land, so to speak, and I was achieving absolutely nothing. I later visited another of these night clubs, accompanied by three of my colleagues.

"Unfortunately, earlier that evening and unbeknown to us, members of the Strike Craft Force down at Salisbury Island, had caused major ructions at this particular night club and had promised to return that same night with a larger force in order to flatten the place. As a result, the bouncers had contacted all the other clubs to call in reinforcements in preparation for the looming showdown. They armed themselves with long rubber batons.

"So when we walked through the door no prizes for guessing who they thought we were. Those batons were in hand and they were watching when one of my friends got into an altercation with a civvie on the balcony of the aforesaid night club, and of course the three of us went over to inspect.

"That is when the amalgamated Bouncer Force dropped in on us, and all hell broke loose. I was involved in a proper bar brawl with one of these fuckers, who grabbed a chair all movie-style, and tried to break it over my head. I blocked it with my forearm and drilled him with a right fist. Around that exact moment things went a bit wonky. I felt like jelly. My head had been smashed in with a baton from behind, but despite a cracked skull I managed to stay on my feet until someone tackled me low and took my legs out from under me. Once on the ground they leaped onto me like a pack of hungry dogs onto a carcass and all I felt was batons, blows and boots, breaking my ribs in the process.

"Paul (Mugger) Swanepoel saved my sorry arse. This tough, unstoppable pitbull of a human being dived in, batons raining on top of him, yanked me to my feet and pulled me out of there. I still think he saved my life because this crowd of cowards seemed intent to keep hitting until I stopped moving altogether.

"The force with which we were being attacked literally pushed us out of the night club, and into the street. With my head echoing like a sea shell, and my eyes slanted from the broken nose and cracked skull, I was trying to stay out of the way of blurred figures of bouncers swinging batons when I staggered onto the pavement. Then I was on the street, moving backwards through the cars, trying to avoid them, but then a car hit me and I can still remember the sensation of flying upwards before crashing down onto the tarmac. There was no pain because the adrenaline was pumping – I was beyond pain but somehow still fully conscious.

"Somehow the four of us made it into my Silver Mazda 323 and fired it up. I drove with my left hand, because my right hand had to hold my right eye open so I could see the road. It was completely swollen shut from the smashed-to-pulp nose. I remember vomiting blood at home. At some stage an ambulance picked me up and took me to Addington Hospital. They found multiple fractures, including several ribs on both sides, a cracked skull and busted nose. I was in hospital for about five days, with a neurosurgeon attending to me because of my fractured skull. I was released from hospital just before Christmas 1985.

"Whilst lying in hospital, in this pitiful state an officer of 1 Recce, who hated my guts, made claims of having enjoyed an orgasm at the thought of my injuries from this altercation. He took further pleasure in spreading the nonsense that Mike West got fucked up by one solitary civvie. Utter rubbish; I recall at least 12 cowardly fucktards, armed with big batons, being needed to take me down.

I later heard that it was the black night watchman, who belted me from behind with a knobkerrie. This is what cracked my skull. Had he not done that, I would have still been on my feet and deep in the fight.

"The fake information spread to the Commanding Officer. It reached him before parade that particular morning, and it seems he too took pleasure from this, because he announced it to the entire unit. *"Die heavy Mike West is deur die civvies opgedonner en hy le in die hospital…"* (The heavy Mike West was fucked up by civvies, and is presently lying in hospital). Mugger Swanepoel came and told me all the recent news, including the uncouth Military Parade announcement.

"Once discharged, and back at base, people were dismissive and ignored me. Two of my fellow operators, both officers, went and investigated the altercation themselves, and reported the factual events to the Commanding Officer. They explained the dog-pack attack. It was understood that nothing was fair about this fight, and that I held up impressively, considering the odds against me. However Bestbier made it clear that he didn't care. He dismissed their statements, and said that it didn't matter. So it was allowable to lie and tarnish my reputation at a Military Parade, but you cannot rectify this by telling the truth afterwards?

"Merely because he despised me. It was at times like this that I missed Rhodesia; there the RSM would have rounded up the men and they would have gone with me looking for the cowardly crowd, and we would have taught these cowards a very important lesson: don't fuck with the SAS. They would have flattened the place. We had *Esprit de Corps*. We had camaraderie. As an English speaker I felt I did not have that same brotherhood in the Recces. Watching me fall brought some of them immense joy.

"This added insult to injury and my rage and urge for revenge went to another level. I set about gathering information on the fucking swarm that attacked me – including names and addresses – and I planned to visit them and hospitalise them, in the most painful and gruesome way that I could conjure up.

"But someone knew (I believe it was my wife) what I was up to and some 'little birdy' sang to the Commanding Officer about my activities. I was immediately called in and sent for urgent psychiatric assessment at 2 Recce Military Base in Voortrekkerhoogte. There I was attended to by a panel of four psychiatrists, the head 'shrink' being a Dr Phil Meyer.

"I was bombarded by many a question. There were inkblots. I was analysed and assessed. I was also asked how I felt about the families of the enemy that I killed. I was blunt; they felt fuck all for my family, as was clear by the war we fighting, so I felt fuck all for their families. Apparently, in their view, that makes you a psychopath. I was declared unstable, a threat to my own, and in need of treatment of some sort.

"I was then taken, by vehicle to 1 Military Hospital (Pretoria), and transferred to the top floor, where the injured Unita troops from Angola were kept and treated. I was placed in a room with a steel door, which had a cell grid built into it. That door was promptly locked and that was a big mistake. I kicked that fucking door, I yelled through that grid, I swore at them. They had literally locked me up like the criminally insane.

"I demanded to be allowed physical exercise, by means of running, which is part and parcel of a soldier's life. It is one helluva stress release. I was causing such a ruckus that they decided it was best to allow me this, obviously with the permission of the psychiatrists. The gear I carried always had running apparel.

"I enjoyed my first isolation run, followed at a distance of approximately 50 to 100 metres, by two Military Policemen in their puny little fucking military jeep. On one occasion I turned around and looked square at them. They stopped dead. I advanced. They reversed. I flung the bird, both hands, and told them to fuck off. I continued jogging. They continued to follow me at a distance. When I turned around to run back they took a detour to allow me to pass, before following at a safe distance once again. It was clear that they had been warned about this supposed lunatic.

"I was held in a locked cell that night, released the following morning, and taken to the railway station, booked to return to Durban. I noticed two MPs boarding the same train. No puny little fucking military jeep between us now. I waited till the train was on the go, and then went looking for them. I found them sharing a compartment, and when I bellowed at them, the blood drained from their faces. I loved it. Fucking cowards, claiming that they didn't know me from Adam. I threatened them, and they left me the hell alone.

"I was angry. Betrayed, humiliated, and labelled. I had put my life on the line for my comrades. I had put my life on the line for my country. Countless times. This was the thank you I got, all because I decided to visit vengeance on another set of cowards who attacked me?

"When I arrived at Durban Station a military vehicle was waiting to transport me back to the 1 Recce Base on the Bluff. I had to report to the Commanding Officer, Andre Bestbier, who took pleasure in telling me that my wife had taken my beloved children and left me, that I was a nut case, and that I would be leaving the next day, from Waterkloof Air Force Base in Pretoria, to 5 Recce in Ondangwa, as I was desperately needed there.

"I was not in a good place; my home was gone, my family was gone, an empty house greeted me. Nothing but my clothes were left behind, and my bedroom curtains. The next morning I was transported to Waterkloof Airport, with all my operational gear, and off to Ondangwa I went. Arriving there, I reported to Major Koos Verwey, the Commanding Officer of 5 Recce, Swapo Operations who duly informed me that I had been transferred permanently – and that I would not be returning to South Africa. My world bottomed out. He also instructed me to prepare immediately, as they were deploying me on operations that evening to join a group of black former Swapo Operators on the ground.

"I was put in a Casspir (a mine-resistant ambush-protected vehicle) with Koos Stadler in charge. They dropped me in the middle of fucking nowhere. It was at this very moment that I realised that I was completely rejected by one and all. They didn't give a fuck what happened to me. I just got angrier.

"A few days in, we ran into a fire fight, in which we killed numerous terrs. This really lifted my spirits. The smell of cordite and actual combat were the only home I had left, and I revelled in it. It was like a child getting sweets. I had gone quickly from criminal to warrior. A number of days later we returned to the base. It was great to be back at war and the beginning of many more deployments.

"Through the whole of 1986 I was deployed almost the entire time. I became convinced they were trying to get rid of me because I got virtually no break from operations at all."

CHAPTER 10

Counter Insurgency Operations 1986

"I open, with this quotation:

"You've never lived until you've nearly died. And for those who have had to fight for it, life has a flavour the protected shall never know." – Guy de Maupassant

"Deploying from Fort Rev, Ondangwa, our mission was to find Swapo insurgents who were infiltrating South West Africa, destroying communication lines in and around Ondangwa, and randomly attacking soft targets, as well as bombing Ondangwa with mortars.

"Adjacent was the big SA Air Force base where pilots with their designer shades hung out around a filtered swimming pool and their air-conditioned huts. Nearby was the Ondangwa Golf Club which had sand greens. The standard food for us grunts was pretty ordinary, but for the fortunate few there was good 'graze' supplied using the best meat, fruit and vegetables.

"I was in command of a group of 15. On some occasions it was only me with one or two other white operators, the other 12 being Swapo Operators (SOs), most of whom were former enemy combatants who had been captured and 'turned' in the same way the Selous Scouts operated.

"Before deploying, we would make a fire, specifically for the amount of smoke that it would emit from the wood used, in order to kill off the smells on our bodies and uniforms, as the enemy could literally smell you a mile away. Toothpaste, deodorants and soaps were dead give-aways, as those smells tend to linger on the body. A sweaty smoke smell was natural to the environment that we were entering and had to infiltrate.

"We flew out on a Puma and were dropped at the designated point in southern Angola. We then proceeded northwards, in various formations, depending on the terrain. In our order of march there would be two scouts in front. In thick bush, we would walk in single file formation, and in open areas in an extended line.

"The bush was free of animals. Mass slaughter, hunting, and the encroachment of farmers and pastoralists had thinned out both mammals and reptiles. Birds too, were seldom seen. All in all it was a pretty bleak place.

"But our SOs were gifted with bush skills and they were superb trackers. They would read the sand, twigs, dust and plants, a world of clues that were invisible to my eyes but carried stories of who had passed that way, when they came through, what they were carrying, how quickly they were moving, what sort of condition they were in, even what they ate for their last meal. All this knowledge that would be completely lost to most soldiers. As former enemy fighters they also knew the tactics of the people we were looking for so they knew where to look and what to look for.

"My normal regimen, I would let the men walk for 45 minutes, which covered roughly three kilometres, and then rest for 15 minutes, in a well-concealed Lying Up Place (LUP), only taking in water if necessary.

"Standard procedures for eating: Usually between 12 and 2pm midday. This was because any smells from food would be drawn upwards by the heat of the day. Anything eaten early morning or late afternoon would result in smells lingering in the vicinity, detectable by the enemy, should they be moving through that area.

"Upon departing from the LUP, nothing would be buried or left behind, and the area would be camouflaged, disguising signs of our presence. Thanks to Darrell and my time in the SAS, I had ingrained in me the need never to follow the same procedures when entering and leaving a LUP. The lesson learned was repeat your pattern at great risk; don't do the same thing twice. We had a 'dog's leg to the left' or a 'dog's leg to the right'. By taking a circuitous route to where we would settle and rest, we were also ambushing our own tracks. We were resting, refreshing but also fighting.

"Another tactic would be to set up in extended line, on our own tracks, facing the direction in which you came from. If the terrs managed to find our tracks, and attempted to track us, they would be hard-pressed to locate us, as the follow-through on our LUP procedure was complicated and confusing. To track and attack, you need a pattern. We left little or nothing viable to work with, which created uncertainty in their ranks. If nothing else, they knew we were alert and that made them nervous. A nervous terr is a vulnerable terr. To add to our security and to inflict as much damage as possible, we invariably used Claymores on trip-wires that were set up on our tracks to detonate in the event we were being successfully followed.

"The more we deployed, the more we saw their numbers increase to counter us. They had learned hard lessons from taking us on. Despite our small numbers we were punching way above our weight and they knew this so they did not come without plenty of firepower. I took this as a compliment. Our flexibility, unpredictability and aggression had earned their respect. This is only possible when you have years of combat experience. This is not Rambo, there are no stunt doubles, there's no coming back from a rain of bullets. No one yells "and CUT!" when the shit hits the fan.

"Us white troops fully understood our bushcraft limitations so during deployment, without SOs, all movement on the ground was strictly at night, and only when there was moonlight to work with. Movement in the day was too risky. The unfortunate reality was the white man was going to be detected by terrs in the area, regardless of his 'Black is Beautiful' camouflage, which we all applied. A point to note, our packs differed from those of the terrs as we had to carry large quantities of water, up to 100 litres, to remain clandestine.

"The SOs came to us from different angles. Some were captured and turned, some came to us voluntarily, some were disillusioned with their cause, some came for the money. Killing or capturing their former comrades paid a rich bounty and the money mattered more than any ideology.

"Leading these guys was not easy. I felt I had to be absolutely dominant at all times but never too distant, and key was consistently leading from the front. Where they came from discipline was brutal, they were used to it, so showing too much empathy was misunderstood for weakness and that could be fatal. They were also pretty shrewd in analysing their leadership; if they sensed someone was out of his depth they would soon lose interest. These guys wouldn't follow a turkey.

"I saw this with 'Danger', one of the Swapo guerillas armed with an AK who tried to kill me by coming at me in a flanking attack but I was too quick and took him and some of his comrades down. When we were back at base I sat Danger down and spoke to him very firmly and convinced him it was a good idea to switch sides. He agreed and I took him with us on our next operation but took out his firing pin to see what he did but he performed well. Next deployment his weapon was live and we went on to work well together. A special loyalty grew between us but when I was sent back to South Africa later, he was tasked to operate under another commander and that was that, he just disappeared and was never seen again."

Lessons in War

"As with anything, there are measures and preparation prior to any undertaking. What do you do before you go on holiday? Car serviced. New tyres. Spare fuses. Wheel jacks. First aid kit. Sunscreen. The works. You plan your holiday in advance, as well as fail-safe procedures. Going into combat is no different just a damn sight more complicated. Planning is crucial. Here, though, people die, and unnecessarily so, if you don't prepare adequately. The old adage about the fine tooth comb, and rehearsals, to boot.

"Lots of detail went into operational planning but here is a very brief summary of events, prior to an Operation (minimum info only) so wannabe bullshitters don't quote me:

Situation: As Team Leader, you are called in by the Top Brass, and given a Warning Order of an Operation for the preparation thereof.

Having received the order, you now have to collect and study all previous Intel on the area in question.

Do an appreciation.

You prepare the orders for your team, which begins with a briefing of the enemy, the terrain and the situation turned operation.

The mission is then detailed.

1. Execution on the ground: Which includes emergency procedures, infil-tration, on the ground and exfiltration. Experienced Team Leaders are experienced combatants. We know what can go wrong on the ground. We plan for it, we prepare for it, we rehearse it.

2. Emergency procedures to deal with what to do when things go wrong have to be planned and rehearsed. This is where operational experience counts.

3. Administration and logistics.

4. Command and signals.

5. These are all detailed. Top Secret. Unique to the situation, operation and area. There has to be no margin for error, because even with the best planning, paw-paws fly into fans."

"As a Team Leader I tried to draw more on my personal experiences and what I had learned from Darrell rather than on what was written in the text-books. I had survived some hair-raising events and I had learned something from every one of them. All fighting soldiers do but how you interpret them is unique to the undividual. 'The best laid plans…' as the saying goes. You can break it down to the last detail, but if something can go wrong, it most certainly will, irrespective of the best planning, preparation and rehearsal. One must remember that, when deployed on a mission, we were going up against trained soldiers, trained to use that weapon he carried, and he would willingly end you. Something that you both had in common.

"Whoever said 'all is fair in love and war…' has clearly never been in love and certainly doesn't know a damn thing about war. I have seen daring men, seemingly invincible, overrunning and defeating the enemy, then suddenly drop dead from a single bullet. Proving that the best man doesn't always win. But maybe also proving the good guys go early.

For Pseudo Operators

"You deploy in all the gear and kit that a terr deploys in. They don't need it, but you need 'Black is Beautiful' cream, literally in every crevice, including your inner ear. You have to smoke yourself in a wood fire to rid yourself of all the nice smelling branded creams and soaps lingering on your person. No ratpacks. Only enough mielie meal to get yourself started. Once out there, you become 100% dependent on the locals, eating Mahangu porridge, and drinking Mahangu beer, which they prepare for you.

"We, as palefaces, would never go to the kraal to collect food or drink. One of the former Swapo members would go. He looked like them. He spoke their language. There were operations with these SOs, where no food was taken into the field. We all wore Fapla boots, uniforms and webbings. We carried little

Swapo-issue backpacks. You must remember that the enemy on the ground were not issued with rations and seldom carried food. They would be dependent on the local population, which is exactly what we did. This is called Pseudo Operations.

"We, the white Operators in our 'Black is Beautiful' cream, would hang back in the bush, and our SOs would go in to the kraals, as resident terrs in the area, to get food and water. The food that they normally brought back was porridge, crushed from the actual plant. It was dirty brown to black in colour and normally filled with grit. They would also bring a cut-open 20 litre container, containing local beer. Regardless of the fact that this meal and beverage were majorly unpalatable, to say the least, a man must eat.

"One of the highlights of such an operation, was when we would sneak into the goat kraals at night, suffocate a goat, bind the legs up, put a branch through and run off with it, dangling by its bound legs. The goat would be slaughtered and cut up, with the bare-minimum wastage buried in a spot in the bush, and then we walked several kilometres from there, where we used the art form of smokeless fire to cook our hearty meal.

"For a smokeless fire you start off with small, dry, bark-less twigs, as well as larger pieces, until you have a raging fire, with zero or minimum smoke. Anything with bark causes heavy smoke.

"We built a grill over the fire with wet branches, to cook our goat. While the 'chef' prepared the meat, the rest of the team was in an all-round defence to prevent any unsuspected attacks. This smokeless fire was made under a tree that had more canopy than the rest, so that if any smoke was emitted from the fire it could absorb it. Obviously, there would always be a smell of burning wood and the scent of cooking meat. Hence our 50 metre all-round defence perimeter around our cooking area.

"A point to note, the smell of wood-smoke and cooking meat was not associated with SADF clandestine operators, as these are the methods used by resident terrs. The enemy knew that the military provided ratpacks for their soldiers.

"Regardless of the criticism received for these eating methods by inexperienced fucktards, we were never ever attacked whilst busy cooking, nor did we ever find and attack terrs whilst they were doing the same. Think about that.

"Afterwards, the cooking area was always dismantled. The ashes were buried. Exactly like the terrs do. On the odd occasion, in different areas of Angola, and from experience, we would find remnants of a suspected cooking area, so this method was further cover, and certainly not compromising in any way, as we literally practiced their methods, to stay alive. Goat theft was a common, and accepted method, of survival.

"That was the 'in' part but for food there has to be an 'out' and this was quite a complicated process. Our toilet habits had to change significantly. When soldiers take a dump in the bush, they dig a hole, clean themselves with toilet paper, and bury it. Then they camouflage the spot. Along comes a local's dog, sniffs the location, the local moves the bush or whatever was the camouflage and the dog digs it up. Boom! Busted. They know immediately that this is the dump of a soldier and NOT a one of theirs, regardless of all the best dress up and blending. Why? Because they do not wipe. They don't have toilet paper. They don't bury. So you don't leave the toilet paper, and you wrap it up and take it with, and you also dump on the ground, right? Still not good enough. The texture and contents of your turd can give you away. Eating Mahangu pap, and drinking Mahangu beer gives your turd the same smell and texture as that of a terr's. Yes! They scratch. And they check. And the wrong smell, texture and content will give you away, and you will literally be found and killed over an ill-placed dump. This sounds funny, but out there it is no laughing matter. A dump can literally cost you your life. And when taking a dump, you have to be observant. Your troops have to be at your back, so you can look outwards. You don't want to die with your pants around your knees. You have to keep as low as possible, and you need to have your weapon at the ready. No leaning it against the tree so you can squeeze. Your face may be painted, but your white arse glows like a Day-Glo panel. Keep it facing away from the direction that the enemy may come from.

"On one occasion on an operation in Zambia, I took out a Zipra fighter taking a dump. I could see him, because he was well elevated, on an ant mound, with his weapon lying over his knees. That was his very last dump, and he attained a 3rd eye. Later on, the local wildlife began snacking on him. I don't think anyone wants to be remembered that way.

AK47 (Avtomat Kalashnikova)

Avtomat = Automatic

Kalashnikova = the surname of the Russian designer, Mikhail Kalashnikov

47 = the year of completion (1947)

"This weapon fundamentally rewrote the rules of modern warfare and changed the world. Its existence has ensured that even the poor, the small-statured, the dim-witted, the illiterate and the untrained can maintain a weapon, for it requires literally no maintenance. You can pick this weapon up out of water, cock it and fire it. Perfectly engineered to not jam, so stoppages are not a concern. All the bearer has to worry about is which way is front, loading it, and remembering to hold on when firing. Just like that: You have weaponised a new soldier-to-be. It fired a 7.62 x 39 round, rimless bottlenecked cartridge. The round travelled at 750 metres per second, and its effective range was 350 metres. We very rarely shot anyone further than 50 metres from us. This weapon could be fully stripped, from the loaded position (round in the chamber), cleaned and reassembled to a fully loaded position, without a sound; something I mastered.

John Brokaar

"One of the great men I met was John Brokaar who became my trusted second in command through this period of the war. A giant of a Hollander, who I took under my wing and introduced to 'My Bush War'. He was a truly brave, gutsy and a phenomenal Operator, who took to this war like a fish to water. I was so proud to have this brilliant soldier fighting by my side, and together we completed many successful missions.

"He had done some boxing in the 1 Recce gym in the past, and figured he could cut it. The name Mike West was synonymous with violence, so he had heard about me. One afternoon, he approached me with a set of gloves, and asked if we could go a round on the grass, in front of the wooden structure that I slept in. My old friend, Jim Lafferty from the Selous Scouts was present, and cautioned John against this action, but John was adamant.

"Gloves on, facing him, I realised that this kid was no Rocky. He threw a heavy right punch at my head, exposing himself entirely, making it easy to drop him with one right punch. That was that. A rematch was not requested.

"Until one night, whilst consuming an 'Airport Special' (our own nastily fermented pineapple ale), at Oshivello, John's drunken *persona* reckoned we should fight bare fisted. He was obviously still smarting, emotionally, from the first time that I had dropped him. There were quite a few operators sitting in this tent when he issued the challenge. He was standing by the entrance. I too had enjoyed a few toots, and I got very angry at this challenge.

'Now I'm going to fuck you up…' I said, leaving the tent and following him. When I got outside, he walked off and didn't want to pursue the matter. Telling this story about John, someone I respect immensely, is not meant to humiliate him in any way. This is merely the retelling of a moment in my military career. There was another incident where a good friend of mine from SAS challenged me to a fight at 1 Recce Single Quarters. He came horribly short, I dropped him in the blink of an eye. Unfortunately that was the end of our friendship as he never spoke to me again.

"It should be noted that I forewarned anyone wanting to take John on. He was a big lad, and had no fucking fear. A good example: John and I went to a spaza market near the base. There were at least 50 black people there. We went in through the exit door, John in front, and immediately a huge black security guy, armed with a knobkerrie, stormed down on John, swinging it and swearing at him in his home language, because we had not used the entrance. Without breaking a sweat, John closed ranks with him and effortlessly disarmed him, dropping him to the ground like a rag doll. Within minutes, military police arrived and fuck knows who else. We were in our Recce gear. The whole story was sorted out. We were escorted back to base without any further altercations.

"Naturally, we landed up in front of Verwey, who blasted us, chased us out of his office and told us to prepare for deployment. The following evening, we were happily deployed, and returned to our ecosystem, which was the bush. Here you could fuck up people without being berated for it. Just the way we liked it."

Ambush and POW capture

"It was early 1986 when I deployed from Fort Rev with my team. It consisted of John Brokaar, my second in command, 'Oosie' Oosthuizen and 12 SOs. Before going into Angola we made a fire and stood in the smoke to suppress the smells that might give us away on our mission.

"On reaching the target area I laid my team out in an ambush position, on a dirt road that led to Lubango in south-western Angola. According to our information, Swapo engineers and insurgents were exfiltrating along this route by bicycle, having completed their dirty work in South West Africa. This ambush position had to be done in-depth. In other words: You had to have eyes to the rear. There was no given time as to when these insurgents would be travelling along this road, and therefore this ambush had to be extremely well-concealed. There was no room for error as there was a strong possibility of a much larger force, such as Fapla or larger Swapo groups traversing this route during our wait. According to our information, the terrs were only using this route by day, and by bicycle.

"Whilst in the ambush position there was no eating and obviously, no smoking. We were pretty paranoid about noise when on these operations. Even taking a pee was risky, so we pissed where we lay so as to not expose ourselves. Snorers were returned to their units (RTU), no matter how good a soldier they were. Smoking was a big 'no-no'. Very few of the guys smoked, and those who did never did so when in the field, which meant that might be up to a couple of weeks if in a long ambush. Some operators brought smokes with, obviously to have a fag if an opportunity presents itself. A good time for a smoke was after a punch-up with the enemy; 'after action satisfaction' as the Lexington advert went. It helped release the tension.

"Our first day in this ambush position resulted in nothing. No movement at all. Around 08h00 on the second day, having relocated to a new ambush position further up the road, three insurgents cycled up this road, with AK47s slung over their shoulders. It was a walk in the park. We slotted all three in a matter of seconds, dragged their bodies into the bush and cleared the area. We removed all documentation, weapons and equipment from the bodies, and we also photographed the dead for identification back at HQ, upon our return at a later date.

"We obviously used their ammunition to replenish ours as we all used the same weapons. We used their 'liberated' bicycles where and when necessary. Three of our SOs saw fit to use them in order to obtain water from a village roughly three kilometres away. They were the perfect cover, whilst acquiring a critical necessity, as they were in full gear, and on the bicycles, as these people expected them to be.

"Once this first task was completed, we moved 100 metres to the rear of the ambush and travelled a further kilometre up the road in a northerly direction to set up another ambush. No further incidents occurred after our initial success and movement.

"With the arrival of last light, we moved a kilometre to the rear of the new ambush position and set up an LUP for the night. As with all operations, we were up at the crack of dawn and moved to a new LUP until there was sufficient light to set up a new ambush position, as there had been no moon phase to assist us.

"The reader may be wondering why it is that we keep moving? We move, because there is always, and I mean always, a chance of compromise. Being cautiously optimistic in the bush saves lives.

"When it was light enough, I decided to move a further three kilometres, in a northerly direction, back to a thicker fringe of bush behind us that provided a bit more shade from the searing heat and in order to be well clear of the area that we were in. We really struggled with heat and dehydration. Whilst moving towards our new ambush position, approximately 50 metres from the road, in the event of a very large force coming along it, four Swapo came racing by on bicycles in the very direction that we were headed! We ran as fast as we could towards them, and obviously opened fire, trying to annihilate them, but the surrounding bush on our side of the road was relatively thick, and prevented success in this endeavour.

"We ran into the road, firing as we ran, but they were already at least 80 to 100 metres ahead of us. One of them turned off to the right, into the bush, and Oosie ran after him. This is an extremely dangerous manoeuvre as we had no idea where the guy was, and who would now have had time to position himself and fire, or continue on the run. I yelled at him and ordered him to return to our position as I was convinced that this fucker had high-tailed it into the bush, and we were wasting our time.

"Having compromised our position, I moved my team over the road in an easterly direction, and deep into the bush, away from where the action had taken place. We moved for another three or so kilometres, and set up our LUP in an all round defence. I didn't want to move in the daytime now, as the targets had managed to evade us due to the fucking thick bush and bicycles. It was wise to lie still.

"Roughly around 11h00 that same morning, and from our well-concealed LUP, we spotted 10 to 15 Swapo approaching from the north. They were headed straight towards us, seemingly unaware of our position. They were approaching very cautiously, and in an extended line, AK47s at the ready. We let them get as close as what the bush would allow, which was roughly 50 metres, before they spotted something and opened fire. We opened up at a helluva rate, raining bullets on them, and killing some.

"Their line dispersed and bomb-shelled backwards, left and right, as they ran in crouching positions in order to escape. All of about a dozen terrs then emerged from the cover of the bush, and from an easterly direction, attacking us on our right flank. This was unexpected, and most unwelcome. It was, at this point, that I realised that the bastards had pinpointed our position as their firing was very accurate, taking bark off the trees right by us.

"We turned towards the new incoming attack, and once again opened the gates of hell. I could see them dropping after taking our hits. To prevent them from once again bomb-shelling, and running away, I launched a full scale sprint and fire. We ran right into them. Many threw their guns down, dropped to their knees and put their hands in the air. We fucking nailed them with this show of aggression in Darrrell Watt style.

"Of the eight we captured there, four were wounded in one way or the other, but nothing looked critical, and four could walk unaided. We gathered all the weapons, rounded them up, and made them walk in a southerly direction. We had to clear out the area as quickly as possible because we were heavily compromised by this time. Had these troops of mine been SAS operators we would have stayed in the area to take on any other danger that was coming... Darrell Watt style.

"At first, the Prisoners of War (POWs) were reluctant to walk, but they were persuaded by both my gun to a head, and one of our Swapo Operators confirming that I would happily pull the trigger if necessary. They were so won over by this display, that they were kind enough to drag their own wounded with them, as this lot had a lot of trouble walking. I don't want to give all the credit to the round that John fired over their heads shortly afterwards, as motivation. All I can say is that asses were in gear. There wasn't time to treat their wounded, as we were in an incredibly dangerous situation now, post the days firing, and fuck knows what else was headed our way thanks to all the noise.

"As we headed south, and for only about a kilometre, it became glaringly apparent that our POWs were struggling with their wounded comrades. Some were bleeding profusely. I decided to deploy my men in all-round defence.

"John and Oosie, who were supremely competent soldiers, set about treating the wounded. Some of my SOs, who brought cigarettes along, but knew not to smoke during the operation, handed out cigarettes to the wounded, who were happy to receive them.

"It took us about half an hour to wrap up treatment, at which point we'd gained new friends, who were happily smoking and smiling. Some of my SOs made a makeshift stretcher, on my command, in order to ferry the more severely wounded chap along our passage and another wounded fighter was carried on the shoulders of the others. The walking wounded continued to carry those who couldn't walk. At this point, we had discarded the bicycles. We hightailed south, and we could hear the engines of vehicles, travelling towards us from the north. We picked up our pace substantially. I managed to message our HQ informing them of the situation at hand.

"My SOs, whose instincts were unparalleled, stopped the whole group, and 'listened' to the sound of the vehicles in the distance, gauging their approach. We then moved along, more swiftly than before, for about a kilometre, before my SOs stopped us again, in order to gauge the situation once again. I was not a lot of use here as my hearing was impaired from all the explosions and I had become tone-deaf.

"The vehicles were moving up on our left and right flanks, from behind, to try and cut us off, much like a Scorpion approaching with claws spread. My one RPG7 Operator had Anti-Personnel rockets on the RPG7, and proceeded to fire them, in a mortar roll, in the direction of the vehicles' approach.

"It is important to note that the RPG7 Anti-Personnel rocket only detonates upon impact, as with a mortar round. You cannot imagine the shrapnel coverage of this beauty, unless you've seen it firsthand. He fired three rockets, one after the other, towards the sounds, which definitely slowed the enemy approach.

"Major Buks Buys, of the Ondangwa Base, called on the Air Force for aerial support. His request seemed to have been met with a bit of reluctance, so he informed them to get choppers and body-bags ready, to pick up what would be left of us, if they didn't move their asses.

"This, somehow, hastened them into action. Two Impala[11] fighter jets were dispatched in this endeavour. According to Major Buys, as stated at the time, this was the first time that Impalas were used across the border for the evacuation of their own forces.

"My comms with the aircraft, via my VHF 'Small Means Radio', guided them to our position. When they were relatively close, they asked that I mark our position with a white phosphorous grenade. They confirmed the sight of smoke, and I gave them rough directions, from the smoke, to where we estimated that the targets were.

"Take into account that it is fucking hard for a pilot to pick up targets, coming in at that speed, and from that height. The cover of trees screws you up. That, and a rough estimation.

"Their airstrike was nothing short of magnificent. All vehicle movement ceased to exist, much like the hour before Christmas Day. Then we heard the fixed-wing overhead and then the sound of the choppers, it was like a sound from heaven. We threw a smoke grenade and with the airstrike delaying any further approach, Puma helicopters arrived to uplift my team and our POWs. Soon these much-loved machines were overhead, and morale surged. We scrambled aboard the helicopters, and we were on our way.

"We were safely extracted, and taken to back to our base in Ondangwa. We were all relieved to be alive, but it was a very long journey back. This was one very daring and successful operation. We brought out more POWs than any other team before us in this war.

"But I received no recognition except for a letter sent to Fort Rev from the commander of area Ondangwa 51 stating it was the biggest ever success in the

---

11   Impala

area, using former Swapo fighters – and I conducted it. I got fuck-all recognition but the base guy, Koos Verwey, got the praise because we were his fighters on the ground even though he was never part of any of the battles.

"Obviously, big bonuses were paid to our SOs for the killing and capture of their own. The highest rollers were those who brought their own in alive. A lot of valuable documentation and information was gathered from our POWs, as well as from their dead comrades, and handed over to our Intelligence. This helped immensely with tasks given to us in the future. Naturally, the interrogation of the live POWs, by any means necessary, filled in the gaps.

"All credits to John and to Oosie, for the manner in which they conducted themselves under immense pressure. These are two phenomenal, brave and bloody gutsy Operators who stood back for nothing, notwithstanding their sense of humour throughout. Just another day at the office, boys!

"To my SOs: This is how a day starts, without coffee. I know you were fucking glad to be back at base, because your capture would have resulted in extended, brutal suffering prior to death. If it were not for the Air Force, we would have been fucking toast."

'Frankenstein'

"On another operation from the same base, John and I once again deployed with more or less the same SOs. In the group I had one newly captured Swapo fighter, who could take me to an area where he used to operate alongside his comrades.

"He was not issued a weapon as I still regarded him as a potential threat, having been newly captured. Instead, I made him carry a TM46 Russian Landmine, which Willem, a Tiffy (mechanic) at the Transport Park, helped me to customise.

"The base of the landmine was covered in body putty, with nuts, bolts and ball bearings. This I intended to use as a booby trap should a large group of enemy attempt to hunt us down. This landmine was my own creation, and it was the first of its kind. I made a test model a few days prior, which I tested in an open piece of veld, with targets ranging 5, 10 and 20 metres from the mine. It was placed on its side, with the body putty, nuts, bolts and ball bearings facing the targets. I detonated it via a long piece of string, attached to a pull mechanism, from behind good cover. To my surprise all 12 targets, set up in the aforesaid distances, were hit, and the ones placed even further, were substantially damaged from the shrapnel reach. I had just constructed the biggest, deadliest, Claymore on the planet; my very own initiative. Koos Verwey had no idea what I had done; he would have shat himself. I named it my 'Frankenstein Claymore'. It was wrapped in camouflage material, and of such a weight that my newly inducted terr cum gunbearer preferred to carry it on his head, instead of in a backpack.

"At this time I was armed with a East German-made folding butt AK47 as my weapon of choice. But this too I customised, in that I modified the 30 round to a 60 round magazine, the only one ever in Special Forces. It was the only one of its kind – a 60 round monster. I also designed a system that allowed my weapon to move from safety to fire by pulling the trigger – a system that I point blank refused to share with anyone else. It made me the Fastest Gun in the West! I removed it the day I handed in my weapon. It will go to my grave with me.

"I also honed my skills in knife and axe throwing. I previously trained a few white operators in these special skills. Not that it was ever needed, because we carried guns – but I liked to be prepared, regardless.

"To commence the operation we were deployed by means of a Casspir armoured vehicle to the designated point in southern Angola. My SOs kept our recent inductee amongst them, so that he could direct them, specifically, as to where we had to go. Such was their loyalty to me.

"It was a long slog, and it took us roughly two days to get close to the area in question. Once we were in the vicinity, we found plenty of suspect tracks. I decided to form an extended line, and start sweeping forward as we had done with Darrell in the lowveld of Rhodesia.

"We were on the move when my VHF Radio crackled to life. The Group Commander of 101 Battalion, Lukas Laubscher who was in the vicinity roughly ten kilometres away, warned me that he had intercepted a communiqué, stating that a platoon of Fapla troops, plus minus 20-50 were heading directly towards us. They were fully aware of our presence in the area, as they had been alerted by one or other bush telegraph system.

"I was headed in a westerly direction at the time so I immediately about-turned, high-tailing due east, away from the incoming enemy and towards Lucas, who was heading towards us as fast as he could to save my fucking bacon. Once again if it was Darrell and the SAS we would have taken them on but these were SOs.

"Passing through an area that had heavy foliage, John and I decided that this was the ideal spot to give Frankenstein a chance to do her thing. I positioned (let's call her) Frankie against the base of a young thorn tree, to the right side of the area we had just passed through. I had a soldier sit dead still in the tree and pick up any movement coming our way (You would be surprised to know that Swapo used this tactic against us and I never knew about it). This tactic I had learned from Swapo, as they invariably positioned well camouflaged sentries in trees on high ground to keep watch. An excellent early warning system.

"Then John walked a 30 metre tripwire, weaving it between the foliage and over our tracks, so that it would not be detected, securing his end to further foliage. I carefully placed the trip mechanism and detonator on Frankie. The delicate procedure of trip mechanism and detonator insertion being placed into the Frankie claymore, was one of the most dangerous things I've ever done, this side of kissing a puff-adder hard on the lips.

"Whilst Johnny and I were busy with this operation, we ensured that the rest of the team remained at least 50 metres away from Frankie. Imagine my relief, as Johnny and I walked away from my highly volatile creation, as opposed to being spread all over the bush from an accidental or premature explosion. We rejoined the team, and continued our high-tail move eastwards.

"Capture was always our biggest fear: being skinned alive was likely as was being hanged publicly in Luanda for the entire world to see the racist South Africans getting their just rewards! We reminded ourselves that being taken prisoner was just not an option; we would fight to the end rather than take that chance.

"Roughly 20 minutes later I breathed a greater sigh of relief as Lucas appeared, and uplifted us with a heavily-armoured Casspir. Then as we turned the vehicle to vacate the area, there was a distinct rumble, not only heard – but also felt. Someone had disturbed Frankie. A glorious plume of dust and black smoke erupted in the distance above the trees and flooded the sky, approximately a kilometre from us. We burst out laughing, as Frankie had excelled in her task.

"For the duration of our trip out of the area on the Casspir, not one crackle was heard from the Fapla platoon that Lucas had listened in on. Nothing further was heard for the week that passed thereafter.

"At this point, I made two assumptions:

Either many, if not all, of the Fapla team were Marmite-spread over the bush, having disturbed Frankie; or the Radio Operator, and the poor bastard carrying the radio, as well as any unsuspecting bystanders, had joined their ancestors quite unexpectedly.

"In most cases, a claymore will stop a platoon in their tracks, but there are the stubborn types, who will send the remainder of the platoon after you, only to eat another Kaboom. This pretty much sends a clear message about a possible 3rd and 4th claymore to the leftovers of the remaining platoon, and that puts an end to their pursuit. This, however, doesn't always work. Frankie was designed to take claymores to a new, higher level.

"I am eternally grateful to Lucas Laubscher and 101 Battalion, for ensuring that our bacon was not fried that day. What we did, after that day, will also go down in history. If it had not been for him intercepting that communiqué, who knows which way that battle would have gone, as we were grossly outnumbered. Thank you, Lucas and 101. You have balls of steel.

"On a later operation with former Swapo fighters, at first light after deployment we walked into approximately 15 terrs. It is difficult to say, for sure, as these bastards could disappear in a flash. Both sides opened up on each other almost simultaneously. During the ensuing contact, we took no casualties. Our fire power and accuracy was by far superior to theirs, and we dropped seven of them in what seemed like a mere second or two. Those that survived, high-tailed it in every possible direction.

"Soon we were in extended line ready to sweep the killing zone for bodies and equipment. Corpses were strewn along the road and in the gully beyond lay a wounded terrorist, who was well-dressed and well-equipped, who we deemed to be a Political Commissar, and quite possibly the leader of this group. His webbing, AK47 and magazines were clearly brand new and straight out of the box. That kind of luxury doesn't happen for your average enemy fighter. He also had a wad of documentation on his person, in a pouch slung over his shoulder.

"Badly wounded, he had blood coming out of both his nose and mouth, which indicated a hit to the lungs, as well as an abdominal wound that was bleeding profusely, but he still looked very much alive. His uniform was new and neat. I remember looking at him, and his blood was already covered in flies. He mumbled something. For all I knew, he had been press-ganged into going over to the other side, like a lot of them were but I can't say I felt sorry for him.

"Difficult for many to understand because I am not a mad killer but by this time I had seen up close awful cruelty and unnecessary violence meted out to innocent men, women and children by an enemy that knew no compassion. I became convinced that many of those we were fighting against were barbaric and had to be eliminated as soon as possible, by whatever means. I was always quick with a violent response but what I had seen had taken me to a new level and I was to all intents and purposes a pumped up killing machine. I reminded myself what he, and others like him, right throughout Africa, have done to their own people, who were invariably tortured to death, and are beyond comprehension and forgiveness. I had seen too many examples of this cruelty and it had had a big impact upon me.

"After collecting all the information, weapons and equipment, we moved out of the area in a southerly direction, to get uplifted by Puma helicopters, as our time on that specific operation was done.

"At one point Major Verwey summoned me to his office. He asked me if I possessed any religious principles. I stated that from years of combat experience, I had seen the worst of Man visited on the innocent and soldiers, alike. I had never seen one moment, in any day, when any terr had stood back and done the right thing, because of religion. I was showing the enemy that we too were capable of similar inhumanity, when pushed too far. He told me to get out of his sight. He wanted to have me transferred elsewhere, but the fact is they needed me in the field and he had to keep me there. He had to have asked himself where was he going to send me anyway.... back to Durban?

"Just give me a team. I'll train them, then let me go to war with them. Give me cordite, napalm, the sound of war. I'm mad for it. I love it. I think my over-confidence was the reason many disliked me."

Capture of Swapo Commander

"But back to the war. The fact is bounties were being paid to the former Swapo guys and Swapo Commanders were, obviously, more pricey than your Swapo foot soldier. A live captured Swapo Commander, as scarce as that was, was the definition of a Christmas Bonus, and with a cherry on top! Which is why I decided to develop a new way of capturing live terrs, as this way was more beneficial to the pocket. Needless to say, I was later heavily condemned, and widely criticized, because of my unconventional, yet, new and effective, methods.

"The first day of a further deployment I decided to implement this method. The ambush on the road was set up in-depth, as before, but with my new brainchild. The ambush was planned in the same way, with the enemy travelling from the south to the north, as had happened before, with them fleeing South West Africa.

"I positioned myself, and my SO Commander, to the right of the ambush, about 20 metres away, on the southern point. My plan was as follows:

"Once our Sunday cyclists came ambling up the road, keeping a distance of about ten metres apart, as if no one would guess that they knew each other, a tactical move we had already seen in a movie. As per usual when returning from operations they invariably dressed in civilian clothes. I positioned myself so I had a clear view of the road allowing me to see what and who was coming and count numbers.

"We had reliable information, which confirmed that these pedalers were seldom more than three at a time, which was yet another tactical move during their exfiltration up north to safety. If there were three, I would hand signal their number to the killing squad, who would react as follows:

"Once the first two cyclists entered the killing ground, the ambush team would take them out but leave the third guy. My role, in this play, was then to dash from cover with a 9mm pistol in hand and unceremoniously dismount this third cyclist. Remember that this poor, clandestine, misunderstood murderer would have his weapon slung over his shoulder, or firmly strapped to his handlebars, rendering it useless during his surprise dismount. My plan, if successful would ensure kills, captures and better bounties.

"I lay in this position on the first day of my cunning plan. A hot uneventful day, nothing moved near us. That night I moved the men to a safe LUP some distance away.

Early the next morning, whilst once again moving into the ambush position, three Sunday cyclists were spotted pushing their bicycles alongside each other, chatting casually.

"It should be known a lot of insurgents who infiltrated South West Africa donned civilian clothing in order to frequent bar lounges, which is where they gained their information. Once the deed was done, they fled in the same civilian clothes, thwarting immediate capture. But it was pretty obvious that a guy on a bicycle, with belt webbing, chest webbing, and an AK47, to boot, was anything but a civilian. Hence, they had no idea that we were there, clearly, or they would have Tour de France'd out of there.

"The natural reaction of any seasoned soldier is to eliminate the enemy on site – which is exactly what my over-achiever SOs did when they spotted this bunch. There I stood, hands on hips, wondering what to do with my very dead silent Sunday cyclists, spread-eagled in their civvies blotting the road with their blood, and now only half their worth in bounty. One interesting fact is that they were so lackadaisical, that whilst strolling, they hadn't given any thought to unstrapping their weapons from their handlebars. It really takes all types. If my over-achievers had given any thought to the situation at hand, they would have realised that walking out of the bush, into the road, weapons pointed, we could have taken three Sunday Cyclists just like that, with not one scratch nor a single shot fired, which would have resulted in mega bonuses.

"Instead, we had two very dead terrs, and one wounded, hit through the right shoulder, which meant he would make it, severe pain and all. We dragged the bodies and equipment into the bush, and removed everything necessary. There was a rucksack filled with goods, obviously purchased in South West to take back to their base.

"I radioed back to HQ, to let them know what had just transpired, and that I had a live capture. Somehow, my brainchild plan had been leaked at base camp, and I was openly criticized over the radio and accused of endangering the men in my team for the sake of live captures and bigger rewards. I was told that they would be sending an Alouette Chopper to uplift the survivor, and that there would be no bonus paid for this live POW.

"The reader will by now have established, that I was not the 'Cool Kid at Camp'. The fact is, Special Force soldiers are incredibly well-trained, competent killing machines. They are trained to use their own initiative (there's really no time to call a friend mid-mortar for a second opinion) and have to act on their instincts, the use of which is pummelled into them during their training. Any commander, leading a team and walking into combat, was required to ensure that the lives lost, whilst we are annihilating the enemy, would occur only where completely unavoidable. This due to circumstances that they, themselves, went out of their way to prevent. And with all due respect and honesty, quite a few SOs died, and were recaptured during other operations, but never under my command.

"I have a wealth of hair-raising skirmishes and incidents in this head that would keep the reader riveted, but these recollections would have to be tabled in a set the size of the Encyclopaedia Britannica. Yes, that many; forty plus operations in one year!!!

"I'll end off with this quote that is dear to my heart, and which speaks for itself:

"Far better it is to dare mighty things, than to take rank with those poor timid spirits who know neither victory nor defeat." – Theodore Roosevelt

With Johan Roots before downing the chopper

Downed chopper

The Strela team. Rassie Erasmus, Anton Benade and Mike

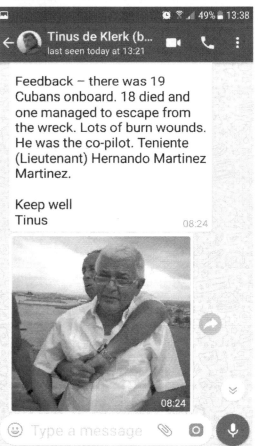

Feedback – there was 19 Cubans onboard. 18 died and one managed to escape from the wreck. Lots of burn wounds. He was the co-pilot. Teniente (Lieutenant) Hernando Martinez Martinez.

Keep well
Tinus

Left: Cuban Pilot. Lt. Hernando Martinez in later years

Chow time with Pseudos

Abandoned Buffel from Op Firewood

Flying into trouble; a happy Mike on the left

Op Boomslang operators

Right: Medic going to work on wounded fighter

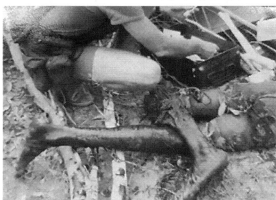

Pseudo group on the move with wounded prisoners

Schalk Kruger, Jim Lewis and Mike at Ruacana

Left: Tony Viera. 'Small Teams Operator' with M203 - AK47 with M79 below. On Epupa Falls operation

Anton Benade and Paul Swanepoel laying a landmine

'Danger' just after being captured

Right: Colosseum camp attack

Mike and John Brokaar with Swapo pseudo team. The operation was a huge success in the Ondangwa area

Pseudo operator on sentry duty

*Left: Mike with Johannes. PKM gunner
who was originally a storeman and who
requested a combat deployment*

Aboard a Strike Craft with Frank Tunney

On our way to look for aircraft to shoot down

Danger on ops with RPG 7 and a big smile

With Lt. Peter Bowles in Angola

Right: Anti-tracking footwear

Johnny de Gouveia on left. En route to Unita training base

Mike assisting with Unita para training

Mike decorated by General Kat Liebenberg

Mike (right) relaxing on the river while serving with Savimbi's men

Strela training

Unita anti aircraft drills

Left: Unita leader Jona Savimbi

Lecture for Unita

Sean 'Mad Mac' McHaffie. Exceptionally brave soldier who was wounded on Op Firewood

Op Coloseum. There were trenches under the bunkers

Unita Special Forces about to jump from a SAAF C130

Jan Breytenbach. (Rear 3rd from right) with instructors and Unita trainees

In later years with Wynand Du Toit (middle)

CHAPTER 11

Operation Colosseum

The Background

During the mid-1980s, the Angolan Civil War was reaching its crescendo. Fapla was being massively reinforced by the USSR, while Cuban combat troops poured into the country. Meanwhile Unita retained strong support from South Africa and covert support from the USA. Both sides (and their foreign backers) were gearing up for the final confrontation; one that would culminate in some of the largest battles fought in Africa since the end of World War II.

Despite successes, by 1986 Angolan air defences had been expanded with the arrival of hundreds of the latest Soviet SAM missiles and radars, backed up by Cuban-piloted MiG-21s and MiG-23s that posed a serious challenge to the South African Air Force which could no longer guarantee air superiority. Consequently, it was now virtually impossible to mount large-scale airborne operations, and the emphasis was now placed on deep-penetration by highly mobile columns of shock troops.

In late 1986, plans unfolded to attack the Swapo-Plan training base only 30 kilometres from the scene of the earlier Cassinga raid, some 300 kilometres inside Angola. Swapo considered it a safe area for its training purposes, mainly because of its distance from the South West African border, and it being completely under Fapla's protective air umbrella. Furthermore, some 20km to the west was a Cuban base with some 1500 troops.

The Swapo HQ base and adjacent training base comprised of rudimentary grass bashas, pole and mud huts, some permanent structures and extensive entrenchments, all well camouflaged and difficult to spot from the air. The attack was to be led by 5 Recce Commander Colonel James Hills.

The Mission

- Assault the Swapo-Plan training camp with the intention of killing as many guerillas as possible.

- The main assault group to remain mounted in Casspirs and trucks and at the 'Go' signal they would conduct a fast, mounted assault on the camp via one or both of the bridges.

- 52 and 53 Commandos would infiltrate across the stream during the night and form a blocking position covering the roads leading north and west out of the camp. The objective was to ambush any attempts by the guerillas to escape, as well as being early warning of any enemy relief forces coming from the north.

- Fire support included a troop of 81mm mortars, and 51 Commando was amply supplied with heavy machine guns and 106mm recoilless rifles.

The Attack

Enemy Forces – The Swapo training unit was at battalion strength. Heavy weapons were fairly minimal – some DShK 12.7mm heavy machine guns, as well as some 60mm mortars, RPG-7 and SA-7 Grails. They also had a fairly well-stocked motor pool, with various types of Soviet soft-skins, so they could mount a quick getaway unless the motor transport was first neutralised.

Although there were a number of other Swapo units and encampments nearby, no coordinated reaction was expected from them. The real threat was the Cuban garrison some 20kms to the northwest, consisting of 1500 men, including a company of tanks, a battery of D-30 122mm howitzers, a regiment of mechanised infantry, and a flight of Mi-24 'Hind' gunships. The plan called for 51 Commando to deploy hidden in the area of dense bush south of the river, whilst 52 and 53 Commandos would deploy in the dense bush north of the river.

The first group designated 51 Commando under Captain Buys, was the main assault force and would at dawn conduct a surprise mounted assault in Casspir APCs against the main camp with 11 Casspirs armed with 12.7mm and 14.5mm roof-mounted machine guns and eight Unimog trucks, each mounted with two 14.5mm machine guns except for four mounting the 106mm recoilles rifle. There were also four 81mm mortars that could be mounted on four trucks. Also in the assault force was Regimental HQ, 53 Commando, under Lt Waal de Waal from 101 Battalion. His Casspir would be fitted with SATNAV, and he would have operators from 2 Recce and the Reserve Force contingent that had been called up for the operation. They would follow just before first light. Sergeant Da Costa of the Recces would do the navigation to the forming-up point.

The assault force would form up and advance to contact. At first light, the mortars would open fire to soften up the target. 52 Commando was to attack from the east while 53 Commando would deploy on foot, infiltrate north across the river under cover of darkness, to establish cut-off positions on the main roads out of the camp, this with the intention of ambushing fleeing guerrillas or Cuban reaction forces approaching from the north.

The attackers left Oshivello on the 30th October and arrived at the forward assembly base at Cachueca on the 4th November, two days ahead of schedule. On the 5th November, a two-man team consisting of Lt Koos Stadler and Sgt Da Costa was tasked to recce the enemy position. They were to report back on the estimated enemy numbers and establish approach routes for the the different assault groups.

On the 7th November, 51 Commando was tasked with doing a motorised reconnaissance on the Bale River looking for the most usable crossing points. They found three around the confluence of the Cubango and Bale rivers. The next day the three Commandos moved north and stopped six kms north of the Bale River. The Echelon remained behind with orders to follow after the attack had been initiated.

On the 8th November the force moved further north, halting roughly 35kms south-west of the target. Further teams were deployed to check for enemy movement and saw no sign of the enemy. A further move closer to the camp took place on the 10th and the following day they linked up with Stadler and Da Costa. Stadler reported the target was actually two kms north of the original position where they had seen movement and heard gunfire. All three Swapo companies entrenched at the target had heavy machine guns mounted at the bunkers and road entrances. They were also equipped with 60mm mortars.

Colonel Hills set D-Day for the 13th November and H Hour at first light. He led his HQ Group, plus two attached platoons from 51 Commando to the east, with the intention of rushing across the eastern road bridge, to assault the eastern gate of the camp. His 81mm mortar platoon was deployed, ready to lay down the planned barrage on the unsuspecting camp, while Captain Buys led the rest of his Casspirs in a frontal assault across the drift.

As quietly as they could, 51 Commando's support weapons moved into position along the treeline, ready to provide supporting fire for the assault. The Fire Support Group had two Unimog trucks mounting ZPU-2 twin 14.5mm HMGs, another two Unimogs mounting B-10 107mm Recoilless Rifles and a GAZ-66 mounting twin .50 Cal HMGs.

At H-Hour, the 81mm mortars, recoilless rifles and heavy machine guns opened up on the camp and the Casspirs roared at full-speed across the river.

As Buys' assault group charged the camp, the 81mm mortars managed to silence the DShK bunker guarding the south gate. The truck-mounted heavy weapons meanwhile caused devastation within the enemy tent lines. Buys' leading Casspir crossed the river and then used its second action to disembark two sections of Recce Commandos.

Hills' assault group closed in on the east gate. The sentries desperately fired their weapons at the armoured Casspirs, but to no effect. There was now utter pandemonium in the camp, as guerrillas attempted to extricate themselves from their tents.

At the south gate the Casspirs, bristling with machine guns, laid down covering fire as two sections of Recce Commandos assaulted the DShK bunker. A further four sections of Recces dismounted and threw themselves into the cover of the trenches.

Due to the vastness of the enemy base, there were many contacts and incidents that played out, respectively. Each and every individual was so deep in his own battle to survive and succeed that there was no way for anyone on the far southern side of the base to know what was transpiring, simultaneously, on the far northern side. Soldiers were wounded. Soldiers died. Dead and wounded were taken to the Mobile TAC HQ, and in that way other teams would be kept informed of events during the battle, outside of their own.

"I was advancing from the southern side with John Brokaar," remembers Mike. "I was leading 53 Commando, through a massive, wide-spread enemy base. It consisted of bunkers (deep trenches) that were covered with corrugated steel sheets and grass, that also served as living quarters, a labyrinth of trench formations, a few huts, and various large tents, which were well concealed beneath large trees. This made them hard to spot from the air.

"This enemy area was relatively deserted, but we proceeded to throw M26 Grenades to clear out the bunkers. The risk was way too high to stick your neck in there. We also began torching these bunkers. However, in reality, burning these bunkers served no purpose, as the trenches were the real target.

"Huge plumes of smoke billowed from the burning. There were MiGs in the air. I contacted Colonel Hills. I told him that I was going to cease with the burning as the smoke was giving away our position, and I was concerned about an aerial strike. Colonel Hills concurred.

"There was sporadic gunfire as we moved through, but there was minimum resistance with the main force already having fled. The attack lasted about an hour. It was only the odd Braveheart/Rob Roy/Rambo who emerged, having not joined the mass exodus. They were dealt with swiftly. I cannot even estimate a figure as to the number of terrs who ate grenades in the trenches. A point to note: I, alone, had five M26 Grenades on my person, in preparation for trench clearing. I cannot recall what the recommended quota was per person or per group at the time, but that was my personal stash. I exhausted my supply."

Meanwhile, at the east gate, Colonel Hills personally led the assault on the dug-in sentries. Aided by suppressing fire from their Casspir, two Recce sections dismounted and assaulted the DShK bunker on the north side of the gate, while a further two Recce sections dismounted and occupied the trenches on Hill's left.

At the east gate a few moments later; Colonel Hills' supporting section was suppressed by small arms fire from the Swapo sentries, but his HQ section successfully stormed the trench and eliminated the enemy. On the other side of the road however, the Recces weren't quite as successful, being beaten off by the suppressed DShK HMG section but the enemy was in disarray. Seeing movement in the truck-park, Captain Buys called the 81mm mortars down on the parked rows of GAZ-66 trucks. Under pressure the enemy fled as their transport went up in smoke! On the south side of the camp, more of the enemy fell victim to SADF fire. At the east gate, Colonel Hills, with help from his

Casspirs, successfully knocked out the machine gun bunker and pushed on into the enemy accommodation. Fighters attempting to flee across the road, were killed by a Casspir racing down the street in pursuit of the fleeing guerrillas. Hill's HQ Casspir meanwhile, drove into the forest on the north side of the camp, in an attempt to cut off the fugitives' escape.

With the eastern side of the camp now cleared, Colonel Hills called his Fire Support Group forward across the river in order to more closely engage the remaining DSHk HMG teams and bunkers.

The Casspir in the road managed to spot and destroy a B-10 recoilless rifle team before they could engage the Casspir. However, a guerilla section did manage to fire an RPG at the Casspir and suppress it, but those fighters were soon eliminated.

Meanwhile, as the battle played out in the woods near the north gate, the Swapo 1st Company spotted an opportunity, and launched an assault on the Command Casspir which didn't have the same level of firepower when compared to the other Casspirs. However, it still managed to break up one of the three attacking sections. The Command Casspir got the worst of the incoming fire and was forced to retreat.

This was a decisive moment in the battle for Colonel Hills – there was the possibility of becoming bogged down in the woods and if that happened while withdrawing there was a possibility of them being captured and a huge propaganda victory to Swapo. Hills checked the landscape and eventually managed to escape their clutches.

With this threat to their lines of retreat temporarily beaten off, the surviving Swapo guerrillas made good their escape down the northern and western roads and straight into ambushes, courtesy of 52 and 53 Commandos.

As the assaulting Recces swept through the camp, mopping up any Swapo units that resisted and driving the rest toward the waiting ambushes, it was clear that this had been a good day for 5 Recce Commando and a bad one for Swapo/Plan which lost several senior commanders and suffered heavy casualties.

Mike West recalled: "Three or four days into the operation, I was part of the convoy with Mobile TAC HQ, moving in an easterly direction, returning to the ambush sites to conduct further checks for abandoned weaponry. The convoy came to a halt, and I was told to report to the HQ vehicle. We were a few kilometres from a T-Junction, and I was instructed to take a team and proceed to this junction and clear the area of ambushes. I had a team of 11 members on my Casspir. I left the gunner behind to man the Browning.

"It was raining, lightly at first, but this soon became a torrent, turning the veld into a quagmire. I gathered a team that comprised of my remaining ten, as well as the team of Jannie Wools. If I recall correctly, we were approximately 16 in total.

"I informed them of the task at hand. My orders were as follows:

"I would lead the mission, with my team in an extended line, with Jannie and his team following in single file behind me, thus forming a 'T' Formation. My instructions to Jannie and his team was that if we were hit from the left, they would move to my left flank, joining our extended line, in line with my team, and the same applied to the right.

"We proceeded to the west in 'T Formation'. John Brokaar was approximately five metres away, to my immediate left, as we advanced. If I recall correctly, we had advanced about 50 metres when we met fire directly from the front. Something exploded about a metre in front of me, throwing me over backwards. I immediately got to my feet, and as I did I saw John come running up shouting: 'Are you okay, Zaccanucchi?!' (Combat name)

"I shouted 'Yes!' as I was coming up, already firing my weapon and leading a counter-attack. There was a large amount of unfriendly fire exchanged with the unseen terrs. My extended line put down one helluva rate of fire, and we rapidly advanced upon the position that the unfriendly fire was coming from. The blast had left me fairly deaf and covered in grit, with my right eye heavily soiled. The terrs gapped it. We unfortunately didn't rack up any enemy casualties. They put down heavy fire, and then ran, without us seeing neither hide nor hair of them. We moved into their position, picking up gear that they had left behind.

"My quick appreciation of the scene: This was an ambush party, of approximately ten to 20 terrs, lying on the side of the road, waiting for unsuspecting vehicles. My appreciation was supported by the discovery of what knocked me over. It was a Yugoslavian SKS 59/66 HEAT (High Explosive Anti-Tank) rifle-grenade fired by an enemy soldier which landed in front of me. Thankfully it was not an anti-personnel rifle grenade, or I would have been prematurely cremated. I know this, having been in contacts where soldiers were killed by anti-personnel rifle grenades.

"It was clear that we surprised their right flank, where they were lying in extended line to ambush the vehicles. Their anti-vehicle grenade was loaded and ready for the vehicles. This is what they fired at me, when we dropped in unexpectedly. The rate of fire laid down by the enemy was fierce, but it fortunately passed right between us in our extended line, and hit the Casspirs approximately 50 metres behind us. This resulted in the simultaneous, rapid low cover of the soldiers in the Casspirs. After completing the clean-up, we returned to the vehicles, with no losses on either side.

"The rifle grenade that exploded directly in front of me wounded two men to the right of me. Once again I believe I had Divine Protection, since it should have killed me.

"Approximately five kms away from the enemy HQ on the way to the evacuation area, the Casspirs were ambushed and took a serious pounding. One of the vehicles caught fire when hit by a rocket, the shrapnel smashed into the back of Corporal Andre Renken's head, killing him.

"I'm sorry to say it but an officer in a Casspir coming behind reacted to the hit on Renken's vehicle by immediately ordering his driver to turn around and get the hell out of the killing ground when he should have assaulted the enemy.

"What all transpired, simultaneously, when this occurred, is not known to me. All I know is that I ended up next to Lieutenant de Waal of Romeo Mike (RM), when we were sweeping through the bush on the side of the road. The lieutenant, the gunner of his own vehicle, nailed three terrs with his Browning. It is important to note that most Casspir vehicles are manned by a gunner, outside of the Team Leader. Lt De Waal was the Team Leader of RM, and also manned his own Browning. One incredibly brave, daring and gutsy officer, who stood back for nothing, he was absolutely fearless!

"When this operation was over, and we finally returned to the Base Camp in Phalaborwa, James Hills stated that the Captain in question, he who had bolted from the ambush, had been transferred to HQ Phalaborwa with immediate effect. There was no Court Martial, nor any form of punishment, for his cowardly actions. I well remember this asshole walking around like he was the white on rice. Not a sign of his conscience troubling him.

"There was another incident in Angola, with another one of these Textbook Heroes, who took Operators out on a mission. I was not present, but many of the Operators present at the scene of the incident were friends of mine, so I am relaying here what was told to me.

"The team was under heavy mortar attack. They were tickets. This officer, straight from a recently completed course, and now Manual Champion, asked his team members:

'What do we do now???' My friend responded: 'We've got to get the fuck out of here!' And they ran for their lives. If they had told him to stay and fight, they would have been mortared to death.

"When you study to be a pilot, do you just climb in after your theory and study courses, and fly away into the sunset? No. You actually have to fly with an instructor and learn the ropes.

"That, Dear Reader, is critical in combat, too. You don't grow a set of balls, garner courage, defend or lead your team by passing a goddam course. You learn it on the ground. You learn it in full combat. You are meant to harness and hone this, gain respect in the field and then – and ONLY then – you can be considered for the position of Team Leader."

CHAPTER 12

'Operation Hooper'

In mid-1987 Fapla, with Russian and Cuban assistance, prepared to launch another major offensive aimed at Unita's stronghold in south-east Angola. More arms and equipment poured into the country. Moscow was looking for a knockout blow to finish Savimbi off and end a war that had dragged on too long. At the time all was not well in the USSR; the economy was tanking and American pressure on the Soviet leadership for political reform was increasing.

The first phase of 'Operation Saluting October' began in August 1987 when eight Fapla brigades deployed to a region east of Cuito Cuanavale where they halted and awaited resupply. Pretoria looked on grimly, it was clear to them Unita alone was outgunned and outnumbered. If Unita suffered a comprehensive defeat, there would be no buffer preventing a large scale Swapo incursion into Namibia. While the Angolan commanders hoped that the South Africans would not intervene, their hopes were dashed when President Botha, recognising the stakes were high, ordered an immediate response and 'Operation Modular' was launched to block the offensive. Into the fray went 32 and 101 battalions along with a mechanised battle group.

Complicating the Fapla advance was movement through swamps and flood-plains interlaced with rivers that forced them to concentrate forces in order to funnel them through select crossing points. These points had been identified by the South African commanders and they seized the opportunity to strike at these targets, much to the dismay of the enemy. Despite this, in terms of numbers and firepower the Fapla brigades should have prevailed, but their South African adversaries were better trained, better led, and more mobile and this led to a rout, thousands of casualties and a hasty retreat, back to the relative safety of Cuito Cuanavale. South African losses in men and equipment were relatively light; 17 dead and a handful of armoured vehicles. National Servicemen performed with distinction and played an important part in the South African victory.

News of this turn of events went back to Gorbachev in Moscow and it was understandably not well received. Some senior Russian commanders started to question their country's commitment to a war far from home and in an alliance with troops that did not always impress them. Only on the battlefield did they come to realise they were up against a well-drilled, well-equipped, and motivated enemy. Some reportedly told their political bosses this war was unwinnable as long as the South Africans were involved. President dos Santos summoned the Cuban and Soviet commanders to an urgent meeting in Luanda where the Cubans explained they had opposed the offensive but had been overruled by their Soviet counterparts.

In November the SADF presence in Angola was condemned in the UN Security Council which called for the unconditional withdrawal of the South African military. This was rejected out of hand by Foreign Minister Pik Botha who reminded the Assembly, that a South Africa withdrawal was conditional on the exit of the Cubans and Soviets from the conflict.

Far from withdrawing, buoyed by their initial success, President Botha authorised 'Operation Hooper'. His generals planned to go on the attack north of the Lomba River, aiming at encircling and destroying what was left of the Fapla brigades. But a crucial delay followed while National Servicemen who had completed their commitment were withdrawn and replaced, and tanks and artillery were dispatched to bolster the offensive capability of the force.

During this time Fapla, along with another large infusion of Cuban support, shored up their defences and recalibrated. Into Cuito came an additional Cuban armoured brigade and several air defence units. Their perimeter was ringed with heavy wire, minefields were laid, and likely approaches were well covered by artillery and tanks. This broke the South African momentum and the combined SADF/Unita attacks that followed were successfully repelled. Frustrating the attackers was loss of air superiority and the fact that their big guns were positioned out of range.

'Operation Hooper' was eventually terminated after the SADF had killed several hundred Fapla troops and destroyed a significant number of tanks and armour but failed to dislodge the enemy. While the SADF reported 13 dead there were reports of Unita losing hundreds, if not thousands of troops.

It appears the South African planners might have underestimated the strength of the force awaiting them and over-estimated the value of mobility when the target was a static one. The effectiveness of air-strikes was diminished by range which gave the SAAF aircraft mere minutes over the target before they had to make for home. Forced involvement in air-combat came with the possibility of aircraft being left with insufficient fuel to return to base. Adding to their woes the deployment of advanced fighter aircraft, some flown by Russians, altered the airborne balance of power considerably and this was a serious problem that could not be easily overcome due to the arms embargo on the country. Air superiority gave enemy MiGs a license to roam the skies in search of targets and this was particularly problematic for the G5 and G6 howitzers so vital to the success of these operations. It was clear now that large-scale future conventional attacks would be ever more vulnerable.

Although the SADF counteroffensive was stalled, the Angolan government, more dependent than ever on the Cubans and Russians, made it known it was open to negotiations. The snag to progress was the timetable for Cuban withdrawal and Castro made it clear he wanted the final say on this issue. In a bid to maintain the peace momentum the Americans agreed to meet the Cubans on equal terms. But while the warring parties circled the negotiating table Castro was looking to up the ante. Acknowledging a stalemate on the battlefield, he wanted to launch an offensive involving some 40,000 troops with armour and air cover that would strike south and threaten the SWA border.

In an effort to find a middle-road solution to the problem, 5 Recce Regiment was tasked to harass Fapla's 59th Brigade located near the Nianei River on their advance south towards the Lomba River. To stop them it was decided to carry out an 81mm mortar bombardment on the brigade positions with all 65 operators.

"We were equipped with Unimogs and Casspirs," remembers Mike. "A big threat at this time was from enemy tanks and the Brass were looking for ways to counter this threat without utilising our armour or heavy guns, so we were re-trained in the use of portable anti-tank weapons. Men on foot against tanks is always a big call, and as it turned out they seldom moved their armoured columns without infantry support, so the chances of getting in close enough to take a shot was remote. Eventually the plan was abandoned. However I did hear that Major Bert Sachse did get into a punch-up with a tank while trying to take it out with a 40mm shoulder fired rocket, but he ended up seriously wounded in hospital.

"The alternative plan then kicked in which involved 52 and 53 Commando from Phalaborwa. We did the advance with Unita to the riverline and from there towards the brigade base. We were issued with six 81mm mortars for the task. We all prepared our bergens for extra weight as each operator would carry three 81mm mortar bombs in addition to his normal SF ops kit. And the mortar tubes, base-plates and bipods had to be carried as well. Team leaders had to carry four bombs each. We walked through the night. Getting into the target area undetected was not easy as they had patrols out looking for us. Duncan Rykaart was in charge on the ground. Once we were in position, James Hills came in with his Tac HQ to take over command. James Teitge was in charge of the mortars.

"On the night the bombardment was set to take place the group reached a position just north of the brigade, about 50km from where they had left their vehicles. The area was a flood plain with the ground surface consisting of soft sand which was not ideal for firing mortars. The tubes were quietly set up and readied for firing. Each operator then came past the mortar positions and offloaded his cargo of bombs. The group then went into all-round defence to protect the mortar positions.

"Jim Maguire (previously in the US Marine Corps, Rhodesian SAS and who had also served in Northern Ireland) and I with four Unita soldiers were tasked to crawl into forward observer (FO) positions on the brigade perimeter and to direct the mortar fire. Jim and I as part of a group of 12 were constantly being deployed during this phase. Sometimes, apart from trying to get us killed, I was not sure what the hell we were supposed to be doing out there because we were constantly in the vicinity of brigade-strength enemy contingents with air support. Our pilots were getting understandably edgy about flying in some of these areas so we could not rely on air cover. At one stage James Hills told me that Jim and I must split up! I was fucking angry; there were only twelve of us anyway, and he wanted us to break up into two smaller groups. I flatly refused the order, as we were a fighting patrol with a Fapla brigade heading our way and it was madness in my view.

"This particular assignment was very dangerous and it is interesting why James Hills selected two English speakers from Rhodesia out of all those teams taking part for this job. Was it because we were so fucking good, or that we were a pain in their arse and would not be missed if something went wrong?

"James Hill ran everything by the book, strict military doctrine, whereas I was an out and out soldier, full time combatant, having served in Grey's Scouts, RLI, SAS, 1 Recce, 51 Recce, Swapo Operations and numerous missions with the 4 Recce Seaborne Unit in Langebaan. I had extensive first-hand combat experience – tons of it – and James Hill (with all due respect) had books filled with rules and regulations, having attended military colleges, whilst command-ing Peace Time Units. To them I must have appeared arrogant, a hopeless loose cannon, unorthodox and a non-conformist. "I studied the map closely; we were four kilometres away. Our Unita guides were good men, knew the lie of the land and were experts in bush craft. We did a check and count of the distance. We had sheep tally counters with us, which were very accurate, recording each step which we clicked.

"It was getting dark when we went in because you cannot approach a brigade like that without being in darkness. The Unita guides walked in front. Walking at a speed of four kms per hour I estimated we had done three kms when suddenly, one of the Unita guides dropped to his knees. He was pointing and I closed with him but could not see what he had seen. 'There – there – there…' he repeated, but the bush was dense, and I couldn't see through it. Only when I brought my binoculars up did I pick up the outline of something that didn't belong there. Then I saw the faint glow of some light about 100 metres away. All credit to the enemy; for a brigade-strength position they were damn quiet; and they had been well trained and were disciplined. I figured out what we were most likely looking at was an early-warning section of four or five personnel but just how far they were from the main body was impossible to know.

"As we closed on them, we saw the flicker of small fires through the under-growth and could hear the faint sound of voices. I was pleased to note they appeared to be relaxed but I was reminded this was no walk in the park where you bomb them and get out of Dodge City. There were thousands of heavily armed, well-trained troops nearby, and there were all six of us with AKs.

"I motioned to Jim and he and I quietly climbed high in a tree with the binos and night-vision equipment. Scanning the area from north to south and plotting the fires I came to the uncomfortable conclusion we were actually within the brigade's perimeter. If there had been perimeter patrols, we must have evaded them. And thank God for small mercies because if we had got into a firefight the response would have involved hundreds of men using APCs armed with BRDMs to mow us down and we would not have had a hope in hell of getting out of there.

"Despite scanning the area from the tree I was still unsure about the exact location of the heart of the base which is what I needed to know to plot the ranges for the mortar men. But the Unita guys seemed to know and after talking quietly to them I followed their instructions and figured out the distances. Then I radioed back and gave the information they required. The plan was for the incoming mortar bombs to sail roughly one kilometre over our heads and onto the enemy leaving us a safe distance from the explosions.

"On receiving the range from me, the bombardiers would then look at their tables which would give them the angle that the tube should be set. Depending on the distance they might have to add secondary charges to increase the range. Being on soft, sandy ground they know there will be movement of the base-plate and therefore the tube, caused by the recoil, the moment the first bomb is fired. This beds the weapon in but an immediate check must follow to reset the angle. Once that is done the full barrage must proceed at speed. Remember, no bombs fall on exactly the same place. They fall over a large area as the base-plates and the mortar pipe actually alter with every shot, so the explosions form a large area known as the 'beaten zone'. The beaten zone is perfect to throw at a brigade as it covers a large area, especially using six mortar pipes, which will cover an area big enough to cause havoc. In amongst the ordnance were air-bursts designed to inflict maximum harm on the fleeing enemy before they got to their trenches or into better cover.

"Once the FOs (Firing Officers) had confirmed by radio that they were in posi-tion and ready to fire we heard the shells coming but our joy was short-lived because all of a sudden, mortars rained down on us. I remember seeing trees split by the blasts and the shockwaves blew Jim and I out the tree we were observing from. We fell a long way to the ground, and we had been totally deafened. We both lay there conscious but dazed. At least eight mortar bombs hit our position. It was lit up like daylight. It looked like we were standing in a dust storm. We were covered in sand, our clothes, our eyes, and our hair, covered in a mat of dirt.

"Clearly we were in the 'beaten zone' and we should not have been. I know our ranges were right so can only think it was the soft sand. Jim, ever the cool dude, gathered his senses, reached for his radio, and calmly but firmly told them to 'stop... stop... stop'. I reckon he said 'stop' about 10 times before they reacted. James Teitge was in charge of the mortar crew, and clearly he was not listening to his radio as he should have been. But I take my hat off to Jim on the radio. He was so calm, clear, and loud, delivering an order with pauses as we were taught to do. I looked over at him and shouted: 'We're fucked'. During the bombardment we were fortunate enough to flee out of the beaten zone, how we did it I dont know, another Divine intervention.

"So maybe they reset it, maybe they didn't, but I've got a funny feeling they just fucking let go, didn't redress the mortars, and we got nailed the shit out of us. They adjusted the range and within a few minutes some two hundred 81mm mortar bombs consisting of a mixture of HE and red phosphorous were delivered on the brigade. Fapla must have shat themselves, the place was lit up like daylight and the earth was shaking under our feet.

"But our problems were not over, I don't know how far we had withdrawn before we were hit again, as just then Unita on the south side started firing again, and we were fucked as they hit us again, overshooting their target. We couldn't move because we were inside the perimeter. Of course it could've been the enemy shooting their mortars, but why hit us? By now we were 150 metres outside the 'beaten zone', and I didn't know which way to go. We had early-warning groups either side of us so we were trapped in a sense. Initially we went to ground because of the shrapnel, and one of our Unita guys got hit in the hip.

"I really wasn't sure what was hitting us. It felt like a 122mm Stalin Organ (Katyusha rocket launcher) shooting a barrage of 40 rockets. We held our hands over our heads, fingers in the ears, and opened our mouths as wide as possible, with our eyes tightly closed. We were literally shaking on the ground covered and choking from the dust. We were so fucked!

"The moment the 'beaten zone' moved west we legged it back to our lines as fast as we could. Full moon and the stars were up, but there were no reference points. Luckily, I had watched the stars and saw in the moonlight going forward an isolated tree I had seen on the way in, so I knew we were not going towards the enemy.

"I managed to lead them back and we walked straight into the mortar team. The moment we got back, I went and approached James Hills and wanted to know if they were trying to kill us. Hills response was 'Staff-Sergeant, why did you put yourself between the enemy and the mortars? You made a bad decision.'

"What did James Hills, the parabat from Bloemfontein, who never did selection or had combat experience, expect? That we would walk over to the enemy and request permission to walk over to the other side because mortars are coming? Their brigade was spread out three to five kilometres long. Where the fuck was I to go?

"We were right there, very, very close to death, and our own mortars nearly took us out. Of course I assume it was never done on purpose. Rather it is likely that the mortar base plates dug into the soft sand after the first few rounds, and no one checked. We did nothing wrong. I had added an extra 1000m to protect us, but I still got the blame. I was told I wrongly calculated the distance, which was bullshit!

"We must be just about the only people who were in the 'beaten zone' who got out alive. There must have been a guardian angel looking after us, because we were goners. This was hell! This was hot! We got fucked up! How we got out I don't know. A cat has nine lives; well I've had more than nine lives.

"There is something I want to get off my chest. I've been told to wind my neck in and not to tarnish the name of the Recces, but every unit has people who make mistakes and we were no different. There were people I have an ongoing problem with.

"When the shooting stopped Jannie was sent in to find out where the brigade had moved to. He had no problem finding them, but he was spotted by a patrol and found himself under fire right inside the enemy position. He was pinned down but managed to make a distress call and support fire was put down near his position which enabled him and his men to withdraw. It was clear by this time that Fapla still had plenty of heavy armour available and with only Casspirs and Unimogs we did not stand a chance.

"At various times during this operation we were calling in artillery on selected targets, with devastating effect. We had lots of big guns and our blokes were good at using them. We called these bombed out areas 'no-man's land'. Pieces of missiles lay strewn all around. Tree trunks were cut off, there were huge craters and ash blanketed the whole area. On one occasion I remember the eerie silence and the only thing that was moving there was a single fork-tailed drongo, which is a little black bird that flies around an area, after fires, to chomp the surviving insects. No bodies, no body parts.

"About 500 metres past 'no man's land', I spotted what looked like a base camp, comprised of grass shelters. I had no idea what to expect because Unita had had a strong presence in the area, so I was concentrating on our advance, when all of a sudden a helluva rattle of heavy gun fire came from above and behind. Two MiG 21s had dived in and were strafing the camp from behind and directly over us. We fell flat on our faces, on the ground, which literally reverberated and bounced with every round and bomb that hit the base.

"They circled overhead to check for signs of life, and then flew off in a northerly direction. Once we were sure that they were gone, and that we were still alive, we moved through the remnants of the camp. There wasn't a soul around. It seemed clear that the previous attempt to bomb them, which had fallen short, had chased Unita off, so the MiGs had just spent unnecessary ammunition and fuel.

'Operation Coolidge'

"Later, in August 1987, we were deployed south of the Mianai River, when guys from 4 Recce under Major Fred Wilke came to join us. They were divers and their task was to destroy the bridge over the Cuito River which would cut supplies to the four brigades that had already crossed the river. The plan was for them to kayak close, and then swim to the bridge to blow it. We in 5 Recce were to infiltrate the vicinity of the target to keep an eye on enemy movement near the bridge, help the divers if they got into trouble, as well as to help them exfiltrate once the job was done. For this RV points were established and manned by 5 Recce. They would be flown out by chopper.

"They were dropped about 70kms from the bridge and started paddling but they had problems near the bridge when they hit barbed wire and other underwater obstacles. Sentries spotted them, opened fire and started chucking grenades into the water. Major Wilke was wounded. Some of the divers still managed to lay their charges, despite the fact they were under fire, and then swim away. Of the 12, ten made it to the RV and by early morning two, Beukman and Wessels were still missing, and the decision was made to leave without them. Swimming downstream Major Wilke survived a crocodile attack, and they were constantly fired upon by foot patrols and from choppers. Beukman and Wessels survived and were making their way to the emergency RV, but because of all the enemy activity they had to keep swimming. Beukman was then attacked by a croc and dragged under, but used his combat knife to continually stab it until it let him go."

Renier Hugo remembers: "With Jim Maguire my team was tasked to infiltrate and set up the RV for the evacuation of the 4 Recce guys. The infiltration with the diving team went fairly well and I cannot elaborate on that as I was not with that group. Our infiltration did not go too well as our Unita penetration group was initially in charge of the navigation to get us to the RV point. As usual they were reluctant to take us straight there and I then suggested that Jim and I take over the navigation. It was hard going and we had to walk through a lot of marshes, but we stuck to our plan, with Jim doing most of the navigation and myself acting as his backup. At one stage Julius Engelbrecht told us that we were lost and that did not go down well because we knew the bush and we knew the area, and in the end we took him to the exact position that he wanted to be. He later on apologized profusely about the incident. We then established the RV point which consisted of a rope with Lumi sticks (stick-on night light) attached to it which we then took across with a Zodiac dinghy. We also established a listening post on our side of the river in the Zodiac.

"I still remember it was Julius and I that were sitting in the Zodiac at around about 03h00 in the morning when all hell broke loose at the bridge, and there were bangs and gunfire everywhere. We knew that the divers must have been detected and in some sort of trouble, so we started a few deception actions to draw the enemy's attention away from the bridge. A little later we heard a large explosion and we knew that the charges had exploded and that the bridge was damaged or destroyed. We now eagerly awaited the arrival of the divers at our location as we knew that we were compromised. At first light there was still no sight of the divers and the whole situation very quickly deteriorated, as the enemy had helicopters in the air and ground forces sweeping the river line looking for us. We had to withdraw back onto a small little hillside overlooking the river, as Fapla ground forces and helis were now trying to locate us. At about 12h00 that afternoon we saw the first divers coming around a bend in the river. At the same time a Fapla group of about platoon strength detected us on the opposite of the river and a contact ensued. Whilst the contact was in progress, we scrambled down and if I remember correctly we retrieved ten divers of which one was Fred Wilke who was wounded in the shoulder. We treated him and destroyed one Zodiac and an engine and threw it in the river. Anton Beukman and Les Wessels were still missing, as Anton had been bitten by a crocodile during his exfiltration, the two of them being held up and separated from the rest of the team. It was then decided that my team and I, with Fred and the rest of the divers would start exfiltrating in order to get Fred to Rundu asap for better medical help.

"We started our exfiltration that afternoon and the South African soldiers carried Fred as Unita refused. Everybody did some carrying – even the 4 Recce divers that had just finished a very long and hard swim. I again did the navigation and initially starting running south, as there were a lot of MI-24 and MI-17 choppers in the air looking for us. At one stage I thought that two MI-24s had located us because they were circling our position for a long time. It was with pure luck that I saw a Unita soldier with an RPG7 wanting to fire on one of these monsters. I stopped him because firing a missile would have been suicide. I then realized that they were dropping stopper groups on our escape route and decided to move eastwards. We walked non-stop through the night and crossed the Vimpolo river and then ran directly south and crossed the Mianai River at first light the next morning. We then went into a hide where my team and I established a LZ for the helicopters later that night.

"In the meantime Anton and Les arrived at the RV where it was determined that he had been attacked by a crocodile, but although badly bitten, had managed to escape. Anton was treated immediately and the team started exfiltrating to a different RV. That evening the choppers collected Fred and his divers from my location and then flew to the RV of Anton and Les, after which they flew the 4 Recce team to Rundu.

"The choppers returned and collected my team as well as Julius and his team, and we were then flown to Mavinga to rejoin our forces and carry on with our original task. One Zodiac engine was left behind where Julius was collected and the funny part of it is that that specific engine pitched up in Rundu a couple of months later at the CSI base and was eventually handed back to 4 Recce. Needless to say the 4 Recce boys got their medals for bravery, which they deserved, but I think there were quite a lot of heroes that night. For the 5 Recce guys it was business as usual and we did what we were trained to do. Another interesting day in the life of a 5 Recce operator."

CHAPTER 13

'Operation Firewood'

The Plan

The aim of 'Operation Firewood' was to locate and destroy the Swapo HQ for the central area near a small place called Indungo, about 50km north-east of the town of Techamutete in Angola. The plan was to hit the enemy while they were training in preparation for their 1988 rainy offensive. It would be the deepest penetration into Angola during the conflict.

The actual attack would be preceded by an extensive reconnaissance operation involving members of 5 Recce which would take place between July and late September 1987. This was be conducted from Unita-controlled areas near the target.

After getting the green light to go the force began assembling at Oshivello at the beginning of October 1987. Equipment was prepared, marrying up was done, rehearsals were held, and briefings were presented. The force, which totalled 750 troops and 153 vehicles, consisted of:

- 5 Reconnaissance Regiment and echelon.
- Members from 2 Reconnaissance Regiment.
- Four companies and an echelon from 101 Battalion
- Support elements including an 81mm Mortar Fire-Group, paratroopers, engineers, drivers and medics.
- A Mobile Air Operation Team. (MAOT).

Key personnel included:

- Operations commander Colonel JR Hills.
- Commander 51 Commando: Cmdt. AJ Verwey
- Commander 52 Commando: Maj. D. Rykaart.

- Commander 53 Commando: Maj. SN Du Toit.

- 5RR Echelon Commander: WO1 Koos Moorcroft.

- Commander 2 Reconnaissance Regiment: Maj. J Van der Merwe.

- Commander 101 Battalion: Maj. J. Kruger.

- 101 Battalion Echelon Commander: WO1 C. Schutte.

- Commander Medical Detachment: Maj. R. Berry.

- Commander Paratroop Detachment: Capt. P. Pienaar.

- Commander MAOT: Maj. P. Carrolan.

The battle group would use Infantry Fighting Vehicles and Armoured Personnel Carriers: Ratels, Casspirs and Buffels.

- The attack would be preceded by an air bombardment using F1 Mirages. Air support during the attack would be provided by Impalas.

- 101 Battalion was tasked to deploy three companies to the north, east and south of the base to act as stop groups. The fourth company was to deploy on the Indungo/Vila da Ponte Road as an early-warning element.

- 5 Recce, 2 Recce and the paratroopers would approach the base by vehicle from the west, debus and assault the base on foot.

- The 81mm mortars were tasked to provide fire support.

- It was then planned that the force would attack the Eastern Area Headquarters once the target area had been cleared.

The force departed Oshivello on the 25 October 1987 and all had arrived safely at the forward staging base by the 30th, five days later. D-Day was set for 31 October and H-Hour 10h00.

Rumbling in the Ranks

Mike West: "Prior to this attack, James Hills had come to ask my opinion. I read him, correctly I believe, as a textbook soldier and theoretical thinker, and that was a problem because here we needed to think local, and adapt to the reality of what we were up against. Commandant Jaco Kruger, Commander of 101 External Operational Forces, was just such a soldier; an experienced, courageous soldier who had no time for books and orthodoxies.

"At the time we were in a forward holding base, from where we would advance for the attack. I was the oldest Operator there, and based on my experience and understanding of trench warfare, Colonel Hills wanted to know how I saw this playing out.

"It was simple, I told him, I saw two scenarios:

1. They run, and all is well.

2. If they stay in the trenches, we are going to bleed.

"I was pretty sure the latter scenario was more likely. We were headed into their domain. They were lying in wait for us. As it turned out, we had attacked this same area a few months prior, on 13 November 1986. It was now 31 October, 1987. We heard later that intelligence had been leaked to the enemy that we were headed to this area once more, and they were waiting for us. Colonel Hills disagreed vehemently, and called the enemy a bunch of 'garden boys' (his words) and that they would run.

"Moral of the story is no commander should ever hate his adversary blindly. Try and understand his motives, recognise and respect his strengths, and you will be better prepared to confront him and win."

Sean McHaffie remembers: "My mate Sean Froud who was the PKM gunner in our stick was rather pissed off that 2 Recce was allocated Buffels instead of Casspirs. I had just had a brew with Mike West and Eddy Edwards. Mike said then there was going to be a lot of bleeding because he had been down this road before as had a lot of the guys from 2 Recce.

"So this request for questions from the commander as well as General Sabie van der Spey was a God-send for Sean who immediately stuck his hand in the air and waved it vigorously but he was ignored. Frustrated, he came to his feet waving frantically and eventually the general acknowledged him.

'Yes Sergeant, what is your question?' he enquired.

Well you could hear a firing pin drop; all horrified eyes on Froud.

'General,' said Froud standing up defiantly, clearly showing his Boys Scout scarf tied by its woggel around his neck. 'On our drive into Camp we noted many unused Casspirs at a police depot. Having noted this the men are at a loss as why they cannot be allocated to this operation. As it's obvious based on experience we are in for a rough ride.' Well the general's answer was crisp and sharp: 'We have military vehicles and that is what we will use. Those Casspirs belong to the police. Any other questions?'

'Yes Sir' said Froud, looking at me with a wink …..

'Why is it that we always end up sucking the hind tit?'

Froud was told to sit down and shut up."

Mike West: "Colonel Hills was a very religious man, and in this view, he wanted us to know he had the full support of the Dominee present, who actually knew squat... absolutely fuck all about combat. And all this tension when the Command Vehicle delivered the Dominee, complete with pulpit and purple scarf, handing out Holy Communion and wine, in order to bless the Operators and the mission. The Dominee actually came over to see me. None of my team operators attended either. He brought light wine with him for Holy Communion, which we stole and drank. It was good wine. They had lost the plot! No amount of biscuit and beverage and religious bullshit will stop a bullet. Something my team and I knew first hand, but it was frowned upon when we declined the light meal and fluffy words. We were preparing for battle, and I knew we were walking into some major shit. While I was not interested in listening to this Dominee and all his bullshit, I did have my own beliefs which I preferred to keep to myself. This was a kill or get killed operation and not a church service. Men had to be psyched up for fighting not for going to church.

"The reality at the time was that I was well aware it was my team I was leading out into war on 31 October, and not all of us were coming back alive. We watched from our Casspir. I worried about the young Parabats; this was a first for many of them and they had no idea what they were headed into. My fears were soon realised when so many of these great youngsters lost their lives. My mood worsened on the way in as our vehicles were kicking up dust clouds that could be seen for miles.

Into The Fray

"When we closed in on the camp we were in thick bush and debussed to head into the fight on foot. A navigation error *en route* meant we were an hour late so the air-strike was postponed to 12h00. We also had 81mm mortars giving us fire support.

"The first contact was with a vehicle that drove into the column, and that was soon taken out. There was another punch-up a little later with another vehicle which was also taken out. The bush was thick and we were slowed up in getting to the camp. The enemy knew we were coming, and they were ready for the fight. The incoming fire was intense. It occurred to me that being over 40 years of age I was probably the oldest bastard around. The Paras were slightly ahead and they got hammered; four of them being killed in the opening assault. The fighting was extremely intense and many men that we greeted that morning would not be there to answer a greeting when night fell on the silenced battlefield.

"As mentioned in previous stories, we were under incredible fire and people were dying. The 101 guys were ordered to close in on the camp and provide covering fire for us but they ran into another big battle with a Swapo reaction force.

"My friend Sean McHaffie, better known as 'Mad Mac' was in the thick of it. The Buffel he was in was hit by mortars and rolled. A B10 had a go at them but fortunately missed otherwise they were toast but they were still under intense fire when Mac and others in the group got wounded but he fought on, laughing all the way. Balls of steel, brave, honourable, one of the very best, I would have gone anywhere with Mac. Unbelievable sense of humour – a real nutter."

McHaffie remembers: "I was with Jan van der Merwe during the de-bus when the one Buffel got stuck on a tree stump, through the front wheel-struts – our wounded were not as a result of the hit by the B10 strike but from accurate incoming mortar fire. The enemy were expecting us and they had marked the trees for aiming purposes. The mortar bombs were exploding in the saplings above us. We also had incoming air-bursts and direct fire coming at us with the 12.7s and 14.5s being very effective. The enemy was well prepared and well trained.

"After being wounded the third time, I clearly remember seeing the leaves falling around me like surreal confetti in a burning cathedral. We learnt later that most of the radio antennas had been either shot off the vehicles or taken off by shrapnel.

"The ambulance that came towards the Red Smoke indicating the wounded was also an enigma – it came in from the wrong direction – arriving from the direction we were attacking in. Later we heard it had got lost in the confusion of the fire fight. I clearly remember my surprise seeing it coming at us from our front.

"Later in the day when we were moved to the TB (Command Base) after being redirected as the ambulance came under heavy fire – we debussed and the doctors and combat medics started patching and psyching us up. Unfortunately I could not get morphine due to my head wound so no relief from the pain but luckily the Doc pushed a drain into my left lung after assuring me the large needle he was about to stab me with would miss my heart on its way to the lung. We had a smile at that once the lung started draining. His expert skill took a hell of a lot of internal pressure off the gut wound and lungs and relieved the pain. He then also drained my stomach.

"Later in the day our rear came under possible attack from the second enemy base that was not indicated as a threat – we received early warning – and formed up to defend the rear – that was when the two Casspirs from 101 came into the fight – they formed up and started firing on the advancing enemy. We could hear and see part of the engagement – we later heard most of the crew that were defending the Tac HQ and medical post were shot out and killed. I strongly believe they knew they were outnumbered and outgunned – but they stood and fought – salute to those brave soldiers who sacrificed there all to hold their position against what was not known to be a threat. One wonders what the outcome would have been if that unexpected enemy movement had not been slowed and stopped to allow tactical countermeasures to possibly save the day."

Mike West: "Meanwhile we were in and out the trenches, I had to lead the way followed by Jim Mcguire and Clement Kunaka, it was close-quarter fighting. After clearing numerous trenches we came under heavy and accurate fire from a line of trenches we could not see. The reason we could not see the trenches was because the terrs, when digging the trenches removed the soil they dug out giving them a flat trajectory to shoot from. We got pinned down from the heavy firing we were taking from the trenches. One black operator got hit through his upper right leg. We were now lying in a extended line putting fire down on these trenches. One of the defenders in the trenches had my number, on two or three occasions the rounds hit about 30cm from my head. My line had already advanced and we were giving covering fire for my troops to move forward to my position. They did not move forward because they were pinned down by heavy fire and one guy was already wounded. Due to us being exposed on open ground we had to leopard-crawl backwards to get out of the killing zone. We found cover in uneven ground, I managed to grab the wounded guy, throw him over my shoulders and then carried him to safety. My friend and officer, Jan van der Merwe of 2 Recce, one very daring and gutsy operator, managed to reach the trenches on our right flank, but he too could not proceed any further. A RPG 7 was fired from the trenches, it hit a tree and Jannie Meyer was badly wounded in the shoulder and neck by the shrapnel. Another one of Jan's troops also took a round and went down.

"Jim Maguire and I went over to the Senior Battle Commander, who was safely sitting in his Casspir conversing on his radio, as we could not find our 53 Commander who was obviously engaged elsewhere in the battle. As we were approaching the command vehicle Jim Maguire angrily shouted out to the commanding officer, whose head was protruding above the upper lip of the vehicle and said: 'Sir, we are pinned down and they are shooting the shit out of us, we need armoured support'!! The officer replied, in very broken English:

'Sergeant Maguire, don't tell me how to do my job!' And then went straight back to talking over the radio.

"I then raised my voice and said to him: For fuck sake, we are taking casualties, we need support! His reaction was to turn his back on us and continue speaking on his radio. I was totally gobsmacked. When I carried the wounded guy to safety this officer came from his Casspir, took the wounded guy from me and just said, 'thank you Mike'. My first thought was 'Why the hell was the commanding officer of 52 Commando sitting in his vehicle and not leading his troops. Secondly, I was wondering where the commander of 53 Commando was, because I was leading both 52 and 53 Commando in the attack on the trenches. At the time, Major Jan van der Merwe, the commander of the ground attack force, was leading his 2 Recce troops into combat.

"Commandant Jaco Kruger, Ops Commander of 101, had a clear view of what was transpiring. He too requested that support be given, via his own fleet, and was instructed to hold his position. Jaco and I have a history in combat and he was in a 'fight for his life'. I named him 'Machine gun' as he was a very brave and gutsy commander, an excellent tracker, who led from the front and who had a huge number of firefights. 101 was a killing machine and along with 32 Battalion holds the record for the most kills in South African combat; Jaco's guys once drove into an ambush by 56 soldiers and killed 54, captured one and left one badly wounded behind, but I digress... men were falling like cannon fodder. We collected our dead, and gathered in the laager (circle) of vehicles, with more terrs flooding in to join the fray.

Retreat

"Whilst standing in the laager I was staring directly at James Hills – he could not look me in the eye. He then decided that we must retreat. And his next instruction was rather interesting. Me... Mike West, the big-mouth, number 26 in the convoy, was told to lead the line of vehicles out of the combat area. At the beginning of the operation my vehicle was 26th in line. Target on my head? On the way out I was placed right in front as the lead vehicle; so if there was an ambush, guess who was most likely going to get whacked first? Why do I think someone was quite keen to get me fucked up. And he had reason, because you see, I had called this. Which is why I am sure he picked me, like Moses, to lead us out. Bad things can happen to you when you are in the front.

"We then retreated for approximately 30 kilometres without incident. A great place, according to James Hills, to hold a debrief on what had just transpired. Only the Recces and surviving Parabats were lucky enough to attend. Jaco's 101 was still in the thick of things, and had further missions.

"His first words were directed straight at me: 'Staff-Sergeant West, you keep quiet.' You could hear a pin drop as everybody at the debrief was staring at me wondering what was going on. Unknown to them I had called this. I told James Hills before the time 'if they run, they run, but if they stay we are going to bleed,' and his reply was that 'they are just a bunch of garden boys'. I would have loved to be able to add my bit by asking him what he thought of the garden boys now? But I was ordered to keep my mouth shut. And then he tried to put a positive spin on this continental fuck up, by saying that we had succeeded in being able to penetrate and attack the enemy, to a degree, without being detected. I don't know what course he missed, or which textbook he didn't read, but he was deluding himself. They dealt with us on their terms; they let us in, shut the exits and shot the shit out of us. They knew we were coming.

"To add further insult to injury, the Senior Officer in charge of the attack, Verwey, our Radio Shack Man, called my team and I for further orders. Only us. He then began instructing us in full-blooded Afrikaans – not a strong point for the expats in my team. I immediately respectfully interrupted, and explained that although I understood what he was saying, none of my team did. His words, in very broken English: 'That is not my problem. They are in my army. They must learn to speak my language.' And then he continued in Afrikaans – which may as well have been Russian. I was left with the task of translating what I picked up, after he was done. When I explained the orders to my troops their jaws dropped because they could not believe what we were being tasked to do.

"We had just retreated out of a battle where we were losing hands down, men were dying, yet my team and I were going to be taken back five kilometres so we could monitor the enemy activity on the ground as well as the enemy following up on the convoy. The orders were foolhardy, dangerous and stupid to say the least. This was akin to lighting a match in an open gas factory. My team was completely dumbstruck. The place was a hornets nest of enemy activity.

"All I said was: 'Orders from the top. We have no option.' And there we were, dropped off like farts in the wind.

"We moved away from the drop-off point, and lay down in a defensive position. There was no way in hell that I was going to serve my team up to the enemy, and with chips, by just walking in. And down came the mortars, but an hour later, clearly indicating that they were searching for our convoy. I notified James Hills by radio that his so-called 'garden boys' appeared to be advancing with aggressive intent and there must have been a lot of them. I wasn't about to pull a Kamikaze and advance on an army with nine other people. The terrs were clearly having a good time, with us retreating and them pursuing.

"There are propellant rings, which we called incendiaries, which you place on the mortar base, to increase the range of the mortar, so it was near impossible to gauge their distance and position without venturing out and being shot to shit. You could set these to hit a target at a distance of anywhere between 180 metres to 4.6 kilometres. These fuckers, their location and their numbers, were a mystery to us, but based on our collective experience, we garnered a guess at anywhere between one and three kilometres from us. We held our position, because the mortars were landing about 100 metres to our right. James Hills finally saw reason, and told us to move in a southerly direction in order for a Casspir to pick us up. Our convoy was to move further south.

"Commandant Jaco Kruger and 101 were still in combat and we were forced to move south. Had Jaco, with all his armoured vehicles and many years of combat experience, led this assault, we would have been victorious. But that did not happen.

My Thoughts

"When we arrived back, I went to the Command Vehicle to report on what had transpired. I was told to go straight to my vehicle and move with the convoy. No interest in what had happened, nor what we had seen.

"The Recces, a specialised unit who appointed Textbook Heroes as Commanders, were given the task of leading real combatants into poorly planned operations, because they were not trained in conventional warfare. 101 was the most professional and highly skilled mobile unit, fully trained in conventional warfare and tactics, with more kills on the ground than any other fighting force in Africa at the time. They were the best of the best, and on par with 32 Battalion, yet they had to follow instead of lead. We had not trained enough with them. We went in blind, led by the blind. Good men died, unnecessarily. Young, inexperienced Parabats lost their lives too.

"After the attack MiGs appeared on the scene but thankfully they did not find us. The SA Air Force did another strike on the camp a day later and drew heavy anti-aircraft fire so the enemy was still there and still defending.

"The fact is the base was not successfully taken by the SADF forces, who withdrew when Plan reinforcements were understood to be on their way. The SADF incurred 16 killed and 56 wounded, and a 101 Battalion Casspir knocked out by a RPG7 anti-tank rocket and burnt out with the men inside. On the Swapo/Plan side they captured a SADF Buffel Armoured Personnel Carrier (APC) belonging to 2 Reconnaissance. It was lost fully intact in that battle. Three 101 Battalion Casspirs were also lost. The men on the ground fought bravely and Swapo also took a big hit, losing at least 150 fighters.

"All the SADF dead and wounded were casevaced to AFB Ondangwa during the night of October 31/1 Nov 1987. The last Puma helicopter departed at about 03h30 the following morning and ferried the remaining dead and lightly wounded. We eventually made it back to Ondangwa on the 11th November.

"In my view, 'Operation Firewood' was a tactical loss for the SADF; obviously this was not widely circulated, and thus relatively unknown to many SADF servicemen. I believe for the enemy it was a qualified victory and a 'tactical' defeat for the SADF in not meeting its objective, part and parcel of waging war. The leadership sought not to dwell on what went wrong because it would have damaged morale but in any military campaign there are always setbacks, and 'Operation Firewood' qualifies as one of the very few real setbacks that the SADF experienced during the Border War.

"Despite the passage of time, I remain very angry about the way I and my men were treated. All this after we had lost so many good men in large part to poor planning and poor leadership. All they had to do was listen to the fighting men and use the armour that was available to them.

"There was Jim Maguire, a brave soldier committed to the fight being humiliated because he could not understand Afrikaans. If being bilingual was a requirement why was he allowed into the army in the first place? We were sent into a situation that promised death; ten of us against fuck knows how many of the enemy. There we lay having the shit shot out of us while the command sat in their vehicles on their radios. There was a helluva lot of firing going on in the general area. They were busy on that fucking radio, in all likelihood singing *Sarie Marais*. Jim and I looked at each other, and felt an intense sense of bitterness. I'm not lying when I tell you, so angry were we, both Jim and I thought of turning our weapons on one of our officers. This is not something I'm proud of but both of us felt they were quite happy to see us getting the shit shot our of us, so why not return the favour.

"And let's not forget: To add further insult to injury, when we survived their nonsensical orders, with terrs advancing and mortars falling around us, they weren't even interested to hear what transpired upon our return.

Roll of Honour 'Operation Firewood'

Year	Force Number	Name and Rank	Date of Death	Unit	Service
1987	.	Abraham W., Rfn	1987/10/31	101 Battalion	South West African Territory Force
1987	83587345BG	Botes D., 2 Lt	1987/10/31	101 Battalion	South West African Territory Force
1987	83561928BG	Cobbolt D.C., 2 Lt	1987/10/31	5 Recon-naissance Regiment	South African Army
1987	82513110BG	De Rose H.N., Rfn	1987/10/31	1 Parachute Battalion	South African Army
1987	.	Epafu P., Rfn	1987/10/31	101 Battalion	South West African Territory Force
1987	82437369BG	Ewels W.V., Rfn	1987/10/31	1 Parachute Battalion	South African Army
1987	81033292BG	Light R.M. , L/Cpl	1987/10/31	1 Parachute Battalion	South African Army
1987	83219139BG	Olivier N.S., Cpl	1987/10/31	1 Parachute Battalion	South African Army
1987	.	Petrus V., Rfn	1987/10/31	101 Battalion	South West African Territory Force
1987	76330893PE	Rademeyer A.H.du B., Capt	1987/10/31	101 Battalion	South West African Territory Force
1987		Sheepo T., Rfn	1987/10/31	101 Battalion	South West African Territory Force
1987	84533793BG	Steyn E.A., Spr	1987/10/31	101 Battalion	South West African Territory Force
1987		Uushona M., Rfn	1987/10/31	101 Battalion	South West African Territory Force
1987	83247502BG	Van Rooyen D.W., Rfn	1987/10/31	1 Parachute Battalion	South African Army
1987	.	Wateka, Mufitu, Rfn	1987/10/31	101 Battalion	South West African Territory Force
1987	83271031BG	Schuurman J.M., Rfn	1987/11/01	1 Parachute Battalion	South African Army

CHAPTER 14

The End is Nigh

Military College, May 1988

"After moving to 5 Recce, my new home was Skiettoght Military Base, Phalaborwa. The two operational units were 52 and 53 Commando. I was working mainly with 53 Commando. These were black troops, comprising of ex-Portuguese, ex-Swapo and ex-Selous Scouts from Rhodesia. I may not have been the Commanding Officer, but I believe I lifted morale and initiated positive change in that outfit. To this day, my war cry in ChiShona: *Pamberi ne Hondo*, is remembered – it means: 'Forward with the War.'

"It is still being used and was printed on the back of our red team T-shirts. However, the logo on the front was changed because the powers that be deemed it to be pornography. It was changed from an eagle's head with a pair of enemy testicles in its mouth, to a scorpion. The resident Dominee apparently decided it was pornography. What a laugh. The Eagle, the beloved symbol of Rome's greatest conquerors, holding the strength of its enemy in its beak depicts victory against all odds. I wonder what the hell they have been watching

"As far as being a rebel is concerned I must admit that they were not wrong. I was living in the Single Quarters and it was time for mischief. I got busy and the next thing the Dominee presented himself to explain to me the error of my ways and to tell me how promising my future was if I would only stop being rebellious. I just couldn't stomach being preached to by this self-righteous bastard.

"They decided that the solution to the problem I was presenting was a spell at the Military College in Voortrekkerhoogte where they would turn me into a real soldier with a book under my arm and a better attitude. They even sweetened the pot by assuring me of a promotion from Staff Sergeant to WO2, should I pass the courses. I'm certain they were setting me up for failure, and had banked on it. They knew my history, and wanted to humiliate me by labelling me a dumbass. Challenge accepted!

"Arriving at the college, I understood instantly what being shackled in slavery and having your spirit broken must have felt like. Everything was literal military precision. By the book. To the 'T'. Neat. Pressed. Marching in twos wherever you go. Short hair. Ever clean shaven.

"As a Special Forces Operator, having led soldiers into combat and having to use initiative and training at all times to stay alive… I had never felt so out of place in my life. I was secretly hoping that some world leader would declare war, so that I could be ripped back into the world I understood.

"There were around 80 entrants for this particular course. We had to write an entry exam that required a pass. Here sits Mike West, behind a desk, with note-pad and a pen, all neatly dressed. Coached by non-combatant, office-working, 'Jam Stealers'. The world had flipped on its fucking head. Their puffed chests, as they imparted their great knowledge, riled the Viking in me. The entry exam trimmed about 15 people from the course, who were RTU'd (Returned To Unit), no doubt back to the safety of their heated offices. Guess who was still there? Guess who hated his commanders more by every boring minute?

"Those of us who had survived the 'Jam Stealer' entry had the pleasure of being military-marched to another building, where we were issued the following:

• A huge steel trunk

• Lock and Keys

• A mountain of manuals on every conceivable military anything and everything.

"The only use I could see for these fucking manuals, in times of combat, was to wipe my arse in the bush. Who references a goddamn manual when you're being fucking shot at?

"To add to my growing claustrophobic state, I was given a room in the single quarters, outfitted with a single bed and a cupboard to hang my clothes in. Because when we combatants pack anything for anywhere, we always have fucking hangers, right? I had brought all the required military attire for this particular shit show, and put them in the future firewood. The next day, the

9ᵗʰ Circle of Hell swallowed me whole, as classes began and studying became my only nocturnal activity.

"I deserve a medal for the amount of self-restraint I enforced in order to not Hulk Smash the entire goddamn place, storm out of there and disembowel anything resembling the people who put me there. But I channelled my anger into meeting the challenges that came with having to sit still and study hard. I decided that I would fucking pass so well that they'd have to eat any stupid commentary they may already be making about me and my progress. I would return victorious, trump the twats, and express my utter, seething, unquenchable contempt for them.

"If these were Special Forces commanders, I was the fucking Easter Bunny. I had served under real officers in Rhodesia. Men who cracked tough Special Forces selections. Survived war. Moved up the ranks and became commanders. I did not hold Hills or Bestbier in the same regard.

"Back at the course: There was an exam every single week. If you failed one, you were out. Weeks went by. But I was determined. During the coldest part of winter in that part of the world, which is May to July, I wouldn't even wear the prescribed warm clothing, because this hatred's fire burned wildly. I wore my 'Summer Edition' uniform straight through, without a jersey or jacket, to show them I was a fucking operator. The others were 'Jam Stealers'. I had to show them I was a leader. Fellow candidates in class had heaters by their feet and zipped up warm jackets. I had James Hills' pending humiliation keeping me warm.

"I realised that I had to expel some of this tension and rage. I found a hotel conveniently distanced from Voortrekkerhoogte, parked my bike outside, and ordered a Passion Fruit and Lemonade drink in the lounge. Seated to my right, about ten metres from me, were two ladies and a gent enjoying drinks.

"The guy was bald and bloated. He had that drunkard loudness going, having had an altercation elsewhere (which he was communicating to these poor plump women), and just looking at his 'kick my head in face', I was immediately drawn to flattening him. *Decorum* dictated otherwise, but opportunity presented itself when he rather uncouthly announced that he was going to take a piss, this comment in Afrikaans.

"I eased my way to the toilet, quietly following him. When I entered, he was already mid-piss, left arm leaning against the wall, at an angle. He immediately graced me with that drunken fucked up look you give people when you think that you're a tough guy. I walked directly at him, hit him square with a right fist and he dropped like a limp sack of shit.

"A wonderful sense of relief came over me, as the stress began leaving my body. I had just figuratively dropped one of those officers I loathed. I walked straight out, climbed on my bike, and the ride back was blissful. I slept like a happy, fully grown adult and woke energised, ready to star in the circus I had been sent to.

"I obviously didn't tell anyone, so it's anyone's guess as to what happened to Drunkalot next. As difficult as it was for me, my raw hatred for the entity that posted me there fuelled my success. I received an 87.88% Distinction Pass Mark. I was 4th in the class out of 25 (of the original 69) 'Jam Stealer' students.

"This was cream, to me. In 1974, still a civvie, and before going to Rhodesia, I had heard stories about the Recces. Tough guys who didn't eat ice cream nor greet their parents. This was my cup of tea. I hastened to Poynton's Building (the Military HQ in Church Street, Pretoria) to apply. My enthusiasm was shattered when I was told that I didn't qualify because I had no Matric and I had no religious affiliation. I had stated that I was a Free Thinker, but they insisted I was too dumb and I was told to get lost.

"Now, here I sat, having aced this course. With WO2s as company, having out-classed most of them. I had already taken Recce Operators into combat in 1978, on the ground and during camp attacks in Rhodesia, as an SAS Operative. It would have been lovely to find the 'Jam Stealer' who rejected me in 1974 and flash him a medal and certificate. Look where I was, already, without Matric and a Tithe debit order. How do you like me now, Dumbass?

"You won't believe what happened next… I had a surprise visit, after the course, from one my Favourite Four psychiatrists, who had obviously been following the progress of this 'Danger to Society'. You are going to love the question posed by this non-combatant, overfed, pen-pusher. 'How do you now feel about the families of your enemies?' he asked. The very same style of question, dear reader, which originally had me labelled as a psychopath, with a bipolar personality. I responded from the deepest part of my heart, in all sincerity, wanting to be this newly distinction-earning reborn me: 'I would still kill the fucking bastards.'

"He tried to correct me, and I vehemently reminded him that he could never change my outlook on war. I fucking *knew* war. He did not – nor did the moron who devised that question. He didn't bother completing the form he had brought that bore my name. He gathered up his bullshit form and pen, and hastily retreated. I arrived back in Phalaborwa.

"Cue cicadas, because not one fucking word was said about my outstanding success. Not even from the great CO who sent me there to fail so that he could humiliate me. Someone lost a fucking bet. I hope it was big money. I thoroughly revelled in the knowledge of his humiliation at failing to down me further. And he didn't promote me because I wouldn't follow their religion, or join their UCC Church, the United Church of the Conquerors, who gave out church badges to be worn, and they hated me for that.

"They sent me back to the bush to pick up where I had left off before they sent me on the course. The fact they did not honour their promise to promote me says more about them than about me. It was times like this I missed the SAS where religion and politics was of little importance, they respected initiative and results.

"And this is where I missed my hero Darrell Watt, The true God of War."

* * * * *

In March of 1988 a large force of Cubans based at Lobito was ordered south. Their confidence boosted; thousands of Plan insurgents joined their allies on the march. For the South Africans the threat increased when the Cubans formed three joint battalions with Plan fighters, each with its own artillery and armoured contingents. In an effort to slow the advance the SADF launched harassing attacks while over 100,000 reservists were mobilised to prepare for a major onslaught.

While there was no question the South Africans were going to stand and fight, the political leaders were well aware of the need to avoid a protracted conflict that was a drain on the fiscus and one certain to incur more casualties. Public sentiment was a factor and the majority of the voting populace preferred peace. Similarly, Gorbachev in Moscow was weighing up the cost of conflict in a distant place and coming to the conclusion it was not sustainable.

Thus among the principal players there was a fundamental meeting of minds and both wanted an early end to the war. While Castro was in aggressive mood, he was still playing second fiddle to the Soviets; if they decided to end it he would not go it alone.

Early May 1988 talks commenced involving delegates from the Soviet Union, the US and South Africa. The Americans insisted Pretoria commit to independence in SWA and South Africans insisted on a comprehensive withdrawal of Cuban troops from Angola. The offer on the table to Pretoria suggesting this withdrawal take place over three years was rejected with caveats. When the South Africans were promised the presence of a 'verification mission' to oversee the Cuban exit their position softened. Carlos Escalante, who came to head the Cuban delegation in July brought with him an air of optimism. He could read the changes in the global balance of power and showed a willingness for compromise in order to improve relations with the Americans knowing that the Soviets were not in Angola for the long haul.

In August, the Angolan, Cuban, and South African delegations signed the Geneva Protocol, which established the principles for a peace settlement in South West Africa and committed the SADF to a withdrawal from that territory. Plan declared a ceasefire days later. Influencing the Cuban position was the election of George Bush and with that the knowledge there would be little or no change in Washington's approach to the imbroglio.

Three days after the US election results were confirmed, the parties agreed to a phased Cuban withdrawal over the course of twenty-seven months and South Africa pledged to grant South West Africa independence. All hostilities in Angola and South West Africa ceased on 1st April 1989. On 21 March 1990 Namibia became independent under Swapo leader Sam Nujoma, the majority of the South African troops having left the previous year.

Looking Back

"Looking back and realizing what we accomplished over many years of war, 14 years to be exact, and to look at the photos today, makes it hard to believe we survived. Far more than 100 contacts, with many loss of lives, and here I sit and struggle to survive in old age.

"I often think about what happened to the old Recce operators who had my back, and without whom I could not have operated. Some remained with the Special Forces. Some transferred to other units within the SADF. Some retired on pension, whilst many took financial packages and left the service completely. With the advent of peace, some left because they could not envisage serving under people they regarded as the enemy, and some settled in civvy street and have done well, whilst for others, not so well.

"At all times we in the Recces had fantastic support from the Navy and the Air Force. I suppose because of the nature of our deployments we came to know the Navy chaps better and I cannot speak highly enough of them. At every level they were so kind to us and backed us in every way. They went out of their way to give us the best food and to make us as comfortable as possible. And no matter how much trouble we were in they came sailing in to save us. If not for their bravery and professionalism a lot more of us would not have made it home.

"The vast majority of the Rhodesian fighting forces emigrated from the disaster of Mugabe's dictatorship; many to Australia, New Zealand and South Africa, while some went to the UK, USA, and Canada. Those who missed the smell of cordite, the surge of adrenalin, found wars elsewhere as mercenaries with other former soldiers. Some became brothers-in-arms with Executive Outcomes – a private company supplying mercenaries and security protection services in various wars in Africa, or in fighting off pirates around Somalia and the African coastline.

"A sad state that today, sportsmen, celebrities and musicians get greater recognition than fighting soldiers. We were expendable I suppose, cannon fodder, fighting an unpopular war. We could never be ambassadors for our country like sportsmen who received fame, recognition and salaries that were and are still, unheard of. We loved our profession and made sacrifices so that these sportsmen could enjoy their professions. We were not there for the money; nine years of full combat service in the Recces with allowance and all, I never got a decent salary. The highest rank I reached was WO2, but only very briefly before I was returned to the rank of Staff Sergeant because of my persona and my religious beliefs.

"I was fine with most of the Afrikaners, it was the Afrikaners in the senior ranks that did not like me. To say that some of the officers actually tried to get me killed might be stretching it, but the way they kept deploying me, sometimes for reasons I didn't fully understand, I sure as hell got the impression that they were not going to shed too many tears if I didn't make it back. But I never left, I felt I was doing what would make my family and my country proud, and I was literally addicted to the smell of cordite. Combat soldiering was in my blood, and I would die for it if I had to.

"The older I get the more I understand that it's okay to have lived a life others don't understand. There is in war an intensity to the moment that exposes character with the precision of the vivisectionist. No half measures there, no place to hide, with both good and bad starkly revealed.

"What did we fight for – to be betrayed I suppose? When I was in Rhodesia, I was fighting for Rhodesia, and I truly loved that country and its people. In South Africa I did it because I enjoyed it. Who would have employed me other than as a janitor? Today I am a pensioner making a living out of debt collecting. Adrenalin! Will to live and respect. I just wanted to be like Darrell Watt I suppose. He set an example for me that I wanted to follow.

"But people forget, we were fighting against the Russians and their proxies. Without the Russians these so called 'liberation movements' would not have functioned. In Rhodesia and South Africa, when our generals and politicians tried to get the Western world to understand we were not fighting to oppress black people but against communists who were bad news for Africa and the world, they were laughed at. Today, with the war in Ukraine, the leaders of those countries seem to have changed their view. And look at Mozambique, Zimbabwe and what is happening now in South Africa and tell me who was right?

"I often hear and read about war veterans who are not coping in society. Many good men who came through the hard times but are paying a price later in life. Night-sweats, nightmares, the demon drink. Social misfits screaming in their sleep. Institutionalised people who are unable to deal with what they saw and did in war. Men who are not able to cope with what they did in war, or what was done to them. They gave their all, fought like lions, and when it ended nobody said so much as thank you. It was just 'so long soldier', pack your bags, and see you when I see you.

"When I see how many veterans are struggling today and remember the guys who did not survive I get very angry with these posers out there claiming to have been in the Recces and other special forces units. These wannabees be warned, shut your mouths, if I find you I'm going to fuck you up!

"I still wake up having dreamed of the thrill of combat, the adrenalin flowing, readying myself for a fight. But I do miss the smell of cordite, my brothers in comradeship, and the action, and wish I was able to go back to that life. I don't suffer from Post Traumatic Stress Syndrome or whatever they call it. I have lived with violence all my life, and I was prepared to die with a bullet in my front rather than in a car accident.

"I don't fully understand it all, but I have given it a great deal of thought, and this is my take on religion. Hear me out. As a child, you are indoctrinated into your parents' religion. You are told that this invisible friend watches over you, protects you and safeguards you. You are told that if you don't believe this, you will burn in hell for all eternity – or whatever the equivalent is in the other faiths. You are told that this one God is the big kahuna, ignore all other Gods, and you are special and will live eternally.

"Then you enlist. You are trained to be a soldier. Waging war for your God, because he hates the people that you are going to fight against, and you are going into battle protected by him. Wrapped in the proverbial cotton wool of your religion. The pastor/dominee/priest appears before battle to bless you and your mission, to remind you that your God is the good God, and he is with you when you walk into the fire ahead.

"Bullets are flying. There's so much noise. Men that you trained with, the tough guys, are screaming like they are being gutted. Your best friends are falling. They are not getting back up on their feet. The air reeks of blood and war, and you can literally smell death.

"The small bible in your best friend's pocket and the priest's blessing didn't stop the bullet. He's stone dead, right next to you, where you lie, trying to see through the smoke and chaos. No one came. No Angel. No God. No holy cotton wool.

"And there's a good chance you will die here, too, if you don't fight your way out.

You somehow make it out. You put it down to your fervent prayer… but why didn't anyone else make it, those who prayed just as hard as you? Then it happens again. And again. And again.

"You're shot, too. You live, but the injury doesn't feel like it ever really heals.

You are alone. You have been alone this whole time. A lifetime of believing in… what?

Harps and holy choirs don't stop bullets – nor do they make you feel better about being tortured, gutted or shot in the back of the head by your enemy captors.

"Fucking life is what it is. Your paths are already carved into life. If you're going to die, you're going to die. You can pray until you fall off the fucking chair, they can't save you. If you're going to die when you go into a skirmish line, and you attack people in trenches, you must expect to fucking die. You can't pray to some non-existent being, and think he's going to carry you though the fuckin war. Fucking sick fucks!

"The great warriors of old had Gods who supposedly went into battle with them. Strengthened and lauded them. In fact, if I recall correctly… it was better, and more honourable to die in battle than to die of old age. Your name stacked and listed with the other great warriors by the Gods that you served. Gods that relished war, blood and sacrifice.

"If you want the makings of a soldier, take a kid who has bounced from home to home. Find a boy who has seen the ugliness of life, first hand – and survived it. Train a young man who knows that nothing comes easy, has had to fight all his life, and is ready for the fights that lie ahead; he has the heart and mind to find that path and lead his comrades through. A man who will make selection, because he knows that he can depend on himself out there, and he has a country to protect. No cushioning. No coddling. No cotton wool. Take it from someone who knows. But no doubt about it, whatever hardships came my way, I was there because I loved it; I loved war."

CHAPTER 15

Civvie Life

"Having finished at the College I was deployed once again but it was becoming clear that the war in Angola was winding down. They sent me back to the bush to pick up where I had left off before they sent me on the course. The fact they did not honour their promise to promote me says more about them than about me. I ended up sitting around Phalaborwa getting bored and missing the excitement of combat. I applied to leave but my requests were repeatedly turned down. I persisted and eventually they relented and said I could go. It was times like this I missed the SAS where religion and politics was of little importance, they respected initiative and results. And this is where I missed my hero Darrell Watt. The true God of War."

* * * * *

"I joined Herman van Niekerk and the Group 45 Intelligence Group. It looked interesting as there was some work to do out there, but in a more subtle way. I would have to swop my fatigues for civvies and become a different animal.

"I hooked up for much of this time with Corrie Meerholz, an ex-Recce operator, who I liked and respected. Corrie was frightened of nothing and game for any adventure as long as we were after the 'bad guys'. We got up to all sorts of tricks and I carried out several undercover missions. During this period I was arrested twice by the Security Police who did not have a clue what we were up to. The different intelligence services actually had little clue what the other branches were doing.

"I enjoyed the work. Often I was followed by the Security Police but I always knew when they were on my tail. On one occasion outside Pretoria I drove into a garage complex where there was a Steers restaurant I knew well. They did not know there was a way out the back of the restaurant. I came back in another car in the early morning and they were still sitting there waiting for me to come out. Hell, I laughed. Another time I went into another garage complex where I knew someone and while they waited outside I changed my clothes in the toilet, put on a hat and using a walking stick I came out looking like an old man and walked right past them.

"The security people tasked someone by the name of Robert Dean to do a report on us (see below). Little did he know I had pals in the Security Police who knew me and liked me and when this report was delivered they let me have a copy.

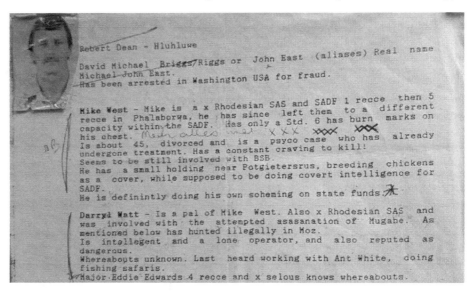

Robert Dean - Hluhluwe

David Michael Briggs/Riggs or John East (aliases) Real name Michael John East.
Has been arrested in Washington USA for fraud.

Mike West - Mike is a x Rhodesian SAS and SADF 1 recce then 5 recce in Phalaborwa, he has since left them to a different capacity within the SADF. Has only a Std. 6 has burn marks on his chest. Is about 45, divorced and is a psyco case who has already undergone treatment. Has a constant craving to kill!
Seems to be still involved with BSB.
He has a small holding near Potgietersrus, breeding chickens as a cover, while supposed to be doing covert intelligence for SADF.
He is definintly doing his own scheming on state funds.

Darryl Watt - Is a pal of Mike West. Also x Rhodesian SAS and was involved with the attempted asasanation of Mugabe. As mentioned below has hunted illegally in Moz.
Is intellegent and a lone operator, and also reputed as dangerous.
Whereabouts unknown. Last heard working with Ant White, doing fishing safaris.
Major Eddie Edwards 4 recce and x selous knows whereabouts.

We were very creative in coming up with new ideas on gathering information. Once I had learned all about these machines, I became a salesman for Kirby Vacuum Cleaner Sales in Garsfontein, and would offer to do demonstrations at houses we wanted to know more about. These were normally places where known criminals were living. I would go in, do my thing, have a good look around and gather information without anyone knowing.

"One of my tasks was to infiltrate an abattoir which was losing a lot of money through meat theft and they did not know who was involved. I learned about the slaughter house and then went to work there while I gathered the information. It did not take me long to work out what they were doing. Once I had all the evidence, I slipped away and arrests were made. Later I infiltrated an organisation where workers were defrauding the company of large sums of money, and I successfully exposed them.

"There were many incidents, with both successes and failures, but too many to name. These jobs also led to my collecting monies owed to firms and such, where the obligation had not been met. There were plenty of these.

"I was also hired to discourage violent husbands from harming their wives – and there were tons of these, as well as protecting relatively wealthy individuals from other relatively wealthy individuals, with whom they had clashed.

"Cage-fighting became an interest. I decided to go and train fighters at one of the clubs. I was already in my 60s, and no longer interested in getting physically involved in this wonderfully violent sport. I started my own fighting team known as 'The Wild West Warriors'.This was a great success. I had fighters coming from other provinces to fight in my tournaments, women included. My son helped coach alongside me, and participated in fights at the club, during training.

"I was then approached by an individual who had an army of large Congolese employees. My job was to train them so that they could protect him, his family and his business. This became VIP Protection.

"These Congolese men were truly sizeable specimens, and had balls of steel. They had basic fighting skills as well as Black Belts in judo, but they had no refined fist-fighting skills, which meant developing proper fighting skills. This was a time-consumimg exercise. I also requested the involvement of another cage fighting club, specialising in Jujitsu and wrestling, to assist in this training. Furthermore, I taught them to disarm someone pointing a weapon at them. Due to their size, strength and determination, they became the most threatening Congolese that I have ever met. I am truly proud of this, and of them. They were a force to be reckoned with.

"They participated in a tournament hosted by Fight Star, in which I had enrolled them to fight. Their employer, who had approached me to assist him, pulled the plug when my top fighter (who was a light heavyweight) fought a heavyweight contender from Joburg, who outweighed him by 15kg. He fought a giant of a man who used his weight to great advantage, tiring my top fighter. My fighter lost, hands down.

"The employer of this team attended the weigh-in, pre-fight. He had no objections at that stage when the two fighters were matched together. Yet after my top fighter had lost, he criticized me for allowing him to fight this giant.

"Unless you've actually been in a ring, you will not understand the necessity of building experience, nor weighing the fight in a man. I wanted him to gain the experience, and I believed that he could take the giant down. My mistake. My mistake cost me the loss of my entire Congolese team. I was so disgusted and insulted by this, that I aborted the entire operation and went back to my old ways, which was solving other people's problems.

Friends Remember

Jaco Kruger

"I started in the armed forces, then went to the infantry as second in command of 101 Battalion SWATF. I was in this position when they went into action in Southern Angola, and I worked closely with 5 Recce, always on standby to help in cases of emergency and to extricate those operators who got themselves in trouble. We also fought in 'Operation Firewood'.

"Two incidents in particular:

1. Mike was being followed by Fapla and I organised to go and pick him up. I went in with 40-50 trackers. Now he had to be very good to lead his men and link up with us while being chased, and without chaos erupting. The enemy was very close to him, but all went well because Mike was a fighter and a bloody good leader.

2. 'Operation Firewood'. In Mike's case, the troops were pinned down. The operation was a total fuck up. I wanted to align a flanking from the south, but high command refused to let me do it. They didn't know what they were doing. Here I was reminded that you can have and train soldiers, but you must be a born fighter and have the instinct. Only a maximum of ten per cent of soldiers have these characteristics, and Mike West was one of them. He had guts. I would go anywhere with him!

"Mike West is a born fighter. Together with instinct comes guts and great training. An outstanding soldier and leader, especially when he was leading black troops. He didn't stand back for anyone. If you fucked up he would speak his mind. You need other opinions so that you can put together a tip-top plan He was in a league of his own!"

Barend van Zyl

"It was an honour to have been able to meet and know a true war legend, Mike West, as well as being able to carry out certain missions in the Rhodesian SAS with Mike.

"Mike was a born soldier – that was his life, his passion, and that was what made him one of the most vigilant, courageous and daring war machines that wore the colours of the elite SAS.

"When war is your life as it was for Mike, there are no limits or boundaries. No lack of being absolutely brutal in combat and physically a power house with incredible strength, needing no invitation to destroy any enemy, nor person finding themselves on the wrong side of a merciless Mike West.

"If ever there were true war words spoken of Mike it would read…

- Mike will never waiver
- Mike will never tire
- Mike will not falter
- Mike will never fail

"As to your impeccable fighting record and missions accomplished, you can only be described as a fighting legend of war. Born a true soldier of war, a legend that should never be forgotten…

"I salute you Mike."

Ben Nortje

"Mike was an old bull; people from the SAS still talk about him with much praise. He is iron. Still looks damn good. Fit and well-built. A good man. Yes, and he looked like a poster boy for a soldier in a uniform. Still so. A hard man. No fear. Good friend.

"Wish I could have trained under you. Salute my friend. That photo taken in the Strike Craft *Oswald Pirow* on the way to the dangerous operation in Luanda. I heard from other sources that you were the best. Not the other guys you praise."

Shaun McHaffie

"Mike West was a soldier of note. He was the guy us younger operators aspired to be. He was seen as a man's man. He was definitely a living legend, the epitome of a fighting soldier. Professional soldier all round.

"Every day prior to, or after an operation he was always working out on his fitness. He was a boxer, a martial-arts exponent, and would not hesitate to take people out – a cleaner. You don't mix it with him. He was simply one level above all of us.

"Insofar as Op Firewood, he was in and out of the Casspir when it required him to lead. The guys felt he was 'bullet proof'. People looked up to Mike West. There were other leaders who would not get out of the vehicle.

"He had a lot of flaws as well, but he was a mentor. Fit and hard, and not scared of a fight. He didn't do a lot of courses, but he did a lot of fighting. He was not well liked by the Afrikaner Broederbond members. They didn't like the Rhodie guys who came down from Rhodesia and who were instrumental in forging the unit because they were seasoned operators. They were bush ready. These Afrikaners were fighting in terms of their Calvinistic-based bible morality. Mike was seen to be cold blooded.

"He did a lot for which he received no recognition. He was never mentioned in dispatches. He was heaps better than a lot of the other guys because he had a lot more experience. Koos Verwey was a good training officer but shit at fighting. Mike liked the bush and working.

"Mike, you be strong like a bison bull, fathered by a lion on steroids who fucked an African buffalo."

Peter Bowles

"I have been telling guys for years that you were the best Special Forces soldier I have had the privilege to serve with, then Frank Tunney, Menno, Paddy (despite his dislike of me), Mugger, Wayne R Smith and Sean Mullen. The likes of Verwey could never separate their hatred of English from the fact that a job needs to be done and I don't care whether you are an atheist or a Buddhist.

"You were a guy I was proud to serve alongside, and when the chips are down, who do you want next to you? A warrior of course, not the Drakensberg Choir.

Mike, stuff those guys, we all know the truth about the real fighters, and in my opinion and a lot of the guys I have spoken to, also say you were the best mate. The fact that they wanted to send you for all the psycho analysis crap says more about them than you.

"I did a recruiting drive once, and Verwey actually asked why it was that more English-speaking guys wanted to join SF than Afrikaners. He actually admitted that there was something wrong with how Afrikaner boys were raised and schooled. Can you believe that?

"Hard-assed, hard-as-coffin nails Mike West means the world to me. I have told my family that in my opinion you were the best ever NCO operator, fighting soldier (in other words not a parade ground puppet). The fight continues Mike, but it is a tough road and we might have to redistribute squad ammo for the next session which I am now dealing with in hospital. Stay safe brother."

Darrel Watt

"I remember so well going to the Matopos with Rob Johnson, the Rhodesian SAS Training Officer, to have a look at the guys on the selection course. I was there only because I had been wounded in the attack on the camp at Chimoio and was unable to operate. Brian Murphy, who was playing rugby for Rhodesia at the time, was also on that course. I don't think they wanted Mike and were putting him under some serious pressure. They had him splayed out on a table holding two bricks in each outstretched hand while they grilled him about his past. I looked at what they were doing to him and thought this is a guy I can work with. Although there was some reluctance from other officers, he passed the course, and I'm very pleased I had a hand in that decision.

"Right from the start with me, he was keen to learn and frightened of nothing. He became a formidable fighting soldier but more than that he was a good friend and loyal to his fellow soldiers. It does not matter what the challenges are, Mike will back you up. Wherever Mike went he made a difference. He put his life on the line for his adopted country, Rhodesia, and I'm sorry he did not get more recognition. Big, brave and ready for anything; that's how I will always remember him!"

Dap Maritz

"When I first met him – in a SAS team from Rhodesia, he immediately made an impact on me! A warrior and fighter!

"When Mike brought his family over from Rhodesia to 1 Recce, I admired him greatly. I thought what a perfect couple! Sorry Mike that things went wrong between you and your wife. Very disappointed. Little did I know that the same fate will hit me one day. We are all human and I knew what a proud man Mike was, and is, and the effect on Mike was devastating. The betrayal – Mike will never ever leave someone behind.

"For us youngsters, we looked up at him – he was our idol! He taught us many things. Mike, I will never forget the privilege I had to meet you. But unfortunately, I never had the privilege to operate with you, or under you!

"Yes, I was part of the boat team who dropped you guys off somewhere. Yes, I had the privilege to see you fuck up, vomiting your guts out on the Strike Craft with Pete jokingly riding you like a horse on your way to the toilet! You never got angry with your fellow soldiers and buddies!

"You were a giant and stood out among us. Strong as a beast and a bit more. You were not the average guys' man, nor do you and we care! The love and care you showed to us, your fellow buds and mates, made a huge impact on me and others at 1 Recce. I was a 'boertjie' who could hardly speak a word of English and trying to communicate with you guys was a challenge but we managed .

"If I may say it, I respect and salute you Mike. Take care 'old man'."

Jannie Wools

"Dan praat ons oor (*then we talk about*) Mike West ... balls of steel. Came to 53 and really fired up the operators. Operated till after he was 40 years old (which takes some doing) ... hard to believe Mike's 72 now. Like Darrell Watt, just a bull. Just wanted trouble."

TJ Brummer

"Mike drove an Anglia. Then one day returning after our outing had been withdrawn, Mike had a flat tyre. He loosened the wheel nuts, then placed his back against the car with his hands under the wheel's fender. He straightened his legs… his small wife or girlfriend then unscrewed the wheel nuts, took off the wheel, and placed the spare tyre on… he then put the car down and tightened the wheel nuts… Can you remember that on his kids' kit, there was always written on his outfit… WEST IS BEST."

Clement Kunaka – former Selous Scout and pseudo-operator

"Mike is a hero. A very good soldier. I worked with him a lot. We did many operations – undercover, bush war. He doesn't play. He knows his job very well. A born leader. Lots of anger. He would even go inside a bunker and take them out. Always going forward. Best Special Force soldier. Good for the team's morale, confidence, enthusiasm, and discipline. Was a good buddy, so strong and tough."

Veenash Naidoo

"I arrived in Pietersburg in 1998 as a 24 year old, where I worked for Body Life Gym in sales. At this stage, Pietersburg was still gripped in the old apartheid ways such that a non-white could not go anywhere, and given that I was an Indian, I was warned not to go to any of the after-hour clubs. So I went to the gym at 07h30 leaving at 20h30. I didn't have much of a life. In 1998 Mike West and his girlfriend signed up at the gym. He would come early in the morning around 07h00 or late around 19h00. He engaged with me and we got to chatting.

"One day Mike invited me to join him. He collected me around 21h30. I had been warned about Mike, and not to get involved with him. At this time, he was in his middle to late fifties, very well built for his age, huge muscled arms and a six-pack, and when he hit the punch bag, it vibrated all over the place.

"We went to the Barnyard Club with his son, 'Little Mike'. I was the only non-white. Mike never drank then, although I drank brandy and coke. An Afrikaner came over full of aggression; 'wat maak die coolie met jou?' (*what's that coolie doing with you*), he asked. Well those were the last words he uttered as Mike smashed him.

"Mike was the bouncer and when there was trouble Mike was lethal. He lived in two granny cottages, where I lived in one. I called him 'pops'. He always referred to me as his 'son'. He would come to the gym and ask for his son, and everyone knew he was referring to me. Mike would sometimes go to Jo'burg and as he didn't want to leave me alone in Pietersburg, he started training me, so much so that he had me vomiting. So when I finally went out on my own to a club the bouncers initially would not let me in, but after the owner informed me that I was Mike's 'son' the doors opened. By then I had an attitude because I knew Mike would protect me.

"Then once, inside the club, someone bumped me on purpose. I fought back, meanwhile the owner called Mike. Suddenly there were two shots fired, and Mike had arrived, wearing his gloved right hand which had lead dust on the knuckles. The next thing he had hit four or five guys, while I was still busy with one guy, and then he came over to help me out. I had lots of fights with Mike, where I helped, but I was not lethal like Mike.

"I was hated in Pietersburg, even by the Indian community, because I was affiliated with Mike, but they left me alone because they knew Mike would come looking for them. At this time I got him drinking brandy and coke, such that he fell asleep on the couch, with his girlfriend and me laughing. He also took to loving a Persian cat. I've never met a more awesome man, a heart of gold, despite being one of the most feared guys. Because of him, I am fearless and still an enforcer.

"One time, Mike had gone to the movies with a girlfriend, so I drove with two of my friends to a nearby park where we were drinking in the car. We were parked near two other cars. Suddenly one guy from these cars came and punched the window. There were ten of them and of the four of us, my three mates ran away leaving me to face them.

"One of them swung a punch, but missed, so I jumped back into the car, and drove as quickly as I could back to Mike's home. Mike wanted to know what happened, then he drove to the park where these guys were still there having beaten up two of my mates. Mike took them all out except the last biggest guy, who he said must fight me. After I had put him down, Mike thought that was not enough and hit him so hard he went flying over the railing.

These guys' fathers were cops and tried to find out where Mike lived. Mike was a very private person, with no friends visiting and he would visit no one. He just looked after people he loved.

"His cagefighters whom he was training never lost a fight. When he was called out to sort out fights at clubs, he never talked to these guys to stop the fight, he simply hit them, such that they stopped calling him to assist. He had a lot of firearms, but I only saw him carry them twice, and then never shoot anyone. His hands were his weapon."

Koos van Zyl (NPA)

"I have been a Prosecutor, in Pietersburg, for as long as I can remember. In the year 2000, Mike West made his appearance in Pietersburg as a bouncer. I had to save his bacon on many occasions, because of the resultant fighting.

"Mike West was never a trouble maker. He disliked drug-dealers, and he was a protector of the underdog. There were so many instances where Mike was called out to sort out trouble at various clubs around town.

"Mike went there to sniff out the troublemakers, and rescue those being subjected to their antics. This is where I stepped in, and kept him out of the cells, because he was helping clean up the rampant, existing problem that had plagued our clubs and pubs for years.

We were particularly thankful for his penchant for drug dealers, because he aided us in nipping a nasty ring in the bud. Mike became a legend, here.

"Some of these 'problem children' would rope in their mates from surrounding towns (as far as Joburg) to come and aid them in taking Mike out, but that always backfired, and they always went home the worse for wear.

"I, as a Prosecutor, visited many of the watering holes, and managed to pick up loads of shit, as I am not an easy person to get along with. When things got out of hand, a call would be made and Mike would appear. That would snuff out the disagreement. I knew, no matter where I went, Mike would be nearby, in the shadows, watching over me quietly. Nobody fucked with me. Mike took on larger groups over the years, and I had to step in to make sure that he was looked after.

"Being the person he was, there were always stories floating around about someone supposedly having gotten the better of him – but that's about as true as Peter Pan. Such is the nature of this game. I can assure you that this never happened.

"Mike is a true legend. Mike will always be my friend."

Callie Snyman

"My name is Callie Snyman, I met Mike West around 1992. At that stage he was hawking chickens which he bought from my late parents. To the eye, he still has a normal appearance and is engaging. He is still like that except I think he is not altogether normal. What I mean by this is that he doesn't have a frightened hair on his head. He is a fantastic, sincere friend, but don't get on his wrong side. Mike can fight, be heartless and at the very least, destructive.

"Nevertheless, according to me, Mike is a fair and an honest person. Mike was a 'chucker out' (bouncer) in many instances such as at dance halls, etc. I last saw Mike fight when he was 69 years old. Nevertheless, he fought as if he were a 30 year old. I, myself was an amateur boxer for about 12 years and can use my hands.

"Luckily Mike and I never bumped heads. You know, every person has his good and bad points. I say this because he sometimes can be heartless and cruel. Mike was also a referee for Cage Fighting and we together hosted a tournament on my premises..

"Mike West remains a good friend and I wish him prosperity for the future."

My daughter Michelle

"We were the children of war. Our fathers went to war. Our fathers brought that war home, each time that they came home – which was maybe a total of three months in a year.

Not exactly lasting, happy marriage material. Not exactly quality time with your children material. But I was lucky, my father did come home, not all of them did. We were the children of parents torn apart by war. Uncles lost. Godfathers gone. Brothers who would never return.

"I remember when we came to South Africa. When my father was still Rhodesian SAS. I remember the rush to get out of Rhodesia as the country was taken over by the people my father fought so hard against. I remember my mother breaking down, repeatedly, with my little brother and I crammed into this small barracks space with her, hoping for word of my father who we thought we had lost. I was five.

"I reminded myself that my father was always preparing me for the worst, but ever promising me, that he would come home no matter what. He never broke that promise. Not even when my parents were lost to each other.

"Now I live in a world where young people who have so little to complain about, but never seem to stop crying; they are posers pretending to be victims and they have no idea. If you want to know about hardship and gut-wrenching anxiety, stop watching junk movies and hear me out. We, the children who survived all of these wars, have this to say to the make-believe wannabee bullshitters:

"How Dare You Complain? Bring out your dead. Show us your failed marriage because of war scars. Show us your broken homes. Show us your injuries.

Or shut the hell up, go make something real of yourself and leave the heroic stories to those who were actually there. Hide your head in shame, pretending to be that which you could never be. It's better to be hated for who you really are than to be loved for what you are not. Rather fail with honour than succeed by fraud. To the reader: Sit with warriors, the conversation is different.

Wait… I forget: The men who survived all of this don't like to talk.

Because they don't have to talk. They DID.

We, the children who survived all of these wars, have experienced more hardship in our left pinkie fingers than you have in your whole bloodline.

"It would be a really enjoyable movie moment for all of you wannabees to watch you try and make your way through an enemy camp. Or just survive in the bush for ten days with little food and low on water. Toting something other than a pellet gun, and having someone shoot back at you.

"We, who have felt the pain of war are disgusted by the many today who have no idea how lucky they are to have so much, who do nothing but complain. These men, our fathers, risked their lives so that spoiled brats remained safe and now they stretch their mouths in condemnation because that is what the world demands. No white heroes allowed today. My father fought not for money nor personal gain, but to protect us and to protect you.

How Dare YOU?
Sincerely,
Michelle West

'Only Daughter of Mike West: True Operator. True Combatant. True Warrior. True Hero.

'(Also known as: Daddy)' "

Bibliography

Printed matter

Battle Scarred: Hiden cost of the Border War – Anthony Feinstein

South Africa's Border War 1966–1989 – Willem Steenkamp

The Silent War. South African Recce Operations 1969–1994 – Peter Stiff

'Iron Fist From The Sea' – Arne Söderlund and Douw Steyn

'The MiG Diaries' – Lt. Col. Eduardo Gonzalez Sarria and Lionel Reid

About the Author

Born in 1956 in what was then Salisbury in Southern Rhodesia (now Harare, Zimbabwe) Hannes Wessels grew up in Umtali on the Mozambique border. As a young boy school holidays were spent with Rangers in the Rhodesia Game department but time in his early teens on safari in Mozambique with the late Wally Johnson were a big influence. During this time Wessels met Robert Ruark whose love of Africa, its people, politics and the written word left a lasting impression.

After leaving school he saw action in the bush-war before acquiring a law degree which he chose not to use. He hunted big game professionally in Zimbabwe, Zambia and Tanzania in a twenty-year career. In 1994 he was severely gored by a wounded buffalo which almost cost him his life.

He has published 'Strange Tales from Africa' in America which is a collection of stories about people and places encountered by him in the course of his hunting days. His biography of PK van der Byl (former Rhodesian Defense Minister), 'P.K. van der Byl; African Statesman', includes a revised history of the Rhodesian political imbroglio. 'A Handful of Hard Men' was his first book about the Rhodesian war focusing on the exploits of Captain Darrell Watt during his service in the SAS. His second book on the SAS, 'We Dared to Win', was written with Andre Scheepers and has been well received in South Africa and abroad. The third book in the SAS trilogy is 'Men of War', written with Richard Stannard. He has also published 'Guns, Golf and Glory' about the great golfers that came out of Rhodesia and later Zimbabwe, which he co-wrote with former world number one golfer, Nick Price.

He is married to Mandy and has two daughters: Hope and Jana and lives in the Cape Province of South Africa. While no longer directly involved, he remains keenly interested in all matters relating to African wildlife and conservation.

OTHER BOOKS BY THE AUTHOR

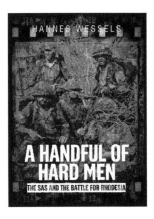
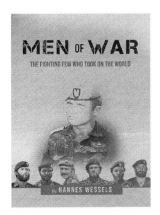

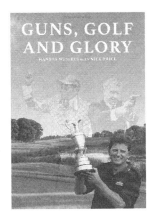

Printed in Poland
by Amazon Fulfillment
Poland Sp. z o.o., Wrocław

40528719R00148